# VENGEANCE, MY LOVE

## E. G. Fulton

TOR

A TOM DOHERTY ASSOCIATES BOOK

Distributed by Pinnacle Books, New York

VENGEANCE MY LOVE

Copyright ©1982 by E. G. Fulton

A Tor Book

First printing, May, 1982

ISBN: 0-523-48035-0

Printed in the United States of America
Distributed by Pinnacle Books, Inc., 1430 Broadway, New York, N.Y. 10018

Published by Tom Doherty Associates, 8-10 W. 36th St., New York, New York 10018

*To My Father*

# PROLOGUE

Horse and rider walked along the shore, side by side, as the sun was sinking into the Mediterranèan. The wet sand gave like flesh under their tread. The rider unfastened the girth of the saddle and let it slide to the ground. Next came the bridle, as Mabruka, the charcoal mare, offered her head for the rider. Then the reins of braided wool, up and over the horse's head. The animal plunged into the surf before the rider could give her a nudge. She galloped down the beach glorying in her freedom, throwing off the lather of the long journey.

The rider scanned the coastline to the north, where the Lebanon bowed eastward before swelling again, taking a last bite out of the sea, close to the Syrian border. The rider's eyes turned southward to see if any goatherds had ventured into the cove. There were none.

At sunset most of the villagers were home washing for dinner. Eyes would be flashing over the cookfires. Fish scales would be scattered as mulch on plots of land that bore tomatoes and radishes big as fists. High ceilings would gather smoke like a curtain being raised, heavy with the scent of onions and coriander. Huddling in the

womens' skirts, barefoot children would watch as
sugar was doled out in cups of coffee "sweet as
sin" to be sipped amidst the stories ever unfolding
from the lips of the eldest of the family. Their
sedentary grandeur, their silver tones and veiled
eyes would silence for a time the staccato
offerings of their sons.

Assured of privacy, the rider stripped down to a
rough cotton vest and shorts and waded into the
water. The sun's reflection was like fire on the
surface as the rider rolled under, embracing the
water's coolness, caressing its silence, diving deep
and stroking seven, then nine, then eleven,
snapping arms, then bursting forth for air,
surprised that feet found sand. The rider let the
water take the weight, then like a comet streaked
through the phosphorescence. The plankton that
glowed green and white trailed through the fingertips like vagrant constellations.

Rising then, the swimmer brought both arms
up, carrying with them sheets of red water that
assaulted the mare's eyes. She trotted down the
beach, tossing her damp mane and swinging her
Arab tail high, true to her bloodlines. The rider
half swam, half walked to her, and as the rivulets
of brine ran down the sleek body of the swimmer,
the image blurred.

Weeks of training showed in the limbs, hard
sinews of the warrior, but the sea finding its own
form ran down the slender lines of a woman
emerging from her bath. Mabruka approached,
pushing with her nose, nuzzling the rider seaward
again. It was clear that, hard hewn and taut as a
bowstring, a woman strode from the water.

As she paced back under the shelter of the ledge

her fingers played against her eyes. In a moment, brown contact lenses lay like sepia jellyfish in her hand. She reached inside the leather pouch that hung from a saddle hook, found the plastic case and tucked them in.

As if negative emulsion had been washed clean from her face, she turned to catch the lid's edge of the sun slipping over the other side of the world. The fire at her feet crackled through the sea salts that crusted the kindling wood. The flames grew. Like a magnet they trapped the heat of the beach before the night could steal it all away.

The woman sat stark still, unblinking. There was no vulnerability there. Only determination. Heart and mind, nerve and impulse, ticked within a network of tensed muscles. As the flames leapt, she closed her eyes against the flash of light that tore at her from the inside of her brain. The image was always the same. The citadel, golden in the sunlight, the falcon with blood on his talons, and the banshee wail of the ambulance carrying her lover away.

It was this ghost that had sent her back to Syria; in her saddle bags, explosives; in her soul, assassination. This ghost that compelled her thoughts backwards in time.

# ONE

Walter Chesterton walked to the podium amid an ever-diminishing chatter of plates. He folded back the pages of his speech and searched the audience for calm. All eyes were on him. Levy was there, Christopher, Morris, all the great names from the war fronts, from the European and Middle Eastern bureaus.

He cleared his throat, looking as great and grey as *The Times*, the newspaper that had carried his byline for forty years. His words crackled over the microphone.

"Ladies and gentlemen, good evening. It is not uncommon to honor women for their reporting skills, for their writing talents, for their intuition in all fields of the quest for knowledge and analysis in this complex world . . . ." He paused a moment, then went on.

"But it is an uncommon woman whom we honor tonight."

"Cassandra Morgan has proven herself a member of the most honored ranks of the fourth estate, not only for her biting commentaries and her perceptive interviews, but for her valor under fire." The audience shifted attentively.

"In an ever-widening conflict in the Middle East,

Cassandra Morgan kept her head at a time, if I
may steal a bit from Kipling, all around her were
losing theirs . . . ."

Cass Morgan pushed back from the table. "The
rest of the Beirut press corps won't think much of
that remark," she confided to a friend. He put a
finger to his lips.

Cass burned to be out of there. "Take the Overseas Press Club Award and run," she thought,
embarrassed to be sitting there surrounded by all
those newspeople, too embarrassed to be proud of
the honor. A blush filled her cheeks, then spilled
up to the roots of her hair. She remembered the
reason for tonight's award, not in the words of the
speechmaker, but in her gut.

Beirut. Jaded, faded, shell-shocked capital of
the Middle East. She traced that memory across
the tablecloth in the safe and staid Overseas Press
Club, over the brocade on the walls stained with
time and the cigar smoke of past generations.

The day had begun routinely enough, well,
routinely enough for Beirut in the midst of war.
The Phalangist Militia had radioed an invitation to
a few members of the press corps.

"Come to the seventeenth floor of the Holiday
Inn."

The hotel elevators still functioned. Cass with
her notebook, and Kodak with his camera, George
from A.P. and Mike McLaughlin of NBC crowded
the cubicle. The elevator doors opened into a
corridor of drab green. Room 1701 was visible.
The door had been knocked off its hinges. An M-60
machine gun was standing on its tripod to the left
where the sun streamed over its cartridge belts.

Shoved against the far wall were the bed, the lamps and the tables of the hotel room. A coffee pot sat percolating atop the pile of unwanted furniture.

Five Phalangists lined the windows, where no glass remained. They crouched against the sill shouldering M-16's. Five more gunners hung back, at ease, waiting to relieve them when their barrels grew hot or their backs started to ache. Of the ten snipers, seven were women.

"They are steadier shots," Gamal said. "They do not waste their ammunition like the young studs do."

One of the gunners pumped a slug into the building below. The young girl giggled. "We are not always the best shots," she said in Arabic, then switched to English as she turned to the journalists. "We are still in school," she confided and turned her eyes to Gamal who had trained them all.

"This is Nadia," Gamal said. "A prize pupil. Nadia, your gun!"

Gamal turned the rifle over in his hands and showed the stock to the journalists, revealing the cross-hatching.

"She has killed nine of the Palestinian pigs. We do not count the wounded," he added, as if he were generous.

Kodak recorded all of it on his camera as Cass observed the young girl. The fleshiness of youth was still with her in the round face, in the soft arms and wisps of hair that broke free from the rubber bands that held her ponytail. The lumpy green fatigues of the urban guerrilla concealed her form.

Nadia surveyed the journalists with equal interest, her eyes stopped on Mike McLaughlin of NBC. Mike was easily singled out. He was tall with an unkempt head of wild red hair. Bright blue eyes pinioned anyone who chose to look at him. Freckles dotted the bridge of his nose and his cheeks.

"I know you," she said mischievously.

"I don't think we've had the pleasure," Mike said.

"Oh yes," she said. "I've had you in my sights three times in the past week, but I didn't shoot."

"Very kind of you," he said. "I'll have my wife send you a thank you letter."

"Enough to curl your hair, isn't it, Mike?" Kodak snorted. He cuffed Mike on the shoulder but the correspondent didn't budge. Cass watched him closely but no emotion played in those blue eyes.

"I think we've seen enough. Seems you stopped the war for a while, eh, Gamal? Just for us, huh?" Cass said.

"It is nothing. The Palestinians are awaiting their arms shipment. They can wait forever. Today they have nothing to throw at us but angry words. We have blocked the port at Junieh. We ourselves are not averse to using Soviet-made arms. But you Americans, you know how to—"

Incoming gun fire burst through the windows, tearing into the asbestos ceiling. Flakes fell on the gunners as they hit the floor.

"We hold the high ground," Gamal yelled triumphantly.

Kodak tugged on Cass' hand.

"Angry words, huh?" Cass said.

"Words of lead," Gamal laughed.

"We're out of here," Mike McLaughlin said, diving for the open elevator. Cass followed quickly. Kodak and George hung back.

"Make it snappy," Mike yelled. "Don't want to get trapped here, do you? I can think of better company."

Kodak and George crossed the threshold together. The doors clanged shut.

"Phew, that's the last one for me," Mike said quietly as the elevator descended. "Too close, they're getting too damn close and for what? To get my Goddamned name on television. Jesus Christ, the bastards, the fucking bastards. It's just a game to them. A fucking, deadly, stupid game."

"Come on, Mike," Kodak said. "You've been through this before. Vietnam was no picnic."

"My salad days, thank you very much. Trouble with you, Kodak, is you've never grown out of it. You can go for glory and be hauled out on a stretcher if you like. Some 18-year-old cunt with a rifle can drill you full of holes if that makes you feel brave. Little virgins who'll make your balls shrivel. Not for me. My last time."

Kodak swung his film camera to the floor. "Mike, come on, can't let them get to you like that. Anyway, she didn't fire."

"Yeah, and what about next week when she's on the rag? Get to me? Hell. What's the matter with covering Washington on the cocktail circuit instead of spending my days in a flak jacket?

When you're six five they'll go for your legs
anyway, or your head. These baby blues are going
to stay mine and I'll see you all later." Mike broke
out of the elevator and ran for the front door.
Kodak followed him swiftly, but more lumbering-
ly with his camera.

"Cass, you go with Samir. I've got to talk to that
boy."

"Right," Cass said.

"Cass, you want to ride with me?" George called
out.

"No, no, Samir likes to feel wanted. See you
back at the bureau."

The gunfire was sporadic, half-hearted. They all
bolted to their prospective cars. Cass jumped into
the last car in the convoy. Samir was gritting his
teeth.

"Come on, Miss Morgan, time to fly."

"Hit it," she said. They had yet to cross Beirut's
green line, the line that separated Christian and
Moslem fighters.

"Safe conduct, they promised." She laughed.

Samir clucked. He knew the same joke.

"Where's Abu Kodak?"

"Gone with Mike. He's trying to talk Mike into
staying."

"He's going?"

"I think so, Samir. Seems he's got the fear of
God in him. Saw his name stamped on some
Phalangist's M-16."

"That's bad," Samir said gravely. "Bad luck. He
should go. What about Kodak?"

"He won't go. He'll try and talk Mike into
staying, because he doesn't want to feel
abandoned. Doesn't want to let his craziness show.

They spent a lot of time together in Vietnam. Foxhole buddies. Brave ol' boys. You know. Kodak won't find another friend like that."

"Kodak *magnoon ketir*!"

"Yeah," she said, "he's loony as a bat."

Samir laughed and slowed the car to allow for some spacing between the convoy vehicles. Cass leaned back against the seat just as a machine gun parted the curtains five floors above them. The bullets ripped into the pavement.

Samir kicked the accelerator, spinning the wheel and breaking rank, but not in time. A bullet shattered the windshield and struck him in the throat. He slumped over the steering column and the car careened into a wall. Cass's lap was full of glass. As she raised her head to dashboard level, she heard Samir gurgling something. There was a lull. The sniper reloaded.

Cass dove from the side of the car, crabwalked round to the other door and pushed Samir over to the passenger side. The A.P. Bureau chief in the car ahead of hers stopped just out of the line of fire. He was kneeling and yelling something at her but she couldn't hear. Steam clouded the windshield. She switched off the car, then sparked the ignition. Three times it failed to start. Three times she ran through her considerable store of four-letter words.

The machine gun tore into a building nearby, sending chunks of concrete over the hood of the car. He was playing games with her now. The killers of Beirut had become capricious. She tromped the accelerator, and the vehicle lurched backwards away from the wall. She held one hand firmly on the wheel and the other on Samir's body so he would not roll forward, then she maneuvered out of the main street, Rue De Damas. The A.P. Bureau chief rose to his feet waving wildly. Kodak shouldered his gear to make a run for her, but Mike grabbed him.

The front axle was twisted, but the car jerked forward and, wheezing, kept going. After an agonizing three blocks she came to a halt behind a row of buildings, away from the gun fire. The others rushed to her aid. It was some time before they could extricate her from the driver's seat. She would not let go of the wheel.

Samir was lifted out of the car and was carried to a field hospital on the Moslem side. He survived. That was the only striking thing about the incident. They both survived.

That evening, after she'd filed her nightlead, Cass Morgan's compatriots prescribed liberal doses of scotch. Best story she'd ever written, she thought, something about mortality and the human spirit, hammered out on the typewriter rapid-fire, no corrections. She predicted her editor would slash it to ribbons, but he didn't touch a word. She saw the night through at the Commodore Bar in the Hamra section of Beirut, shaking sometimes with hysterical laughter. Night shelling lit up the sky like heat lightning.

The sound of the distant artillery gave way to applause as Cass walked to the dais and approached the microphone. Her palms were sweating, and she wiped them indecorously on her dress. At the back of the room, she spotted Mike McLaughlin. He nodded to her.

"We're all taught to be brief and to the point in

this business. This has nothing to do with valor or bravery . . . with all due respect, Walter."

Chesterton raised his head in acknowledgment.

"There are plenty of people who deserve it more, in fact some absent friends who should be here tonight and couldn't make it because they're still slugging it out over there, trying to make some sense out of the madness. And some people who couldn't be here because they weren't as lucky as I was. I . . . well . . . ." She couldn't find any more words.

"Thank you," she said softly, and walked away. Some of her colleagues were on their feet as she left the podium.

"It's okay, Cassie!" one of them yelled.

"Sob sister to the end," she called back as she strode toward the coatroom, shaking outstretched hands as she went. When she got to Mike, he pulled her close and she lingered for a moment.

"Best to Kodak, eh, Cassie?"

"Yeh, Mike. We miss you, you know." He let her hand drop and she walked away. She'd been invited to a drinkathon with the press club members that night, but had opted for a smaller affair, a cocktail party given by a friend

# TWO

The party was well under way as she walked into the room. People sat on the radiators by the windows sipping drinks and smoking cigarettes. The host came at once and encircled Cass in his arms, giving her a hug that rocked her off balance. He took her coat and propped the press club award on the table near the door.

"That could go in a closet, I think, Charles," Cass said.

"Most certainly not. You are the guest of honor. Mary! Andy! Take care of this girl!"

She was surrounded by people she hadn't seen in years. Mary, so much thinner than in their college days. Andy, sporting the paunch of the Wall Street banker. Bobby Westbrook, who had once wooed Cass at Dartmouth mixers, introduced his bright and beaming wife. They were full of stories of kids and diapers.

"Such a long time," they kept saying.

Out of the company of fellow journalists, Cass became reserved, downplaying the war stories, downplaying the Middle Eastern politics that had become her daily diet. She listened intently to her friends, but she felt her isolation growing. In the far corner of the room a domestic political discussion was heating up. The names Richard Nixon, Gerald Ford and Jimmy Carter crashed through the conversation like bludgeons.

Waiting for her chance, she stole away from Mary and Andy and positioned herself near the window, preferring to look out on the river. New Jersey glowed across the Hudson. River barges passed silently downriver, carried by the current. The ramshackle docks of the once great shipping lines looked ghostly without their vessels in port. Forlorn and timeless.

Lawrence Foster had been watching her. She was wearing a simple silver chain around her neck. Her blond hair was trained back in a braid at the nape of her neck. She wore no makeup but a trace of lipstick. The Middle Eastern sun had done its work; the skin was peeling on the bridge of her finely chiselled nose. Her shoulders were squared and broad, inherited from her father. Freckles from the sun wandered down to her small breasts, almost indiscernible in the folds of crepe de Chine. A glimpse . . . as she leaned toward the window.

Foster was intrigued. He asked the host about her. Charles proved a peevish source.

"She was always crazy," he said, "always first to the barricades, the bourgeois revolutionary. And always leaving men like me . . . flat."

"Still nursing it?"

"Be my guest," Charles said gesturing towards Cass. "Just remember, you've been warned."

"Phew. Maneater, eh?"

"Not in the slightest," Charles said. "It's just that she doesn't give a damn. Armor-plated. I think she's still hurting from her Dad's death."

"Father's child."

"All the way. He was a journalist, too."

"When was the last time you saw her?"

"When she went to Egypt."

"Egypt?"

"Yeh. Mummies and Boris Karloff and Anwar Sadat. Take your pick."

"You sound a little bitter."

The host smiled. "She put five thousand miles between us without batting an eye. Go ahead," he said, "looks like she could use some company," then turned to his other guests.

Foster shrugged, and didn't look back.

"Can I get you another drink?" Foster said prying his way into her thoughts.

"Thank you. Scotch on the rocks, please. I'm Cass—"

"Yes, I know. I've seen your stories in the *Herald*. Congratulations on your award."

"Do you live in Washington, then?"

"No, but I go there often on business. Let me have your glass. Don't move. I'll be right back." She gave him an obedient salute then turned back to the window and cooled her cheek against the glass.

"Here you go," Foster said, returning to her side. "Glad to be home?"

"Um," she said. "For a little while anyway. New York seems quite exotic to me now."

"Exotic?" He said. "Mundane, you mean. Look around you. You'd think these guys went to sleep in their ties, with their feet propped up on the ledger books."

"Fed up?"

Foster put his hand to his chin. "To here."

"That's a splendid tie you're wearing."

"Go ahead. Rub it in. I wear the uniform, too. Magazine publishing. I work with Charles, but one more year on Sixth Avenue and I'll be certifiable." He poked at the ice in his glass. Foster looked older than Cass, but not by much. Well built. He moved like an athlete. His tie was askew and his blond hair unkempt. He had a rugged handsomeness, a musculature that could not be completely concealed by the suit that he wore.

"What do you want to do?"

"Travel," he said.

"Where?"

"Overseas. Anywhere. I spent some time in Italy. In Naples. A friend of mine used to sing an old Italian song, "Eat Your Money." Sounded like good advice. At first I thought I'd buy a yacht. A forty-foot sloop to be exact, but I'm not much of a sailor. In fact, I can't keep soap afloat in the bathtub. So much for that idea."

"Why don't you quit?"

"Soon, my lady. Very soon. Just looking for the right sort of partner. Should have a traveling companion, don't you think? Easier that way."

"Don't you have a woman now?"

"Women." He sighed the big sigh. Cass laughed. "Seems I can only talk about women in the past tense, or in some future dream."

"Oh dear," Cass said. "You are in a bad way."

Foster snapped to. "You think we could skip out of here? I hang around these guys all day. They always look the same, always talk shop . . . and their wives. Lovely, but no imagination, somehow. They've been eclipsed, as bogged down as their husbands. Well," he pushed the hair out of his eyes. "How about a carriage ride in the park? A

champagne cocktail at the Plaza, perhaps?'' He
raised his eyebrows.

"You are a romantic wolf," she said. "I think
our host would consider me ungracious if I left the
party so soon."

"I think he thinks you're ungracious now."

"Oh dear," she said, turning full toward Foster.
"Is he still harboring a grudge?"

"Well."

"Well, how about seeing this through with me,
eh?"

"As you wish," he said, "but only under duress."
He tugged at his tie and craned his neck.

"It can't be as bad as all that."

"No," he laughed and looked at her more than a
little lasciviously. He had a lazy eye, and the lid
was just closing when she said, "Take it easy
there, chum. The night is young and you may be
left fraught with promise."

"I'm already fraught," he said. "I've never been
to bed with a journalist."

"Well, that's heartening news," she said. "I
wouldn't like to compete with H. L. Mencken in
the sack."

"You got it, hands down."

She moved away from him, uncomfortable at
the turn of the conversation.

"Sorry," he said and held her hand lightly. She
let it rest there for a moment, feeling his warmth,
then moved farther away.

"You're a very pretty girl. To have gone through
the things you have, I'm surprised you don't have
more grey hair."

"Depends on how I part it," she said. "There."
She pulled back a wave of blond hair to reveal a

streak of white at her temple. "That's what Beirut's done for me. That's what I paid for the award, not to mention this." Her hand shook dramatically.

He grabbed it.

"Only kidding," she said, laughing openly now. She handed him her empty glass.

He took up the cue at once and headed for the bar. As he threaded his way through the crowd, she made good her escape.

He saw her as she passed through the front door, her coat hastily thrown about her shoulders and the press club award held tightly under her arm. He looked down at the two drinks in his hands, then at Charles, who was the only one to notice her exit, and smiled.

# THREE

Cass roamed around her mother's apartment, picking up objects and putting them down.

"Cassie?"

"I'm all right, Mom."

Mrs. Morgan stood in the den, eying the wall. Without much ceremony she hoisted the hammer and pounded in a nail, scattering some plaster. Cass came to the doorway.

"It will hang right next to your father's. He'd be very proud of this," she said, lifting the award to its place on the wall.

Cass walked into the room and propped herself up on her father's desk.

"Yeah, he'd like that." She picked up a letter opener. It was a miniature Bedouin dagger in a silver sheath. A straight blade. She toyed with the point, then dropped it onto the blotter. The point sank in. The blade wavered back and forth. She yanked it out and did it again.

"Want to play mumbly-peg, Ma?"

"No thanks, Cass. Can't you sit still for a moment?"

"Nah."

"Never could. You and your Dad." Mrs. Morgan adjusted the plaque again, giving it a nudge to set it flush against the wall.

"There," she said.

"Looks fine, Mom."

"Cassie."

"Mom, you sound awfully serious."

"Cassie. I know it's kind of close quarters here, now, but I spend my days at the agency and go to the shows at night. I'm never here much, and I'd like you to stay. I really don't want you to go back overseas, you know that."

"Thanks, Mom."

"You've done it. You don't have to prove anything now. You don't have to waste your life on the front line of a foreign war that no one gives a damn about anyway."

"You use that same argument on Dad?"

"Yeah. It didn't work then, either. But Cass. It's different. You're a young girl. I've lost . . . you don't have to break your mother's heart."

"Please, Mom," Cass groaned.

Mrs. Morgan paused, thinking better of it. "Hopeless," she said. "Okay. I'll have your trench coat cleaned and your daggers sharpened and your cloak . . . but I wish to hell . . . I do worry about you."

"Yeah, Mom."

The phone rang.

"That's probably my editor wondering the same thing as you. When am I going back?"

"Maybe it's for me. A boyfriend, perhaps," Mrs. Morgan sniffed, looking at the wall as she said it. She picked up the phone.

"It's for you," she said, covering the mouthpiece. "It's a man."

"Christ, Mom! Don't act so surprised," Cass

said, pushing the hair back from her forehead brusquely.

"Yeah." She spoke into the phone with more than a little exasperation in her voice.

"Ms. Morgan?"

"The same," she said more softly.

"Lawrence Foster."

"Foster?"

"Lawrence. You remember, the party the other . . . ."

"Oh yes, but how did you get my number?"

"I did a little investigating," he said, "spurred by longing and some remorse for my behavior the other night. A little too forward, hum?"

'I'm glad to hear from you."

"It's only, well, I like to be direct."

She chuckled. "Charles had something to do with this, no doubt."

"Dinner tonight?"

"That's pretty direct," she said.

"What about it?"

"I'd love it."

"Pick you up at 7:30. A cocktail dress would do."

"Do you know where I live?"

"Uh-huh," he said.

"You have done your homework. At 7:30 then." They rang off.

Cass sat quietly and stared at the phone for a moment. "Well, what do you know about that?" she said to no one in particular.

# FOUR

Lawrence Foster had just gotten out of the shower. His hair was wet and his face was smooth, just shaven. He turned up the stereo and rubbed his head with a towel, then tossed it over the rail.

It was Golden Oldies Time on the radio. "Twist and Shout" by the Beatles. Foster strode out of the bedroom with a towel wrapped around his hips and looked at the clock.

She was late, he thought. As usual—in the six weeks they'd been seeing each other, she'd been on time twice. He smiled and took a turn through the living room, picking things up and tossing them into the wastebasket from across the room.

The late afternoon sun filled his apartment. He knew she was riding somewhere in Central Park, under the trees and ramshackle bridges, galloping the cinder track jockey-style, scattering joggers and children and winos alike. The sign said NO RECKLESS RIDING. It had been several weeks since they met.

Foster went to the window as if he could hear her galloping by. It was an astoundingly bright day for New York. Alive and benign.

He looked at the clock again. *Late*. He dropped to the floor and began to do push-ups. The doorbell rang.

Foster curled up into a forward roll and came to the door, bounding to his feet.

"Uh, sorry I'm late," Cass said. She handed him a bottle of wine.

"Ugh," he said, looking at her. She was still in jodhpurs, smelling of horses.

"Hey, same to you," she said. "You look awful sweaty for a guy that just got out of the shower."

"Just trying to keep in shape for my baby."

"Yeah, well, your baby's in trouble," she said.

"What's the problem?"

"Taylor, my editor."

"Won't give you another extension of Rest and Relaxation, huh?"

"Christ. No. Hey, save me any hot water?"

"There's plenty," he said. "Get to it."

"I asked for more than R and R."

"Oh yeah," Foster said. "Jesus Christ, Morgan, what's this shit on your arm?"

She looked down. "Oh, horse-spit, probably. One big kiss from one big gelding. He had great lines, Foster."

"Please, Morgan, to the showers, okay?"

"Hey Foster, love me, love my horse, huh?"

"Love you, love your body," he said and pulled her toward him. He held her with one arm and began to unbutton her blouse. She yielded, but as the undressing progressed, her riding boots were another matter.

"No, Foster, the boots come next."

"Christ, Morgan, couldn't you play ping-pong or something?"

"The boots, Foster. The boots. You can't get my pants off 'til you get the boots off. What's the matter, didn't you ever take physics in high school?''

"I excelled in anatomy."

"Mine?"

"Yours," he said hefting one boot off and letting it fly across the living room.

"One more."

"Right. Right."

"What a gentleman," she said pulling him down to her on the floor.

"What a lady," he said picking a piece of straw from her hair. The towel round his waist fell away and he kissed her hard on the mouth, searching with his tongue. He ran his fingers up the insides of her thighs. She groaned as he found his way inside her. The force of his strokes pressed her hard against the floor. The rug burned her elbows and stung her backbone. He put both hands under her hips and held her tight against him when he came. The pleasure resounded from him to her, and they both relaxed in a heap of spent energy. Cass giggled.

"Hey, this is serious business," he said, rolling away from her.

"Uh huh," she said and sighed. He gave her a hand up and caught her in his arms.

"Come on," he said, "got to show you a few things."

"Shower first?"

"Yeah, yeah, go ahead, but hurry up. Important matters to discuss."

She shut the bathroom door without comment.

He collected her discarded clothes and threw them in a pile on a chair, then propped her riding boots against the hall cabinet. He shut off the stereo and listened to her singing in the shower.

"Nothing like a happy woman," he said poking his head in the door.

"Um," she responded, letting the warm water spill over her body. She pulled the curtain aside and gave him a wet kiss.

"Later," he said. "Listen, I've got our itinerary all worked out. First France. Wine country and Mont St. Michel. The Normandy beaches. How's that sound?"

"Wonderful," she gurgled. "I'll be out in a moment."

"Chateaux, champagne, then Greece, Italy, Yugoslavia."

"Wonderful, wonderful."

"So you're going to quit, right?"

"I called my editor today and gave notice."

"You did?"

"Yep."

"And . . . ."

"He wasn't very pleased. Made me promise I'd file some stories along the way if we hit any hot spots."

"Okay. Okay, but no hot spots. All pleasure, understand?"

"Yep," she said. "Sounds wonderful." She turned off the faucets and stepped out of the shower into the towel he held for her.

"Then Istanbul, wild and woolly Eastern Turkey, then Iran, Afghanistan, Pakistan, and India."

"Wonderful, wonderful," she said rubbing against him as he dried her hair.

"The trip's the thing," he said. "The East. When can you leave?"

"Soon's I get my Cairo apartment squared away.

There are a few things to be worked out, Mr. Foster. I've only known you. . . ."

"Centuries," he said. "Centuries. Now get cracking!" He stung her with the wet end of the towel.

# FIVE

Before she met Lawrence Foster, Cass had been a loner, dogging the greatness of her father's byline, trying to play catch-up with his reputation. She had followed the Egyptian tanks into the Sinai and crouched beneath the helicopter rotors of every Kissinger coming and going. She had attended so many red carpet arrivals at Cairo Airport she could hum the national anthems of every Arab nation and Emirate, and a few African ones as well.

In the business they called her a "professional bachelor." For three years she had lived alone among the Fatimid screens and brass lamps of her Zamalek apartment, a moment's stroll from the Nile. The jangle of donkeys' brasses mingling with the morning call to Allah awoke her at dawn every day, though she often pushed her face back in the pillow and slept until ten.

Guests came to her home to visit, to smoke hash and to drink sometimes until sunrise, but never to stay longer than a night or two. Cass Morgan's life revolved around a typewriter, a telex machine and, as the civil war heated up, plane flights Beirut. More often than not she would remain in that war-ravaged capital for weeks on end, leaving the apartment to her maid, Fawzia.

Fawzia was old, wall-eyed, and trustworthy, and seemed more than a little disappointed when Cass called from New York to say she would not be returning to Egypt.

Cass's fixer and research man took on the job of storing her furniture and sending her the journals and notebooks that she had filled with writing in those endless days when there was no story to write about, no deadline to meet, no action to lift her out of the torpor of dusty days and long, fragrant nights.

Lawrence Foster had barged into her psyche, crashing through her professional woman's defenses as if they were paper walls. Her skin gleamed, her moods lightened, and her cynicism fell away. She found herself relaxing all the triggers, standing down from the newshound's adrenaline addiction.

"You're out of the locker room, now. Right, Morgan?"

"Um," she said, stroking his hair.

"Camaraderie's one thing, Morgan, but it's time for you to forget about being one of the guys for a change. You know. A woman. Forget about those rattletrap press buses."

"And the warm bottle of scotch passed around among us. All wondering why we couldn't write like Lawrence Durell. Sipping away the dust and the sweat from our khakis. Sounds poetic, right?"

"Starlit Arabian nights. Yeah. Durell, but bitter lessons, not bitter lemons."

"Something like that," she murmured.

"And slapping each other on the back and drinking away the nervousness, praying for the fatigue, because it's been fear all day that's been driving you. Fear of the bombs, fear that the lead won't come."

"Nah, never that," Cass laughed.

"Fear, though, right?"

"Yeah. The same kind you get on a rollercoaster. The scream that goes away right after you slide down the long hill and swing back to the starting gate, only to do it over and over again."

"Come here," he said gruffly. She buried her face under his chin, against his chest.

"It will always be there, you know."

"Yeah, well, not if I can help it. You just need a new sense of direction, that's all. And I'll provide it."

"I don't know."

"The hell you don't know, hotshot." He tumbled her under him and filled her with his energy, with his pleasure.

The dream of the trip to Asia grew in scope and magnitude daily as he traveled over his maps with red pencil in hand. She sat next to him and traced her fingers over the mountain passes and the wide, golden valleys, the realms of ancient kings and deities from Zeus to Allah to Buddha to Krishna.

Foster quit his job and counted his money. He put his three-piece suit in mothballs, gave away what he couldn't sell, gripped Cass in one hand and their airline tickets in the other, and they were gone, sailing into Orly on champagne and high spirits.

# SIX

Paris was grey. The skyline was stacked up like dirty dishes, but on their first night the lights of Notre Dame and Sacré Coeur dispelled the murky atmosphere. They filled themselves with postcard vistas and greeting card exclamations and happily bedded down in a tiny hotel where flowers writhed through the wallpaper.

The proprietor of the hotel, which they quickly dubbed "L'Auberge Bizarre," had decorated their room with erotica. Silk stockings were draped over the bureau and dresser, and a long, low mirror hung above the bed with a shadowy image of Marilyn Monroe in recline staring out with moist eyes and wet lips. Foster got a big kick out of it. Cass just settled back and gave Foster a "tame kitten" look.

Their trip began in earnest three days later when they bought their car, a 350-dollar special purchased at American Express.

"This car," said Randy from Seattle, "will take you all the way to Nepal, to the foothills of Everest if you like. No lie, man, I sold one of these to a guy who drove it from Casablanca to Nairobi. No problem. Fixed a cracked gas tank or something, that's all. He came back and bought another car from me. Volkswagen. I've got one of those if you're interested.''

But they weren't. The ten-year-old Renault Four, a faded yellow wagon with a dented front end and a Disneyesque flavor, was just what they were looking for.

Cass put her name and passport number at the bottom of the green card. Owner number 9. It looked official anyway. Then they were off, on the road past Versailles, out towards the Atlantic Coast, to the graveyards of the Second World War, then on to Mont St. Michel, Normandy and the Brittany Coast. There they harvested their own scallops for dinner and the fine Percheron mare smelled sweetly of clover and trotted over the pasture with Cass aboard. Like the horse in the circus, with a rump so big you could dance all day and never fall.

Petite Jaune, the yellow Renault, held all their provisions, their sleeping bags and tent, their Boy Scout hatchet, their vodka, their volumes of Henry Miller and their chess set. Cass Morgan was a bad loser at chess. Lawrence Foster was a lousy winner. Somehow there was balance.

When things got rough between them, rough as the roadbeds they traveled, and they felt like throwing punches, more often than not they threw their arms around each other.

In St. Tropez, pride of the Riviera, they waded through the mud together, dragging their soggy sleeping bags with them. They shared sips of brandy under a makeshift tarp in the fertile valleys of Beaujolais as the rain drummed over their heads.

The grapes were late, a month late on the vines,

and Cass and Foster couldn't wait for the harvest. They were impatient for the sun. They moved on to Greece, to Crete, where they threw their clothes and their modesty to the winds at Matala.

Scrambling over the headland clad only in shorts, their shirts tied tight around their foreheads against the sweat, they plunged into the Mediterranean, a sybarite's dream. The sun dried them out and made them tawny brown and muscular.

They eased their way along the torturous cliffs and chased the ancient spirits in the Minoan ruins. They sniffed the sulfurous phantoms of San Toreni, emptying bottles of retsina, giddy, expecting to see everything there was to see from the Mediterranean to the South China Sea.

The winds grew chill and they stalked the sun to Istanbul. There they indulged themselves in the baths, Foster heading to the men's *hammam*, "Now don't chicken out, Morgan," and Cass to the women's *hammami* down sooty streets where cobblers sank nails into leather soles and potmakers banged on their wares.

At the door of the *hammami*, the steam rolled up into Cass' face and she faltered. Foster would kill her if she backed out now, first chance to get the road dust off their bodies, but. . . . A woman with pendulous breasts ushered her into the baths, showing her to a stall. A cigarette hung limp from the woman's lips and she asked Cass for more. Cass gave her the pack and turned away to undress. The woman leaned in the doorway watching.

Some semblance of modesty returned as Cass held the towel tightly around her. The woman shook her head, bored, untied the towel and folded it up on the hard wooden bench. She took Cass' hand and padded in front of her down the marble steps into the heart of the baths, the sound of her feet echoing off the wet stone.

The slapping of flesh reverberated through the chambers. Vapors rose from the steamy pit, obscuring shapes and movement. Cass sat demurely on a marble slab waiting. Watching. Sweating. A great big woman with hairy arms tapped her on the shoulder then pulled her up and laid her out flat, face down, on the slab, her cheek against the wet stone. The woman worked, kneading and prodding, pulling and squeezing, working her way up from the toes to the feet to the calves to the buttocks to the back of the neck.

Vast quantities of hot water splashed over her body as she surrendered to the woman's expertise. With a slap on the rump, the woman flipped Cass over and began to work on her thighs and stomach. She cupped one of Cass' breasts and then one of her own and guffawed.

"Yes, very funny," Cass said.

"Small, small," the woman said and clapped her on the shoulder, then she shook her own breast again. "Good, very good."

"Yes, marvelous," Cass said. A European girl in the corner giggled. Cass laughed and looked ceilingward. The dome of the bath was studded with stained glass and mirrors. Drops of water fell back to the floor as it condensed. Shutting her eyes, Cass lay dreamily as the woman worked over her body with a rough mitt, rubbing the dirt out of her pores, scratching away at the aches in her muscles. Then the woman lifted Cass onto a stool

and shampooed her hair, brushing against her
with her strong thighs, her breasts swinging
against Cass' body, grunting all the time,
humming sometimes, tunelessly, totally oblivious
to any sexuality. Then, again, buckets and buckets
of hot water.

When Cass left the baths her body was tingling
and pink. She ignored the stares of the Turkish
men. Her thoughts soared over the minarets of the
Blue Mosque. Foster. Her heart pounded when
Foster pulled her beneath the covers in their hotel
room, rolling away from the scent of the incense
and the wavering light of the candles at the
window. They tumbled over and over, in and out of
each other, exploring, biting, fondling until they
fell asleep atangle in each other's arms.

In Ephesus, on the Turkish side of the Aegean
Sea, they quoted Shakespeare to each other in a
stadium where the whispers of gladiators wound
down through the centuries. They encountered a
snake along the marble road where the temperature grew chill and the Goddess Artemis opened her arms and held them against her many
breasts.

"Ephesusssssssssss." The stone horses of that
noble city drew chariots through their imaginations, along the ruts that zigzagged back
and forth in the ancient pavement. Marble cows
protruded from the grass, unearthed by time.
Statues stood sedately on their pedestals,
impervious to the breeze that crept beneath their
stiff tunics. Cass and Foster stood enrapt and let
the sun filter down to their pagan hearts. Then
they turned their eyes East.

Along the southern coast of Turkey the winter

warning came down twice, once in Adana and again in Mersin. Snow was already falling in the mountain passes. A blizzard had locked in over the Lake Van area, the southernmost passage to Iran. The Turks said there was a fifty-fifty chance they'd be turned back.

"Fifty-fifty, hum," Foster said, gnawing on a raw onion. It was a habit he'd picked up in eastern Turkey. Cass stood her distance, looking at maps. He leaned nonchalantly against the car. His eyes were watering, but he kept on chewing.

"Ugh, Foster."

"Clears out the sinuses, Morgan."

"Here, wash it down with this, will you?" She handed him a cup of vodka and then backed away again.

"Well, what shall we do?" he said, hurling the last of the onion to the side of the road.

"We could always take a right turn and winter in the middle East."

"Nah. Don't like the Arabs."

"What do you mean, you don't like the Arabs? You've never even seen one."

"Bad press."

She kicked him lightly in the seat of the pants.

"Well," he said, pouring himself another cup of vodka. He shivered. "Would be nice to find some sun again, eh?"

"Yep. We could winter in Jordan, or in Israel by the sea maybe. We could head straight through Damascus. The hadj is coming, feast of the lamb. Should be pretty festive. Hashish? Lebanon? Hum?"

"Enticing, very enticing," he mused. "We'll make the decision logically, okay?" He pulled out a Turkish coin. "Heads we go to the Middle East . . . tails we take our chances with the mountain pass."

"All right," Cass said closing her eyes. The copper coin hit the macadam with a plinking sound and bellied up head.

"The Middle East it is," Foster announced. "Shoot to see who drives?"

"Yeah, okay. Odds, two out of three."

He rubbed his hands together and warmed them in the folds of his flannel shirt.

"Once-twice-three . . . shoot. Ha, ha. I win."

"Foster, you reek of onions."

"Once-twice-three . . . shoot. Hee, hee. In the car, woman."

"Don't come near me!" He grinned and yanked her toward him, breathing all over her.

"I'm going to faint!"

"I'm going to take advantage."

"Foster. Drive, okay?"

"Right," he said. He tapped the roof of the car for luck, then slid behind the wheel.

# SEVEN

Night had fallen by the time they reached the Syrian border crossing just north of Iskandarun. Cass and Foster were both slap-happy as they pulled into the customs checkpoint, but they sobered immediately as the military surrounded their car. Cass and Foster got out of the car; the officers checked it from top to bottom. Cass listened to their Arabic and poked Foster in the ribs.

"They're looking for drugs," she whispered. "You did get rid of that hash, didn't you?"

Foster beamed and patted his stomach.

"Smart move," she said. "I'm driving."

He bowed to her and she curtsied back. The Syrian soldiers looked at them with some amazement. It was the first time in months that they'd seen Americans.

"*Salaam a aleikum,*" Cass said as the lieutenant perused their papers inside the office.

"*Aleikum salaama,*" he answered back grinning.

"*Ezzayak?*"

"*Kuwayyis ketir, al hamdullelah. Enti?*"

"Very good, thank God," she answered back.

"You have been in Egypt, I think."

"A few years," she said.

44

"You like the Egyptians?"

"Sometimes," she answered carefully.

"Not to be trusted," he said. "Nasser was good. Sadat—he is a villain."

"You speak Arabic, too?" he asked Foster.

Foster looked puzzled.

"No, no, it's his first time in the Middle East," Cass said.

The lieutenant went through Foster's passport three times before he said, "Wait here," then left the room. An altercation was brewing outside. A young man who looked European was getting agitated as the military went through the car and his belongings. The car was a Porsche Targa, brand new from the looks of it. Parcels in foil paper had been thrown out on the customs bench and were being summarily torn open.

Foster and Cass wandered outside. The European looked at them imploringly. Cass shrugged in the Arabic manner, raising her chin in question.

"They are taking all my things," he said in English.

"Why?"

"Because I am rich. Because I am Lebanese."

"You're going to Lebanon, now?"

"No, no," he said, tearing his hair as they pilfered another package. The contents were spilling off the bench and falling in the dirt. "To Latakia, in Syria. To my parents. They haven't seen me since summer."

The lieutenant sat on the hood of the Porsche adding to a list that he was writing. He was shaking his head and making tsk, tsk noises, amused with himself.

"Doesn't look good," Foster said with his arms folded. A mink coat, a new stereo receiver, three pairs of shoes and various trinkets were heaped on the bench.

"*Baksheesh*," the Lebanese man said, and the lieutenant scowled at him.

"Could I get a ride with you?" he said.

"You mean they're taking your car as well?" Foster asked.

"Impounding it for military use. Can you believe it? Only in Syria."

"And the coat? The shoes?"

"For my mother. They want duties. Heavy *baksheesh*," he whispered. "I must come back tomorrow and sort it out. The Porsche. I'll see it in some parade."

"No."

He nodded woefully.

"Jesus. Sure, come on. Latakia's just down the coast, right?"

"Right. I am Mounir, by the way. Mounir Najaime. I have just come from Italy."

"*Ah'lan*," Cass said and held out her hand. "Cass Morgan and Lawrence Foster. Americans."

"Very pleased to know you," he said and laughed.

"I'm glad you can keep your sense of humor," Foster said.

"What is left," he said, holding out his bare hands. "I am in Syria."

The lieutenant broke into the gathering and handed them all their passports with the proper stamps. He jingled the keys to the Porsche as he did so.

"Got to rub it in, doesn't he?" Foster said as they

were getting in the car.

"I don't understand," Mounir said, settling into the back seat.

"Bastards!"

"Ah, now I understand. Bastards. Oh, I am very sorry, lady."

"Don't worry about your language with Cass. She's been round the block."

Cass hammered his knee with her fist.

"What does round the block mean?" Mounir wondered.

"Uh, experienced in the company of males."

"Thank you very much, Foster."

"Oh I see," Mounir said.

"He just means . . . ."

" 'Tis a fool who does not spend his money on wine, women, and song."

"Who said that?"

"I did," Mounir said, pleased with himself. "Better a wastrel than an unhappy man."

"Oh no. A Lebanese philosopher."

"Worse than that," said Mounir, "A Lebanese gambler, and not a good one at that. I am bringing presents home to the family, or I was bringing presents home to the family to make amends, you see. I've spent a great deal of my father's money at Monte Carlo. Now I am asking for more."

"Will he give it to you?"

"Of course, he loves me. I studied medicine for a while in Rome, but the books wore me out. Now I am determined to be fashionable and happy."

"A dilettante."

"Exactly."

"I'll drink to that," Foster chimed in.

Mounir's family gave them a royal welcome and

greeted their son with tremendous affection. Mrs. Najaime filled the dining room table with an Arab reza, twenty-odd dishes of lamb and rice, aubergine, and olives, radishes, tahine, grape leaves and mincemeat, pistachio nuts and sweet, sweet coffee served with pastry soaked in honey.

They spent several days in Latakia. Mounir acted as tour guide when they roamed through the archaeological excavations just a little north of the city.

"A Urgarit king," Mounir said. "He became very jealous of his scholars. They knew too much, so he had them all killed. Then he burned their libraries. This was before Christ. See. The scorched walls. But books were made of clay then, so instead of being destroyed, they are still here, today."

Cass smiled at him. Mounir, in his polished Italian shoes, was picking his way over the rubble, flirting innocently with her as Foster looked on, bemused.

In the evenings they went to a nightclub called The Blue Beach to listen to American music played with a decidedly Nubian flavor, Jimi Hendrix on camelback. They nursed their full bellies after the meals prepared by Mrs. Najaime, but they were eager to go again. The winter sun had them running south. The day that Mounir and his Father returned to the border with a satchel full of baksheesh, Cass and Foster left for Damascus.

The road stretched out before them dull as burlap. The landscape was unyielding and the light relentless. Dark slim men wore checkered keffeyehs to keep the sun from frying their brains and shielded their eyes from the wrinkles that came just the same.

They did not squint at the sun in the Middle East. They looked up and under it. To those who did not trust the Arabs, the habit was something sinister. To Cass, who had been there, it was a lesson of survival.

# EIGHT

Damascus was a madhouse. Cobblestones rang with the sounds of wooden flutes and skin drums, of babes wailing for nourishment, brassworkers hammering, and goats' milk squirting into metal buckets. Traffic was held up for miles as thousands upon thousands of lambs were driven into the abattoirs for slaughter. It was the feast of the hadj, the killing of the lamb in commemoration of Mohammed's pilgrimage to Mecca.

The sheep bleated and baaed and broke free of their shepherds only to be herded back by angry businessmen and threadbare children. Chickens and honking geese strutted across the thoroughfares. Foster gripped the steering wheel with a wild look in his eye.

All the big hotels were full, and the smaller inns were packed six people to a room. Cass and Foster fought for lodgings, and the bargaining grew heavy. Foster backed out of the discussions when he realized his bad temper only produced resistance in the hotel proprietors. His eyes glazed over. Cass joined the fray.

At the counter, she was trying to be charming as Arab men jostled her back and forth, anxious as she was to get accommodations. The talking had been going on for some time when suddenly Cass leapt in the air, her eyes big as headlights. Foster burst into peals of laughter and after a respectful silence, so did the Arab men. A chicken pecked furiously at Cass' boot.

"Would somebody get this Goddamned bird off me! Oh, you think it's funny!" she said, trying not to smile. The chicken went flying like a football across the room. Feathers falling, bird clucking . . .

"Well, there goes dinner," Foster said.

"Listen," Cass said, twisting back toward the manager. "Do we get a room or not?"

"Ya, Habib," the manager called out. "Take this lady and her gentleman here to Sister Mary Teresa's." He scribbled down the address. "Madam, we are very sorry, but if you stayed here tonight you would be the only woman among two hundred men. That might be strange, no?"

"Strange, right."

"Strange, oh yes," Foster said regaining control of the laughter that was bringing tears to his eyes. The chicken was still flapping around the room with three Arabs in pursuit. The anger pent up during the day was quickly giving way to exhaustion.

Cass and Foster followed the hotel manager's son to the Catholic Mission nearby. They bedded down for the night on the floor. Foster slept on one side of the stone courtyard, surrounded by young boys all tucked in their blankets. Cass slept on the other side, miserably alone, curled up with her back against the vestry wall, her privacy ensured by a linen curtain hung over a hemp line. All was quiet.

Cass fretted and turned and twisted in her bedding, then stuck her head out from beneath the linen drape.

Foster was grinning at her from across the way. He made the sign of the cross, folded his hands together and looked skyward. Cass let the curtain drop.

# NINE

Snow was falling as they drove through the double ridge of Lebanese mountains, and at Jabal El Barouk the pines were shrouded in white.

Petite Jaune chugged on. The heater on the Renault had broken down long ago; as Foster drove, Cass clapped her hands together again and again. The vapor of their breath clouded the windshield.

The climate warmed as they approached Beirut. They swung down out of the hills and descended along Rue De Damas, the green line that still divided the city into Christian and Moslem enclaves. There was not a building untouched by bullets nor a block unmarked by the pox of war, scabs of melted plastic, bones of misshapen steel, concrete skin torn back and open spaces where washing hung in the winter rain.

Foster pulled over and stopped the car. A precarious peace whispered from the blown-out windows.

"Quiet now, isn't it?"

"Like a graveyard," Foster said, stepping out to take some photographs. "I saw it on television, but I never would have believed it."

Cass sat in the car, tapping her fingers on the lid

of her typewriter case. She had turned out thousands and thousands of words on that machine about Beirut, but still she didn't understand it. Foster never would.

Hatreds smouldering for years, injustices both economic and religious had bubbled to the surface in Lebanon in blisters of wrath, in sniping incidents, in kidnappings and wholesale destruction. Moslems and Christians leapt at each other's throats with abhorrent zeal while the sovereignty of Lebanon crashed about their ears. The Lebanese army splintered. Its factions picked up their weapons and joined sides.

There was no force but the force of the private militias, and one of the most abrasive and tenacious of these armies was Palestinian.

Expelled from their military bases in Syria and Jordan, the Palestinians had taken hold in Lebanon, only a stretch of barbed wire from their coveted homeland to the south. Lebanese Moslems had turned to the Palestinians, their fellow Moslems, to help throw off what they considered was the yoke of the Christian overlords.

Battles had raged in the streets. The hills had thundered with artillery. Neighborhoods were flattened, hotels and offices sacked. Then the rest of the Arab world had thrown their purses on the table and hired a peacekeeping force, some thirty thousand in strength, and predominantly Syrian in origin.

In 1976 the Syrians had marched on Lebanon from Damascus, from the mountain ridges, from the coastal highway, and insinuated themselves between the Moslems and Christians. The Christians at that time were nearly exhausted, their backs against the walls of their traditional mountain strongholds.

The Syrians rumbled through the streets in tanks and beat back the Palestinians, struck out with iron fists at all who broke the thin veneer of peace they offered, and the smoke began to clear. Half a million homeless stalked the streets, buried their dead and set up shanty villages. It was a city that had once been known as the Paris of the Middle East.

The Christians had hailed the Syrian intervention, but now, fifteen months later, as Cass and Foster drove into Beirut the veneer was cracking. The Christians were bridling. Their saviors were now considered an invading army of Moslem strength, and the Christians were stockpiling weapons. "Let's put Lebanon back into the hands of the Lebanese!" was the rallying cry. The Lebanese government, an invisible authority, held onto the peacekeeping troops as its only hired police force.

The Palestinians were biding their time, embroiled in their own lethal game with the Israelis to the south.

Somewhere in the middle were the small militias — Christian, Moslem, Armenian, Druze, rightists, leftist — all with their prospective warlords, all with their domains to patrol and protect. It was anarchy in general, fiefdoms in the specific, with no central authority that commanded respect. The children who survived hummed funeral dirges. Tears fell like spent cartridges.

Cass and Foster had not planned to stay long in

Beirut, but within a few days of their arrival all hell broke loose again.

Kodak found them in the streets, and welcomed Cass back to Beirut with a bearhug worthy of a man past forty but still full of piss and vinegar.

"Morgan!" he said, "they're shooting up Ashrafiyeh."

"Ah Christ, Kodak. You always know where to find it."

"How close?" Foster said.

"Oh, a few miles that way. The Christian section."

"Little firefight?" Cass asked.

"A bloody civil war!" Kodak said.

"Bullshit," Cass replied.

"Firefight," Kodak said. "Come on." He herded them up the stairs and into Lord Kitchener's Pub. It didn't take him long to start in.

"Listen, Cass, the Australian Broadcasting Company, you know—the other ABC—wants an on-camera correspondent just for a few stories. Front-page stuff, you know. You'd do me a hell of a favor if you'd get into it. I've been feeding 'em film for years, but we could put some nice stuff together and make some money besides."

"Sure, Kodak, whatever you say. I could keep the *Washington Herald* happy at the same time."

"Hey, wait a minute," Foster said, spilling his drink on the bar. "I thought you were through chasing fire engines."

"My boy," said Kodak, ordering another round of drinks, "this lady will never stop chasing fire engines. She's just like Sally, my girl. A stewardess for Saudia Airlines. They're both hardheaded. They'd rather spend their weekends pinned down at the airport under artillery fire, than under the covers in a fourposter bed." Kodak chuckled.

"Hey, Cassie," Foster said.

"Eh, Foster, come on. Just for a little while. The story's hot. It's breaking now. We might make enough to get right round the world, okay?"

"Oh, Christ, here we go again. Living with a Goddamned workaholic."

"Foster," she laughed. "I'm a newswoman. You know that."

"Deft mind. Deaf ears," Kodak chimed in. Foster winced. He put his elbow on the bar and felt the spilled drink penetrate. He glared at the bartender.

"Cassie. You're a woman, a nice, soft, wonderful woman. I'd like to keep you in one piece."

"She's all right, Foster. She's got a survivor's instinct, but you know what they say in the Middle East—if a bullet—"

"—Has your name on it," Cass filled in the chorus, "you're done for. It's good-bye, Ol' Paint."

"Charming," Foster replied to the two of them. Kodak and Cass were grinning.

"And what am I supposed to do while you're playing Hopalong Cassidy? Roll bandages? Sit tight while you risk your neck?"

"Foster," Cass said quietly. "Not going to risk this neck. It's been with me all my life. Good friend, too."

"You'll find something to do," Kodak chimed in. "Lots of young ladies at American University who want to learn English. Lots of businesses blooming amidst the rubble. What would you prefer: computers banking, airlines, advertising?''

"I'd prefer my woman."

"You've got her," Cass said. "Just let me stomp out a little of this energy. The story's here, it's a natural."

"There'll be hell to pay if you don't, my man," said Kodak. "I've seen her in this crazed, frenzied, adrenaline state before. Beware getting in the way of a woman and her work."

"Yeah, yeah," Foster said.

Cass was staring at Kodak.

"Just save a little of that energy for me, will you Cass?"

"You got it, Foster."

But as the days passed, Foster paled in her limelight. The Fayadieh Barracks incident of February, 1978, was the first round of deadly bouts between the Syrian Peacekeeping Forces and the Christians. She was wired all the time. The days stretched into weeks.

As she turned the key to the door, Foster flung it open and stood before her, his broad shoulders filling the threshold, his handsome head thrown back so that the cords in his neck stood out. His green eyes caught hers and he pulled her inside.

"When are you going to take a break, Morgan?"

"When the story dies down. Come on, Foster, I'm just doing my job. I like it."

"Reporters. You're all maniacs. You go out there and duck bullets and scare the hell out of everyone who loves you. You'd work for nothing, 24 hours a day. You're driving yourself into the ground."

"I'm not. I'm fine. Happy, even. What can I do? I take a break. We steal a swim, a run on the beach, and boom . . . another bomb goes off. It's a story, Foster. Somebody out there is killing somebody else, and I've got to figure out why. I've got to."

"And what about me, when you're not here? Am I supposed to chew my fingernails?"

"I don't know, Foster."

"I think we should get out of here, now, before you get completely sucked into this place. Either that or go to bed with your typewriter, your telex machine. Don't be looking for me to wait around."

"Foster, I love you. I'm a newswoman, that's all. You knew that before. I haven't worked in half a year, and here's a story tailor-made. We're here, it's here. Would you be happier if I were a waitress?"

"Yes."

"Jesus Christ, Foster."

He shoved his hands in his pockets and looked down at the floor.

"I'm just frustrated, you know. I miss you, that's all, and I can't understand you putting yourself on the line for a Goddamned newspaper story."

"Aw, Foster."

"Have you got time for dinner?"

"I've got all night and tomorrow, too, if everyone would just settle down."

He held her then for a long time, and she felt herself melting into him, into his strength and his stubborness. Her fingers played over his body. They lit candles and drank wine and lolled on the bed and talked about India, the best part of the trip to come.

Kodak's driver knocked on the door. The Israeli invasion of Southern Lebanon had begun. Israeli fighter bombers were aloft. The Israeli battalions

were rolling in, blowing Palestinian bulwarks
sky-high with long-range artillery. Predicted for
days, the invasion was retaliation for an horrific
Palestinian terrorist attack on the Tel Aviv-Haifa
Road.

Cass, still wet from their lovemaking, pulled her
clothes on. Foster quietly helped her into her
khaki jacket. He started to say something and
stopped himself. The decision was already made.

"You look like a soldier," Foster said quietly to
Cass.

"An observer," she corrected soberly. He held
her hand briefly, without saying another word,
then grabbed her and pressed her against him.
Her backbone cracked, all her vertebrae fell into
place, then she was gone.

Foster sat on the edge of the bed. He was bare to
the waist. The muscles of his stomach contracted
as he drew long and hard on the cigarette. Beirut
was deathly quiet. The fighting was all to the
south. The candle by the bed cast his shadow on
the wall and he looked at it with disgust.

He blew out the candle, threw on his jacket and
hit the streets, determined to find a woman.

# TEN

Cass spent several days in a Red Cross bunker in Tyre as Israeli airstrikes and gunboat shelling pounded the shoreline. Hits on ammunition dumps lit up the dawn sky. The cries of the wounded could be heard sometimes during the lulls in the shelling.

"*Déja vu*," Kodak said.

"Yeah, the civil war, only worse. Bombers. Jesus. What are we doing here?"

"Bringing it all back home," Kodak said without much enthusiasm.

"What's that?" Cass said. The morning light was playing tricks maybe.

Kodak spun his lense and focused.

"Hey, François!" he called out to the Red Cross medic.

"What have you got?" the medic called.

"Looks like he's wounded," Kodak said, focusing on an old man on the beach.

"Yeah, or shell shocked." Cass said.

François disappeared for a moment. Cass was on her feet as the old man stumbled and fell on the beach, picked himself up, stumbled again. The Red Cross medic unfurled the flag of his organization. Kodak, Cass, and another correspondent grabbed the corners of the banner and ran as bombers screamed overhead.

The pilots held their payloads at the display of the Red Cross.

The wounded man was muttering about Allah and about his wife. It took some coaxing to get him onto the stretcher. A shrapnel wound had bared the bone of his right shoulder. They ran with him in a stretcher as a 120-millimeter shell thudded into the hillside and sent trees, rocks and human flesh a hundred feet in the air.

Incoming. Outgoing. Cluster bombs. Phosphorus shells. Tracers. Katyushas. It was like a chant. Cass and Kodak swore they could write a song about it, but didn't. Taps would suffice.

# ELEVEN

"Give me two," Foster said and slapped the cards on the green baize tablecloth that lay over one of the desks in the A.P. Bureau.

Farouk scratched his chin. Chuck Vazcatchian and Andrew Pym just watched through the miasma of cigar smoke, awaiting their turns. George, the A.P. Bureau chief, was fidgeting in his chair, uncomfortable as always when away from the typewriter.

The doors to the wire rooms were closed but the machines clattered away.

"Come on, Farouk," George said. "You in or you out?"

"I'll see you and raise you twenty," he said, tossing more Lebanese pounds into the pot. Chuck Vazcatchian's eyes lit up. Foster cackled.

"Poker face, Vaz, poker face, now!"

"My dear," he chortled, "there, and raise you thirty."

Foster leaned back in the chair and pulled hard on his cigar, sending a trail of blue smoke skyward. Andrew Pym, looking fragile after a three-day binge, threw down his cards.

"I'm out."

"I'm out, too," George said.

"Sure you can afford this?" Farouk asked,

peering over at Foster as he threw double the money in the pot.

"You are looking at a fairly successful advertising executive, sir," said Foster.

"You mean that Kuwaiti rag of a magazine actually pays you money?"

"Greenbacks. The best kind," Foster said. "Will you accept four Lebs to one dollar?"

"What's the going rate, Pym?"

"Oh come on, Farouk. Pennies."

"All right. I'll be magnanimous," Farouk smiled. The American money sweetened the pot.

Chuck Vazcatchian sighed and rested his hand on his belly. Then he raised it fifty.

George whistled and Pym leaned forward, peering myopically through his bloodshot eyes.

"You going to take Cass out to dinner if you win this?" Chuck said.

"Maybe," Foster said.

"You may win at poker, but you'll lose your woman if you're not careful!"

"Don't intrude, Vaz."

"She loves you a great deal."

"Is that what she tells you?" Foster said.

"You are trying to make her jealous, eh? The wine glasses. The cigarette butts with lipstick stains. That little cunt from the club. What's the matter? You feel your masculinity threatened?"

"Cass loves war, not me. She's reckless."

"Don't be a fool."

"Foster, you've got rocks in your head," George said. "She's a great gal. You're the one who's being restless."

"We playing poker or what?" Foster said. The muscles in his face had tightened. He spit out a piece of tobacco.

Farouk sighed and fingered his cards.

Outside the office, Kodak and Cass were coming up the stairs. They were both feeling dejected. There was a lot of blood on the sidewalk over in the Christian part of town. The Syrians were getting nasty, and the Christians weren't making things any easier. A Christian hit squad had knocked out five Syrian sentries the night before; now the Christians were eating mortars for breakfast.

It wasn't a story any more. Too many things were going on in the rest of the world. Cass and Kodak were both weary of it as they rounded the last turn. Cass had been running the sound for Kodak's camera, so they were still attached by the umbilical cord of an audio jack and wire. The strap on the tape recorder was cutting into Cass' shoulder, but she didn't seem to notice. Her thoughts were far away.

Kodak brought her home. "He's not worth fighting for, you know."

"Horseshit," she said. "If he isn't, what is? God, flag, country?"

"He's not good enough."

"How the hell do you know?"

"Hey."

"What's with this big-brother stuff, anyway, Kodak? This place stinks, and you know it. Drives everybody nuts. If it isn't the Israelis, it's the Pals. If it isn't the Pals, it's the Syrians and the Christians. If it isn't—"

"Well, if it isn't the Armenians," Kodak said loudly, opening the door. Chuck Vazcatchian snapped to attention, dropping his cards to below table level.

"The scourge of the press corps arrives," Vaz said, relaxing.

"Not you, Cassie, that lout you walked in with," Andrew added.

She leaned against the doorjamb. Kodak kept walking and felt the tug on the audio cord. She yanked the plug, coiled the wire, and tied it against the leather strap. Kodak swung his camera to the floor. Foster tilted back in his chair and gave Kodak a show of his cards.

Kodak folded his arms and peered intently at Farouk.

"Well, has he got a hand?"

"Wouldn't you like to know." Kodak snorted and searched the room with his eyes.

"Cig?"

"Here," George said, tossing him a pack of Winstons. "Well?"

"You had it right, George. No firefight. Syrian mortars. No return fire yet from the Phalangists."

"Playing it like martyrs for the moment," Cass murmured.

"See you and raise you fifty, Farouk!"

"Cass, your man here seems to think he's got a good hand."

"He's got great hands, Farouk," she said, without much enthusiasm. Foster turned toward her and caught her gaze, steadily. She dropped her eyes to the floor. Some blood and hair was stuck to her shoe. She wiped it again and again on the mat.

"Whose blood is this, anyway?" she said to herself. The sidewalk had been sticky with it. Red blood just turning black. Purplish in the sun. Black as tar where it congealed.

"You in?" Farouk asked.

Foster could not take his eyes off Cass. She looked dishevelled, only half there. Not pretty anymore. Beaten, pale.

"Call me or raise me," Farouk said. "Vaz is out."

"Right," Foster said swiveling back to the table. Before he could raise, there was a deafening explosion a city block away. The blast shook the windows.

Cass took a flying dive over George's desk. Kodak was down beside her. George had rolled under Farouk's desk. Vaz and Pym were already moving.

"Jesus fucking Christ!" Foster said rising out of his chair, standing at full height. "It only happens when I've got—"

"Don't throw them in, stupid," Farouk said tugging at his trousers. "Down here."

"Call you," Foster said, banging his head on the desk top. "Jesus fucking Christ!"

"Let's see," Farouk said. "Three tens. You bet all that on three tens?"

Foster looked startled. "You mean you beat me?"

A shower of metal bits hit the tin roof and bounced off.

"Hell no," Farouk said. Foster laughed out loud, unfolded himself from beneath the desk, and started collecting the money.

"Foster, for Christ's sake," Cass called. "Get down."

"No more bang-bang," he said. "Bang-bang's finished."

"Get down, Foster!" Kodak ordered.

Foster marched over to the desk where Cass and

Kodak were crouching. "Come on, you," he said, grabbing Cass' hand and literally lifting her over the desk. She resisted, and he pulled harder, nearly wrenching her arm.

"Whoa, whoa," she said.

"It's okay," George said, checking out the debris that lay in the street. "A bomb, probably. Not mortar. Time device. Vaz?"

"Yeh, a hit probably," Vaz said lifting his bulk to the window, ready to recoil in a flash. People in neighboring buildings stuck their heads out. In a moment, they'd be in the street.

Foster was dragging Cass across the floor.

"Stop it, Foster!"

Foster flung open the doors to the wire room and swung her into the chair. "Get Joe, your editor. Tell him you quit."

"Foster, I—"

"Now! I'm leaving. We're going East. Well, I'm going East anyway. I love you, but this hellhole is driving me berserk. You, too. Look at you."

"You've been fighting dirty," she said rising out of the chair.

"You're damn right I have. Fighting any way I can." He shoved her back in the chair. "Telex," he said.

She rose again and tried to get away from him, but he grabbed her, flung her back in the chair and wrapped his arms over her chest. "Type, Goddamn it. I love you."

"Goddamn it, I love you," she banged out on the telex machine.

Foster cuffed her on the shoulder. "No. Joe, your editor. These words. Joe, take your fucking newspaper and shove it!"

"He's going to love it, Cassie. Shortest lead you'll ever write."

"Deserves it," George said looking up from the typewriter. "They all deserve it. Damn editors don't know a bright line from a bromide." He lit another Winston and let it dangle Bogart style. "We'll miss you, Cass, but you'll be a better woman for it!"

"Oh really," Cass said turning away from the telex. "This is fine, just fine. The Boys' Club here is deciding my life for me."

"That's 'cause you're too dumb to decide it for yourself." Foster barked.

Cass stood up. Foster shoved her down.

"Type," he said.

"Barefoot and pregnant, Cassie. Nothing like it really."

"And how would you know, Pym? God damn it, Foster." She could not wriggle out of his grip.

"Join the P.T.A. Raise a family." Kodak was laughing his ass off.

"Kodak, will you shut the—Oh, never mind!" She spun back to the telex and banged it out.

Beirut to Washington via Telex
Washington Herald
Attn Taylor
Pls place foner to me at buro your earliest convenience.
Morgan
NNNN

"He won't even be in the office yet," Cass said, looking at her watch. "An hour."

"Cocktail hour." Kodak lifted a bottle of Johnny

Walker out of the film cabinet. Vaz was already on his way to the pantry to get ice.

"Doesn't anyone care if anyone was killed down there, down the street?" George asked. Everyone stopped what they were doing and glared at George. He hung up the phone.

"No, I didn't think so," he said. "Well, no dead. Minor injuries. Not even worth a graph. Uh, three fingers for me, eh, Kodak? Let's not be stingy."

"Make mine a double," Foster called out.

"You'll need it," Kodak yelled. "Don't know how you'll keep that girl tied down."

"Like this, eh, Morgan?" He pulled her head back by the hair and kissed her squarely on the lips. Her own lingered there, then she bit down on his lips. He kissed her harder, tasting blood.

Vaz twiddled his thumbs. Andrew stood quietly and watched. Kodak marched up to them with their drinks.

"Listen, you're making me horny. Anyone for a threesome?"

# TWELVE

Tripoli was tranquil. Somehow or another with the tendrilling of vines, the bullet holes had become the hieroglyphics of a glorious if not violent past, obscure and valuable in the mesh of greenery. The Mediterranean sparkled. Sapphire coves dazzled them, and they halted Petite Jaune by the side of the road and dove in. They sipped wine and let the sun dry their hair. They were feeling whole and at peace on the cool, bright pebbles of the beach.

L'Aiglon, Chuck Vazcatchian's farm in the mountains, was not far away. Petite Jaune pressed onward. She had had a patch-welding job on her exhaust pipe, so she no longer sounded like a tank.

Grape vines curled and flourished on their stakes. Tomatoes just taking on the blush of pink peeked out from beneath the lush and fragrant leaves. Onion stalks grew leggy and lazy as the June sun meandered across the sky.

When they arrived, Chuck Vazcatchian waved them into the barn. Foster switched off the ignition, and Petite Jaune gave a final kick before she quit.

As Cass and Foster walked into Vaz's voluminous embrace, Ingrid skipped down the stairs of the porch.

"Welcome, welcome," she cried. Ingrid was big, bony, and blond with galaxies of freckles across her cheeks and nose. She was nearly forty years of age but bucking every wrinkle of it.

Ingrid had met Vaz in Beirut when the neon of Phoenecia Street sparkled like champagne. She had grown up on a farm in Sweden. Her brother had taken off to join the U.N. Peacekeeping Forces in Cyprus. With a burst of wanderlust she had left home too, venturing into the heat of the levantine sun.

Vaz had fallen in love with her the moment he had set eyes on her. Despite some consternation among the elders of his family, he had married Ingrid in the village church at Becharre. The whole town came. And then the civil war cut through their lives like a thresher through a field of wheat. Indiscriminately the blades passed through the mountain towns, the Beirut suburbs, then the heart of the city was cut in two. Vaz lost his sister and his father, and stashed Ingrid away in a Druze community where she learned to handle a rifle and run a dispensary for the wounded. Vaz took on the job of bodyguard to the ultra-right-wing leader of Lebanon, the man most loved, most feared, most hated — Camille Chamoun. Chamoun invited attacks. Vaz laid them to waste.

Now the velocity of his life had slowed. The civil war was over. Becharre in the mountains east of Tripoli was his piece of peace. The spire of the village church commanded the view from the eastern side of the house, standing tall and dark against the reddened stone of the hills. Cedars and olive trees offered some shade from the summer sun and the house itself was cool, made of rough stones, held together by concrete. L'Aiglon included eighteen acres of clear pasture, a vegetable garden and, where the property sloped up to the mountains, grape arbors. The irrigation ditches that ran between the rows of vines were fed by a mountain stream.

Foster and Cass dropped their bundles on the porch and ran for the stable. Foster reached the paddock fence first and screeched to a halt, far as he'd go. Ingrid chased after them while Vazcatchian sat on the porch steps, just watching.

First Cass, then Ingrid, bolted over the fence whooping and swinging their arms at Varmint, the stallion, who was getting cantankerous in his celibacy. They were trying to get the kick out of him. He snorted and stomped, twirling one way and then the other. His eyes were wild but not mean.

He trotted over to Ingrid and bowed his head for a scratch behind the ears. Cass came by and rubbed her hands down his neck and then his legs, calming him down.

"Good old boy," Cass murmured.

"Oh, don't say old," Ingrid said. "Gets him very upset. See. There's some play in the old boy yet." Ingrid pointed toward his hindquarters.

"Horny bastard, eh?" Foster called from the fence. "Watch it, ladies. Remember Catherine the Great."

"Yeah, what a way to go," Ingrid yelled.

"You going to let me ride this thing?"

"Hey, my guest."

"Leg up?"

"Okay, but no promises without reins." On the count of three Ingrid hoisted Cass onto Varmint's back. The stallion broke and ran to one side of the paddock, then whirled again, raising ever so slightly on his hind legs. Cass wound her fingers through his mane and hung on.

Foster's mouth dropped open. Horses scared the hell out of him. Ingrid was dodging back and forth in the paddock as Varmint skittered forward.

"Bumpy ride, eh?" Cass was just beginning to think she knew what he was doing.

Ingrid yelled, "Cass, I forgot to tell you, he's got a habit of—"

Varmint took eight paces into a gallop, stopped short and bucked, not straight up and down, but up and with a dance to the side. Cass felt herself going. One last kick of his heels and the ground came up and slapped Cass in the face.

Foster grabbed the fence rail. Cass picked herself up, brushed herself off, laughing so hard there were tears in her eyes. She spat out some dust and shook her fist at Varmint. He gave her a jaundiced eye.

"My turn," Ingrid said. Varmint rocked back and forth, then threw his head and trotted toward them.

"Up you go," then Ingrid was up on his back. Vaz was on his feet now, running toward the paddock.

"That's my girl," he said, poking Foster in the shoulder.

"What do you think, huh? Let's get out of here before they find out what a coward I am. No cowboy here."

"Oh, Varmint just looks tough. Ingrid's been handling him for years now. Like a baby. He likes to have a good time, that's all."

"Too many teeth. Too many hooves. Later. I'll learn on a dime-store hobby horse."

"Come on," Vaz said clapping his big hand on Foster's shoulder. They walked up to the headland to survey the sweep of L'Aiglon, the stand of cedars to the east, the sea to the west. An eagle flew at eye level, then glided away on a thermal that rose from the sun-baked rocks to the mountain peaks.

Vaz squatted down on his haunches. Foster did the same thing, and as he did so caught the blur of movement in the pasture below. He heard the laughter of the women rise and bounce from rock to rock.

"They are happy," Vaz said. "They are content."

"Happy maybe," Foster said. "Ingrid maybe, but Cass is never content."

Vaz looked at him. "I knew Cass long before you did. I knew her when the only thing she had to look forward to was another rotten telex. Another story. Now she cares about something. Don't underrate yourself. She's a strange girl. Much too strong sometimes. Too willful. She'll get herself in trouble, I think; then I see her smile. No more danger. No more trouble. You must hold her tightly beneath you like a fine mare."

Foster sighed and slapped his thigh.

"I think I'll marry her."

Vaz rose to his feet. "That's the most sensible thing I've heard you say in weeks."

"Wait a minute. I didn't say right away exactly. I mean, you know she's still pretty pissed off at me for the . . . ."

"Little doll with the slim hips."

"Yeah."

"Too skinny for me. Like fucking a chicken."

Foster cocked his head to retort, but found himself doubled over with laughter. "You're right, a chicken with pretty feathers. A wishbone to break over Cass' head."

"I don't know how she forgave you."

"She loves me," Foster said.

Vaz eyed him skeptically.

"Yeah, well, I denied it."

Vaz burst into laughter.

# THIRTEEN

Rain. Rain dripping through the windows of the Renault Four. Foster, alert, watching the road through the slash of wiper blades. Jumping out at the last Lebanese checkpoint. Prayer beads no longer clicking, rubber stamps no longer stamping, astonished Arabs watched two Americans dancing in the rain, sloshing through the puddles celebrating their freedom from the Lebanon, sipping Vazcatchian wine and singing "She's a grand old flag" reggae style.

The rain was still falling when they reached Latakia, two hours later. They stayed in the Helwa Hotel, which translates to "beautiful" hotel, resplendent with unfinished concrete, rust-colored stucco walls and bare mattress ticking. The sheets cost extra.

"Hum," Foster said as he sat on the bed. An errant spring made him shift his weight.

"Come here, baby," he said.

Cass was pacing the ten-by-ten-foot room, running her fingers through her hair.

"Come here." He patted the mattress, hoping nothing would spring away from his hand like . . . crabs. The room was clean, spartan. It smelled of lime, as if they'd just taken the victims away.

"Come here, Cassie."

"Aren't you hungry?"

"Yeah, hungry for you. Come here, will you?"

"Ah, Foster, come on. I could eat a horse right now."

"Well," he said, bouncing off the bed, "that's probably just what we'll get in this town. Blue-plate special." He hooked his arm under hers. His lips brushed against her hair.

"Race?" She broke free and clattered down the hotel stairs. She emerged onto the street, into a fine spit of rain. Droplets clung to her hair and the shoulders of her Air Force jacket. Foster jostled her goodnaturedly and they linked arms again, collaring the first Arab boy to walk by, asking him directions to the nearest restaurant.

They followed his lead to the Namoni Casino, a big, brightly lit place that had nothing to do with gambling. Fair food, fair prices, an old jukebox, and a fluorescent light.

They sat down on the steel and vinyl chairs and ordered a hot dinner as Om Khaltuum belted one of her songs from the jukebox. She was considered by many to be the greatest Arab singer who ever lived. Her vocal cords took on the same timbre as the skin drums that pulsated behind the melody. She always sang high and repetitively in classical Arabic, her tones sometimes sweet, sometimes raspy, but always sensual.

"Be glad to get away from that caterwauling," Foster said.

"I was thinking just the opposite," Cass said. "Kind of grows on you." A young man sitting at another table caught her eye. She looked away.

"I could use a little rock 'n' roll, right now,"

Foster said. Om Khaltuum was fading away. The
jukebox sucked one disc out and dropped another
in its place. Doobie Brothers, "China Grove." Like
sailing down a wind tunnel.

"Not a moment too soon," Foster said. The
young man across the way waved to him.

"Friend of yours?" Cass asked.

"Sure," Foster said. He was bringing a forkful
of rice to his mouth. The man's two young
companions began slapping each other, then
looked in their direction. Cass dropped her eyes to
her plate.

"Sure are putting on a show."

"I think we're the show," Foster said looking
around. He smiled as if it were his duty, then
shoved his plate forward. "That's enough for me.
How about The Blue Beach? Entertainment? Live
music? Amerikani?"

"Sounds good." Cass began to rise from her
chair, but the waiter stood beside her with a dish
of fruit in one hand, pistachio nuts in the other.

"What's this?" Foster asked.

"The boys. Moustafa Sheik and his friends
would like to give you these things to finish your
meal. Arab hospitality."

Cass groaned. "Arab hospitality."

"Oh God, here we go again!" Foster turned to
the three young men and shook his head. He made
to get up, but the waiter stayed him.

"They will be insulted if you say 'no.' You are
visitors here. This is a welcome."

"Yes, yes, I know. We've been through this
before."

Cass bowed in the direction of the young men
and said 'thank you' in Arabic. The three boys

stood up and pulled their chairs over to Foster's table. Foster stood and shook hands all around. Cass did the same thing. It seemed to surprise them.

Two of them spoke English quite well, and within a moment they'd asked all the questions. "Where are you from? What are you doing here? Do you like my country? Where are you going now? What is happening in Beirut?"

Moustafa Sheik, obviously the leader, thumped a bottle of arak on the table and poured out glass-fuls. He then sloshed water in the glasses and watched as the liquid grew milky. A gold tooth flashed. He caught Cass' eye, but she avoided his direct look.

He had an interesting face. Lean. Hollow at the cheeks. His hair was long, very long for a Syrian, and he moved in close, fast. The booze was already showing, but Foster and Cass were curious, tolerant. It was refreshing to see Syrians in blue jeans, instead of drab green fatigues, holding wine glasses instead of grenades, talking about rock 'n' roll rather than trajectory of fire.

They were boys really, past draft age, but younger than Cass. They'd probably bought their way out of the military, she thought. Nahass wore a gold chain and amulet around his neck. There was no hair on his chest, and his shirt was open two buttons from the top. Very European.

Mohammed was a little scratchier than his companions. A fine tuft of a beard grew on his chin. His eyes were half-closed from the arak, but they seemed to glint with recognition as his glance slid from side to side.

Cass tried to catch their swiftly spoken Arabic,

but the dialect was thick and she only caught a few phrases clearly. Foster was more interested in satisfying his belly then listening to the boasting of Moustafa Sheik and his *droogs*, but Cass was getting antsy. She tapped Foster's knee under the table. He got the message and rose. Sheik rose with him, almost shoulder to shoulder, and Foster frowned.

"Thank you very much for your hospitality, but we must be going. Please excuse us." He made great pains to help Cass on with her jacket. "And good night."

Mohammed lurched to his feet, banging the table and knocking over some glasses. A waiter rushed forward, but Sheik commanded him to remain where he was.

"Good night," Cass said, and spun away from them all. She and Foster walked arm in arm to the cashier to pay the bill, but Sheik was aleady there, snatching the bill from Foster's hand.

"No, no," Foster said adamantly. "That won't be necessary."

The cashier froze as Foster snatched the bill back and it was torn in two. Sheik was shoving money at him. Foster was posturing. Cass squeezed his arm.

"Don't fight. Don't fight, Foster. It's a no-win proposition."

Foster and Moustafa Sheik pressed against each other, each trying to pay. Cass felt a flush of heat rise to her face. Claustrophobia was setting in.

"Let's get out of here," Cass said. Sheik threw the Syrian money back at Foster.

"Okay, okay, buddy. Thanks a lot and good night." They broke free and hit the streets with a rush, but the three Arab youths soon closed around them, laughing, giggling, talking about having a cup of coffee, a pastry or something.

"Arab hospitality. Arab hospitality. You are visitors to our town. We must take care of you."

Cass and Foster dove into their car, and the three tried to get in, but Foster locked the doors.

"Not this time, friends. We are tired. We want to be alone, okay? Understand?" He revved up the engine and jammed it into gear.

Sheik was laughing in an ugly way when they pulled away from the sidewalk.

"Back to the hotel."

"Fuck, no," Foster said peering into the rear view mirror. "I'm ready to fight a bull, or dance up a storm. You game?"

"I . . . uh . . . ." She swiveled around.

"Ah, don't worry about those guys. Three spoiled brats on a lark with a big bank roll. Showing off, that's all."

"Yeah. Creepy though."

"Just fuckin' Arabs."

"Right," Cass said, and clamped her hand on his knee joint, pressing hard with her fingertips. She never could make him flinch, but when he clamped the same vise on her knee, it sent her through the roof.

The band was playing "Hey Joe," Jimi Hendrix style, as they walked into The Blue Beach. The maitre d' led them to a table that looked out on the water. A candle shed a circle of light at their table. The place wasn't very crowded—a few military men and their wives and daughters, two couples hidden away at dark tables.

Ozid, the lead guitarist, launched into "Purple

Haze" as Cass and Foster sipped at their scotch and sodas.

As Foster leaned back in his chair, the candle-light caught the curve of his cheek and his proud chin. Cass moved closer to him and he threw his arm around her shoulders, smiling. As he turned to whisper in her ear, the waiter arrived with a bowl of pistachio nuts.

Foster looked up. "Oh, no," he said, "the three stooges are back."

"Oh, Christ," Cass said.

Moustafa Sheik plopped himself down at their table. Mohammed and Nahass joined them. Nahass turned his chair the wrong way round and sat cowboy style, leering over the candle at Cass.

"We really don't want you at our table," Cass said quietly but firmly in Arabic.

"I'm so sorry. I can't hear you," Sheik said. He snapped his fingers and the waiter arrived with a full bottle of Johnny Walker Black, a bowl of ice, and more fruit.

"Waiter. No, thank you," Foster said, holding his arm up to bar the way.

"Some problem, Mr. Sheik?" The waiter ignored the Americans.

"No, no, no," Sheik said sweetly. "They are unused to our customs, that's all." He cleared the way for the bottle. Nahass and Mohammed watched everything he did.

"Please, have your drink," Sheik said to Cass. "I like to look at you. You look pretty in the candle-light."

"Thanks very much," Foster said.

"That's very funny," Sheik said.

Foster had his hand on Cass' forearm.

"*Schweya, schweya,*" she whispered in his ear.
"Slowly, slowly." They sipped their drinks. Cass
could feel the hair prickling at the back of her
neck. She rose from the table, but Sheik grabbed
her hand. Foster leaned forward to stop him, but
Nahass held Foster's wrist.

"I'm going to the bathroom," Cass said coolly.
"Please excuse me." She broke Moustafa's grip by
twisting her wrist through the break between his
thumb and forefinger. He threw up his hands,
laughing.

"She is a strong woman. Pretty, too. You would
do well to watch out for her. In this country many
men would desire her. Oh, do not worry. Not I. We
are just . . . . We would like you to be our guests.
We do not like it when you say 'no.' That is an
insult. It means we are not good enough to take
care of you."

"You're taking fine care of us. Fine, fine,"
Foster said. "You are probably the most
obnoxious men I have ever met," he added smiling
politely.

"What is obnoxious?"

"It's a compliment where I come from."

"That's good, that's good," Sheik said, unsure
but relaxing in his chair. Mohammed got up from
the table quietly.

Cass was leaning over the washbasin in the
womens' room when Mohammed entered. Cass
watched him in the mirror. Her heart skipped.

"Uh, I think you've got the wrong . . ."

"I am just visiting," he said. "I have brought a
gift for you. A gift for a kiss."

"No, thanks," Cass said. He closed in on her and
laid a glassine packet on the sink. She twisted

away and yanked some towels out of the
dispenser, edging toward the door. He blocked her
abruptly with his leg.

"Just a taste," he said, "to make you feel so
much better. So much more friendly." He dug his
fingers hard into her upper arm.

"I don't want a taste," she said as he opened the
glassine envelope with his other hand.

He brought her up close against him, the fingertips of his left hand white with granules. He
rubbed his hard penis against her thigh and put
his hand to her face. She pulled away, and he
jerked her back toward him and tried to press his
mouth against hers. She swung round and
knocked the drugs to the floor, then grabbed the
small finger of his left hand and gave it a vicious
wrench backwards. He howled away, and she
broke free through the door.

She did not scream. Not in an Arab restaurant.
She rushed to the table and said, "Come on,
Foster. Let's go. *Now*."

"I'm with you," he said, throwing a fifty-pound
Syrian note on the table.

"Thanks for the hospitality." He shoved
Moustafa Sheik back in his seat. Nahass reached
for the front of Foster's shirt and Foster brushed
his knuckles across the young Arab's face. Sheik
was still smiling. He held onto his companion.
Mohammed was just coming back from the
women's room as Cass and Foster made their exit.

As the yellow Renault roared out of the parking
lot, Cass looked back to see a white Peugeot pull
up to the entrance. She saw the maitre d' stop
Sheik at the door; Sheik pushed by him and
jumped into the Peugeot.

"Bastards," Cass shouted, "Bastards." She thumped her fist against the palm of her hand.

"Take it easy, Morgan," Foster said. The head-light beams behind him cut crazily across the rear-view mirror. The lights went bright to dim, bright to dim, then double bright, searing into the back of Foster's head.

"Bastards," he said. "They're on us."

"Come on, Little Yellow," Cass said as she tapped the dashboard. "Come on, little Renault."

Foster leaned forward and drilled the accelerator into the floor. They were on the coastal road, one moment spinning on sand, the next catching the pavement again.

The Renault's four-horse engine whined. The Peugeot gained on them. Foster jammed on the brakes and spun to the left. The Peugeot skidded to the right, veering off on the shoulder, then Foster put the throttle to the floor again.

"They're drunk," he said. "That's an advantage."

"I wish I were," Cass said, pounding the back of the seat as she watched the Peugeot. "Stuck. They're stuck."

Foster swung the wheel to the left and cut down a side street.

"Nice little town, Latakia. Scummy little streets. Diesel fumes and soot. Half-built houses. Piles of brick and mud. Grimy, grungy . . . . Which way do we go?"

"There, there," Cass jabbed at the windshield. "To the right, round the circle."

"Why the fuck do they have to change direction every country we get to?" Foster yelled.

"There, on the right. Hurry. Lock the car. Up the

stairs. The hotel."

"Got the keys ready?"

"Yeah, come on," Cass shouted. She slammed the car door and took the first flight of hotel stairs two at a time. Foster followed soon after, caught up and passed her on the second landing. They got to the upper floor, where their room was, and found the outer door locked.

"God damn it," Foster said. He pounded on it. "He's locked it and gone to bed."

"Jesus Christ, he's probably gone to sleep," Cass said. She heard the footsteps on the stairs and banged louder.

"Wake up, wake up," she yelled in Arabic, but the proprietor of the hotel made no response.

"You better stay where you are," Foster said, pointing at Moustafa Sheik and his two companions. They were climbing past the first landing. Sheik's jaw tightened in a grin.

"Now, now," Sheik said. "We are just trying to be polite. Just trying to apologize for being so. . . ."

"Stay where you are."

Sheik took another step. Foster's form blocked the bare gleam of a light bulb.

"That's far enough."

Sheik kept coming, walking evenly up the stairs. He tapped Nahass, and Nahass and Mohammed both double-timed it up the last flight. Foster caught Mohammed's forward momentum and sent him sprawling against the far wall; Nahass leapt for Foster's throat.

Cass was still pounding on the hotel door when she felt Sheik's hand on her shoulder. She spun toward him, but he avoided her thrust and grabbed her shirt. She tore away and the material ripped in his hand. He lunged brutally for her breast. Foster dove for him and pummeled him to the ground.

Cass was up, trying to stop Nahass from helping Sheik. She struggled, kicking and flailing and making a racket, when the hotel door opened. Nahass hurled her against the door; she toppled the astounded hotel proprietor as she fell. They were both on the ground, tangled in the dark, listening to the sounds of scuffling boots and shouts. She raised herself to see Foster's face. Then she saw the knife, the blade slashing downward, then Foster's figure disappearing down the stairs, thundering after the three Arabs. Screaming at them. She was groggy, the bump already forming on her head, but she stumbled out to the landing There was blood on it. She raced down the stairs, propelling herself off the wall at every turn.

"Let them go," she called to Foster. "For Christ's sake, let them go, Foster."

Foster stood at the bottom. Blood ran down his forehead, over his shirt, down his pants to the floor. She could see the drops fall. Hear them. He climbed the stairs slowly, anciently.

Then she was in the street ankle deep in the mud that slopped down the gutter, yelling, "Shurti! Shurti! Police! Police!"

The police arrived ten minutes later when Foster was lying on the bed, shaking. She sat by him, trying to quiet him down, as she explained to the police what had happened.

The proprietor of the hotel was frantic when he saw the blood spattered over his clean sheets. He looked at the Americans accusingly.

"You cannot stay here," the police said. "Please gather your things. We will take you to the hospital, but then a new hotel. This boy, this Moustafa Sheik, he is a bad boy. He has done many bad things. You understand. We cannot guarantee your safety here."

"But what about the night's rent?" the proprietor said. "The sheets."

Cass jumped angrily to her feet and stuffed his hands full of bills. She nearly spit on him. The fat policeman watched her intently as she helped Foster to his feet. Foster was in shock. He wasn't responding correctly. The fat policeman held Foster lightly, then carried him down the stairs.

"A head wound," the doctor kept repeating to Cass. "Much blood."

She nodded and turned away as the doctor stitched up the wound. Seven stitches in the forehead. He looked so vulnerable there on the gurney with nurses around him. The big fat policeman took up much of the emergency room. Big, fat and gentle, tapping a rattan stick against his thigh.

It was the fat one, the sergeant, who showed them the mugshots on the wall. The Scotch tape that held them to the board was yellowed and peeling. The pictures were pitted with thumbtack marks, but Cass could single them out just the same.

"There, there . . . and I think that's, no, I'm sure that's Sheik. Mohammed and Nahass."

"Yes, Sheik. You are right. Bad boys only recently out of prison, on President Assad's election pardon. You are not to worry. They will be caught."

"And then what?" Foster asked. He adjusted the

bandage that now concealed his head.

"We will beat their feet with canes!"

"Wonderful," Foster muttered.

"Now we will find a new hotel, by the police station, so you will be protected. Missus Morgan, if you would park your car in the police compound it will be safer for you."

"All right."

"We are sorry about what happened," the sergeant said soberly. "It does not happen in my country. You were unlucky. They will be punished. Kept in prison for a long time. You must come back tomorrow to file formal charges."

Cass translated for Foster. He nodded.

When Petite Jaune was parked in the police lot and Cass had locked the hotel door behind her, Foster blurted, "Don't inspire a whole lot of confidence, do they?"

"God," Cass said sitting on the bed, then getting up nervously to take a turn around the floor. Foster sat stock still, listening to the sounds from the window.

"Jesus," Cass said looking into the sink. "Looks like they culture bubonic plague here."

"Yeah. Like the walls?" Foster said. "How about that cracked mirror?" Cass shivered.

"Uh, feel safe?" Cass rattled the door against the flimsy slide bolt lock.

"Indeed," Foster said, rising gingerly from the bed. He turned one of the bedframes around, and he and Cass pushed it against the door. She brushed his ear with a kiss.

"Not feeling very romantic right now," he said.

"I'm sorry. My fault. It's all my fault. They were after me."

"That doesn't make it your fault. They were just assholes. Punks. Wanted to throw their weight around. Wanted a blond American woman. You know all American women are easy, huh?"

"Yeah, well . . . ."

"Come here, baby."

"Foster, you've got to get those clothes off. You look awful, like an ax murderer or something. Wear some of mine."

He shook a little as he undressed. They lay down together on the bed away from the door. Foster curled up with his back to her and she coiled her body around him. She felt him trembling.

"Foster?"

"It's okay," he said. "Just a head wound."

"I love you." It sounded so lame. He squeezed her hand.

# FOURTEEN

At Latakia police headquarters the next day, Hassan Khoury was their interpreter. He was a city councilman and owner of a chain of gas stations in and around the Latakia area. He wore a blue suit that had a light of its own. He was grey-haired, big-bellied and kindly in an overbearing sort of way. Volunteering to help Cass and Foster, he explained he had studied chemical engineering in the United States but never stayed long enough to finish. He said he felt a kinship with Americans. With a few flourishes of his own he related what they told him to the Police Colonel. The Colonel's name was Fawzi, formerly of the Damascus P.D.

Foster sat in a wicker chair, fingering the bandage around his head. His blond hair stuck out at odd angles and some blood still clung to the strands. A swoop fan whirred overhead. Flies beat against the screen.

"Moustafa Sheik is a bad boy. He has a bad record. He is an orphan, but orphans are taken care of here in Syria. Sometimes they are spoiled. He and his friends, no doubt, had too much to drink."

"This isn't the work of spoiled boys," Foster said.

"They weren't just kids having a good time,"

Cass added. "They thought 'hum, Americans. Easy prey.' We were attacked. Foster could have been killed."

"These things do not normally happen in my country," Khoury said, turning a ring on his third finger. He nodded at one of the assistants who brought cups of tea.

"They will be punished," Khoury said.

When the police session was over and Foster's wound examined by a police surgeon as evidence of the assault, Khoury took them aside and said he would have to make up for "this perversion of Arab hospitality."

"Perhaps you would like to stay in my small chalet by the sea."

"Thanks, really, but no," Foster said.

"But it is so beautiful. You must see the brighter side of this city. You cannot leave Latakia thinking that all people will try and take advantage of you. It was a strange incident. A very unfortunate meeting. Moustafa Sheik will be caught and punished. That is all. You must have an opportunity to enjoy this town."

"To tell you the truth, Mr. Khoury," Foster said, "it's about time we got on the road. Got out of this part of the world. We've spent too long a time in Lebanon, and now Syria, too much violence to accept any more of it. It's . . . well, I don't feel good here."

"No, neither do I," said Cass, "but what about your head? Doesn't it hurt?"

"No, it's okay. It's really nothing, no worse than I would have gotten on the Lower East Side. I'm just tired."

"There you see, you need some rest. Please

stay."

"Really, no."

But Khoury was persistent. Foster resisted. He
was not about to be dragged into another
compromising example of Arab hospitality, no
matter how persuasive Khoury was.

Khoury talked of his brother in Brooklyn, who
ran an antiques store. They had some sort of
import-export business together. Then he spoke of
his chain of gas stations and how, as city
councilman, he was beginning to call some of the
shots in Latakia.

Though he was a Moslem, he was also a drinker.
He offered them whiskey as they sat in his office
on the coast road just south of the city, but they
refused. A boy worked the gas pumps outside and
brought ice when Khoury beckoned.

The panelled office smelled of rotting fruit from
a little pantry where he kept a bowl of apples,
pears, and oranges. On the shelf above the fruit lay
a gun in its holster. It looked like a long-barrel
Colt, but Cass couldn't be sure. On the walls were
maps of the city and of Syria, pictures of family
members, and books in Arabic and English. The
light was dying outside and Cass wanted to be on
the road. Foster was weakening.

"But it would be better for you to stay. To rest
in a comfortable place. We will take a look. You do
not want to drive the roads at night."

"But I thought you said things like this didn't
happen in your country?"

"You are foreign. They think you are rich. You
stop beside the road and who knows. Can you
speak for all your countrymen? Would you have
them all home to dinner? We are not all bad

people, but being careful is not a crime, here. And you with your blond hair and light eyes are targets. So for tonight, stay. You can swim tomorrow morning. Take some sun, then be on your way in a leisurely fashion. Come, I'll show you."

The house by the sea was uncomfortably close to The Blue Beach nightclub, but Foster was exhausted. His droopy eyelid was nearly shut, and Cass felt it would be better for him to sleep rather than drive the 110 miles to Aleppo.

The red cottage had wooden louvered doors and shutters. There was a damp saltiness to it, but it was cozy. Khoury showed them all the locks on the doors, apologized that there was no hot water, then bade them good night, explaining he would see them at his gas station about midday for a small meal before they left. Foster and Cass opened a can of beans and drank some of the vodka they had bought in Lebanon. Then Cass moved into the bathroom, talking all the time. Foster, too, was talking more than usual. The shower water was cold, but Cass eased under it. While she bathed she also took Foster's bloodied clothes and threw them in a tub with detergent. She stomped around in the tub.

"My feet are going to be immaculate for a change, Foster. You won't recognize them. The clothes will be okay, too, I think." She sloshed around. "God, it's cold in here, but it feels really good. Foster?"

"Yeah, yeah," he yelled from the porch, "I'm just stringing a line to dry those things. You think it's safe here?"

"I dunno. It's awfully close to The Blue Beach,

huh?"

"You think we're paranoid?"

"Yep, but I don't think it's a bad way to be."

"I've got the creeps about this place."

"What? I can't hear you, hang on a minute. I'll be finished in a minute." She dumped the wash water down the drain and began wringing the things.

"You want help with this stuff?" He opened the bathroom door and knocked her forward.

"Sorry." He helped her lug the tub outside on the porch. The sun had set and it was quiet. The cove was still; there were no sounds coming from the other beach houses.

"Have we got a weapon of any kind?"

"For the first time in my life," Foster grinned, "I'd say I'd be happy to have a .357 Magnum in my pocket."

"Come on, Foster, you couldn't keep your pants up."

"I'm not kidding," he said, leaving her to hang the clothes.

"You've got the diving knife."

"I couldn't open a letter with that thing. Shit, what good's a knife against a gun?"

"Now you are being paranoid," she said.

"Yeah, right. What are we anyway," he said, jokingly. "Are we going to let a few Arab punks scare us out of here? Could have happened in New York. Things just got out of hand. We've got water. We've got provisions," he eyed the beans and vodka on the table, "we've got . . . " and he waved toward the Mediterranean.

"Yep. I'm going to take a swim. Shower or no, bandits or not. Moustafa Sheik and his *droogs*.

Just a bunch of thugs, you know, isolated incident, like they said. We were just dumb."

"Boy, were we," he said. He watched her go toward the sea. He hung the last sock over the line and followed her movements as if she were dancing across a stage. He strode down to the water's edge, picking up a stick as he went, weighing it in his hand, switching it from side to side. She bobbed under the surface and came up again, then she went under for a long time and appeared in a place that surprised him.

"Wish I could join you," he said, touching his bandage.

"Be out in a moment."

"Come here, you fish. Christ, you soggy wet thing. What do I want with you?" He wrapped her up in a towel and held her. She shook her head like a dog trying to shake off the wet.

"Cool it, cool it. Come on. Inside. More vodka, then sleep, then onward and out of this place."

But sleep didn't come easily.

"You trust this guy?" he asked as they both lay in bed.

"Khoury?"

"Yeah."

"I don't know. He was pretty nice to translate for us and all. And this place would be really great if I weren't so nervous."

"You think this is out of the goodness of his heart, huh?"

"Ah come on, Foster, you don't think this guy is out for us, do you?"

"No," he said and turned on his side away from her. She draped an arm around him and kissed his shoulder.

"I can't sleep, though," he laughed, twisting back to her. "You hear anything outside?"

"Ah Christ, Foster, don't scare me to death, will you?"

"But if they spot the car."

"Come on, they're on the run. They don't want to be thrown in a Syrian prison. God, if the police station looks like that, think of what the jails are like. I think the cops are on the up and up. They're really pissed off that a couple of Americans got roughed up in their town. As Khoury kept saying to the Colonel, 'This lady is a journalist. You don't want her to publish bad things about Syria. Justice must be done' ya da ya da."

"Yeah," he said, "but it sounds like Moustafa Sheik has nothing to lose in nailing us. Maybe it's out of their control. You heard what they said about his record. He might be thinking, hell, if he's going to go back to prison it may as well be for a good reason."

"The car."

"Yep, our car's easy enough to recognize." He turned away.

Five minutes later they were packing up, tossing their wet clothes in the back seat of the Renault and depositing the house key in the nitch where Khoury kept it hidden.

"He said he stayed in the gas station until midnight. Do you want to return it to him tonight?"

"No," Foster said forcefully, "Leave the key and get in the car. We'll find Mounir's house. His parents will take us in for a night, then we'll travel to Aleppo by daylight. No more twilight arrivals."

They threaded their way through Latakia's back streets, then found the main thoroughfare and drove to number 68.

Mounir's parents were slow to understand who it was knocking at their door after they'd gone to bed, but in sudden realization that the Americans were back, they flung the door wide. Mrs. Najaime immediately set to work brewing coffee. When they listened to the story about Moustafa Sheik Mr. Najaime rose from his seat on the couch and went to the closet. He pulled out a twelve-gauge shotgun and handed his youngest son a pistol. Mounir was away in Europe; the other children were in Lebanon visiting family.

Mr. Najaime, a slim and energetic man in his fifties, was dressed in pajamas. He waved his shotgun toward the picture of Jesus Christ on the wall. Two tapers burned under his image.

"Christians would not have done this thing to you," he said. "Christ was a gentlemen. Even if these criminals are caught they will get out of prison. They have money. That's the way the system works." He rested the gun across his knees. His young son watched him with eagerness.

The only weapon Foster could offer to the family arsenal was a fish knife and his sense of humor, born of the embarrassment, he now acutely felt. He felt foolish and cowardly. The fear seemed to slip away as he sipped Mrs. Najaime's coffee.

The family took their armed precautions with all seriousness and bade them to take care.

"You have fallen in with bad men," they said, "and bad men cannot be trusted to run. In Syria, the law is your own strength. Do not trust the police. They are poor men, meager in spirit, misled by bribes. You have made yourselves some enemies here."

# FIFTEEN

Foster avoided the macadamed highways to Aleppo, navigating due east to the Christian village of Slenfe', a mountain town of farmers in baggy black pants who drove their goats and donkeys by the side of the road. They considered staying there for a night, but the only inn in town was shut down for repairs. Open faces greeted them at the market, where they weighed a handful of cheese and some olives to eat on the way.

They were both agitated. They could be over the Turkish border, well out of Syria, within thirty hours, if they pushed on to Aleppo. They pushed.

The daylight dried up the terror that had sprung from the Latakia darkness. The summer sun played in the grain fields and through the tamarisk trees along their way. They swung back on the main highway at Idlib and gunned it for Aleppo. The road wound in and out of desert patches, gullies of sand and shepherds in black jackets and white *keffeyehs*. Scrimshaw faces peered out at the yellow Renault and the two foreigners with light hair. They even picked up a hitchhiker, whom Foster mistook for a nun. She was an old Syrian woman, draped in black, who carried a gourd of milk at her bosom.

She sat cross-legged in the back seat, calling upon Allah to ease her burden. When they dropped her off at Jisr Esh Shugur, where her son was waiting, she tried to press a coin in Cass's hand, but Cass explained it was not necessary. With a thousand salaams they were on the EM 5, only a few miles from their destination.

Aleppo was astoundingly beautiful. Their imaginations soared. The thirteenth-century citadel built by Saladin's son towered over the town, crowning a mountain of golden earth and biscuit-colored stone. Its turrets and towers were a reminder of the greatness of Islam, of the sultan Saladin. How pale and puny those crusaders must have looked, so far away from their green shores.

The city had winding cobblestone streets and houses built of sandstone and mud cakes. Some were painted swimming pool blue, but most were the color of dung and straw. Moslem domes made up the skyline, interspersed with minarets and ruins.

On Colonel Fawzi's recommendation, they booked into the New Ommayad Hotel near the bazaar. Grand Funk Railroad, an American rock 'n' roll band, was playing on somebody's car stereo, mixing curiously with the evening call to prayer. Cass and Foster hung out on the balcony and saw a falcon glide, then plummet, only to glide again. A small exchange of gunfire many blocks away reminded them that they were not out of the woods, not out of the Middle East where feuds are routinely settled with guns.

They stayed in the hotel that evening, treating themselves to room service and reserving the last of their Syrian sightseeing for the following day.

They would make a short trip to the bazaar to exchange money for gasoline, then visit the citadel that lorded over the city from its golden plateau.

Foster crawled lazily between the sheets. He grabbed all the pillows, piled them up, then propped himself against the headboard. He pulled the covers up over his chest and watched Cass as she sat in the window.

"Hey, nurse, what do you think? May I take this off now?"

Cass slid off the windowsill and sat down on the bed next to him. She took the butterfly clips off the bandage and started unwinding it.

"The mummy," he said, folding his arms across his chest.

"Don't," Cass said. Foster closed his eyes and stiffened, his toes jutting straight up, his backbone rigid.

"Stop it," Cass said. "You're scaring me. You look just like a dead body." His lazy eye fluttered open and shut tight. She let the bandage hang over his right shoulder and left his side. He caught her hand as she got off the bed.

"Sorry," he said. "Aren't you going to finish?"

"Too squeamish," she said. "It's stuck."

"God, some medic you'd make. Just rip it off."

"No, no. You'll open it up." Cass put some warm water in a basin and softened the wound then took the bandage away.

"There you go. You'll live."

"What do you think? Ugly, huh? No longer the handsome young Lawrence Foster. Battle scarred. War weary."

"Whatever you've lost in appearance, I'm sure you'll make up for in bullshit." She turned, and he swatted her on the ass.

"Book, drink, anything?" Cass said.

"What's the matter, baby, can't you sit still?"

"Wide awake," she said.

"Cass. It's okay. It wasn't your fault, do you understand?"

"Yeah, yeah." She paced away from the window to the table near the door and poured out a good shot of vodka for each of them. The only olives available were black, so she plunked those in.

"Thanks," Foster said. They clinked glasses and she sat down next to him again, listening as the springs groaned and the floorboards creaked and cars rushed by in the streets. The desert stretched out dark and forbidding to the east. Fewer and fewer cars passed under their window. Fewer and fewer noises assaulted their consciousness, and they began to drop off to sleep.

Foster rested his head on Cass' shoulder. Turning a few times, she moved him gently and listened. She could feel his heart beating. She held his head against her breast as if he were a child, each time more drowsy, more comfortable in those pristine sheets with his breathing fluttering over her skin. Then she, too, went to sleep.

Morning came like jackhammers through the green shuttered windows. The bright Aleppo sun stole under the sheets and awakened them early.

The manager was not behind the hotel register when they went downstairs, but standing in the doorway between the potted palm trees. He gestured to them and without a word they followed him into the street to their car. The Renault had been broken into, the windshield smashed. Cass' typewriter case lay open like a gaping maw. The machine itself had fallen to the floor.

"Nothing valuable?"

"Just some notebooks. A sketchbook with some notes and addresses. A lot of addresses. . . ."

It was all there, the whereabouts of friends and relatives. Cass' insides flipflopped.

"Something's going on," she thought.

"Oh shit, Cassie. We should have brought the typewriter upstairs."

Once again Cass and Foster went to the police, though they knew little could be done about petty thievery. At the wooden table in police head-quarters, they sat beside a woman whose face was bruised from an Aleppo nightclub beating the evening before. As she explained her case to the police officer, Cass and Foster sat back con-sidering their latest bad luck. It seemed so un-important. Nothing. A few papers.

They told the Syrian cop about their run-in with Moustafa Sheik in Latakia, but the policeman waved it away as coincidence. If he'd heard of Moustafa Sheik it didn't show, but the battered woman stiffened at the mention of his name.

Cass saw the motion. "Do you know this man, Moustafa Sheik?"

"No, no. I thought you said. . . ."

"She is not feeling very well today as you can see, Missus Morgan. Please."

"Yes, of course, I'm sorry."

A police officer in a grey tunic led the battered woman away.

"Coincidence," said the Syrian officer behind the desk. "A foreign car," he said. "There are many poor people here. They saw the typewriter through the window and thought maybe a strongbox with money inside."

"Yeah, I suppose so," Foster said.

When the routine was played out, they asked the policeman for help in finding a mechanic to fix the windscreen. He sent a runner. There were no working telephones anywhere about. Cass asked if there were any stables where they might take a horseback ride while they were waiting for the car to be fixed.

"Of course," the police officer boomed. "There is Mohammed El-Masri's stable by the railway station. A show stable of fine Arabian horses. Purebred. King Hussein goes there to buy. The best in the Middle East."

When the Renault mechanic came, he told them he could fit the glass in a few hours. They left police headquarters and went to El-Masri's stable. It was only a mile and a half away, an easy walk.

The stallions were all tied in the sunshine. Their tethers were thirty feet long so as they moved they spun a ring around themselves. Outside the main paddock area, where a few spindly trees stood, were the mares, some pregnant, many young and unbroken. A groom was hosing them down, wiping the mud from their hocks and combing the tangles out of their manes.

There was to be a sale of stallions that day. The Saudi Arabian buyers would soon be there.

The grey horses were inky and shining, as if they'd been oiled. Soon enough the bleaching of age would come and their hides would turn white. Their legs were strong and their power was delicately restrained within their pale skins.

Cass whistled and put one foot up on the

paddock fence.

"Now, Morgan. Take it easy. Don't want to get any of these stablehands riled now."

"Ah, Foster. A little gallop."

"Oh no, not for me. I like my horses on a track with a few grandstand seats between us. If you want to."

"Nah, it's all right. Beautiful, though, aren't they? Like porcelain. Jesus, what I'd give to take that stallion home with me."

"You've got a stallion," Foster said resolutely.

"You're right," she smiled linking elbows. "How about a stroll, my stallion? How 'bout an ice cream?" Her eyes widened.

"It's a deal."

They walked the streets for a few hours, peering into shops and spending some time in the park by the river, at last doubling back to the Renault shop to pick up the car.

It was a short ride to the citadel through the narrow streets. They pulled into a dusty spot beneath a stand of olive trees. Cass bought some pumpkin seeds wrapped up in a piece of newspaper. Then they climbed the stone ramp. They could feel the smoothness of the masonry beneath their feet.

The massive portcullis of wooden beams and wrought iron was raised high over the arched entrance to the citadel. The air grew cool beneath the arch, where the walls were five feet thick.

They bought a guidebook and strolled into the sunshine inside the fortress walls. They wandered into one chamber, then another. Living quarters here, a hallway there, earthenware jars that could easily hold forty thieves.

They sat for a while under a domed ceiling studded with stained glass, which reminded them of the Turkish baths. They imagined the concubines in silk harem pants sitting as they now were, basking in the delicate light that pervaded the chamber. Foster held her hand.

"How do you think they kept all those concubines happy?" she asked.

"They played chess with the eunuchs," he said, then laughed at his own joke. She bent close to him and kissed him on the cheek. Then she kissed him on the forehead, on the gauze above the cut. He held her closer, then released her as the titters of the other tourists disturbed their intimacy.

"Come on, you. We're on to Turkey and the wild dogs of Anatolia."

"To Genghis Khan," she said. "I'm ready." They picked their way over a stone patch overgrown with weeds and tiny yellow wildflowers, and onto the parapet. They looked below into the castle moat, the water long gone, now peopled by goats and children playing in the dust. They breathed in the air under the Syrian sun and imagined the fallen flags of the crusaders far below at the foot of the citadel.

"Come on," he said. "Before it's dark."

She went willingly after him down the long stone ramp. They were alone, a quarter of the way down, when the first shot rang out.

Cass spun toward Foster, but before the warning could come from her lips, Foster yanked her violently downward. The second shot struck him in the chest. He let out a shriek and she clutched at him. He pulled her down as low as he could go against the stones, but there was no protection. A third bullet struck. The fourth struck him in the face. The richochet shaved off a shard of stone that cut across Cass's scalp. A fifth bullet went wild. Cass looked back up the ramp to see other tourists lying on the ground protecting themselves. She peered down at her attackers and watched them dive into the white Peugeot and slam the doors, gravel spinning against the undercarriage. She turned back to Foster who lay encircled in her arms. Foster. The dizziness washed over her. She looked again and pressed her face against his chest, listening, please God, listening for some kind of heartbeat, feeling for some kind of life, aching for some kind of response. Foster was dead.

# FIFTEEN

In an airless Aleppo office, before three Syrian officials, Cass Morgan sat silently. Sweat dripped down from behind her ears and flowed down her neck, pooling at her collarbone, then descending down the front of her blouse. She did not cry and she did not wipe the sweat away. She looked at the three Syrian officials without emotion.

They could not understand her. They were accustomed to the ululations of their own kin, the wail of their womenfolk when loved ones passed away. They offered her sweet tea and oranges, but she refused both. When they came close she recoiled, so they left the tea and the fruit beside her. She asked to be left alone. They filed out of the office to some other room, to some other problem, to sit and murmur to each other about the American girl and her. . . .

The screen door banged as Cass entered the courtyard. The gallows dominated the geometry of the prison square. She held two oranges in her hands, and looking back, making sure no one would see, she smashed them one at a time against the trunk of a palm, the meat and seeds and skin flying away in all directions. Tears pricked her eyes and she wiped them away. She went back inside and sat rigidly in the wicker chair, her hands folded in her lap. She paid no heed to the flies. All she saw was Lawrence Foster, dead under the blanket, in heat so fierce that any join, any bend of the body was fluid.

Foster. His face. His hands gone white. She lifted her head as if he might call to her from the morgue. A Syrian sergeant ushered her inside the other room.

The U.S. Embassy official had arrived from Damascus. He had "spook" written all over him, from his button-down shirt to his tasseled loafers to his iron-grey three-piece suit and the smell of his cologne.

Cass wandered through the next hour in a trance. Indentification of the body. The surrender of Foster's passport. Next of kin. Explanation. Logistics. The arrangements for getting the body to Damascus, then on a flight. The car, the yellow Renault. "Impound it," she said. "It's yours."

"Miss Morgan. Miss Morgan," Douglas was trying to get through. "I will be accompanying you back to Damascus and then on the United States."

"I don't need an escort, thank you," she said.

"You need some time to think about it," he said and handed her his card. Mr. Douglas, Mr. Peter F. Douglas. Reserve officer Political Section. He was brisk. Much too fucking brisk.

They rode down to Damascus in the embassy car, followed by a Syrian Army ambulance. Douglas made sure Cass was safely ensconced in the Interncontinental Hotel. The management sent flowers to her room in the arms of a doe-eyed Syrian maid.

The next day Cass Morgan left Syria by

commercial carrier. She had declined the U.S. Embassy escort.

The landing gear had barely cleared the tarmac before Mr. Peter F. Douglas filed his report. Interpol was more than a little interested; so was the C.I.A.

# SIXTEEN

Cass held out her hand to squeeze Foster's, but in vain. His absence jolted her. It was a different airplane now. A hum was coming from the overhead vents. A murmuring of voices, then silence. She was carrying his body home. He was dead, that was all, nearly a year after their jubilant departure from New York. The initial shock was over, but the aftershocks kept rumbling through Cass' brain, overturning file drawers and scattering her thoughts like so many index cards. Unreadable. The ink had smeared. The handwriting had gone scrawly.

She picked her heart off the airplane floor and tucked it back inside her chest, and as she did she noticed again that she must change the handle of the Remington's battered case. It would break one day, and then what? The typewriter was small comfort now.

She looked at the empty seat beside her and exhaled. God, Mr. Peter F. Douglas had given her the creeps. She settled back to look out at the clouds.

The 727 was out over the Atlantic, well past its stopover in Frankfurt, when the stewardess broke into her haze with a scotch, compliments of the captain, who had been kind enough to sit by her for awhile and kind enough to be silent. The flight crew knew what lay in the cargo hold for the Morgan girl, and they knew the Syrian government had paid her way home, first class, more than a little chagrined at the American blood on its doorstep.

Cass sipped her drink, smoked a cigarette and let the vapors of it fill the empty seat beside her. She envisioned Foster's volume filling the steel casket. Dead weight. No more rugby games. No more running down the pitch until his socks lay soaked around his ankles. No more Lawrence to tell her what a lousy tennis player she was.

The seat belt sign came on with a muffled gong. She had a two-hour stopover at Kennedy Airport before her Tampa Flight. Mrs. Morgan would meet her at JFK.

"Mom," Cass' voice, like the wail of a five-year-old, startled the other passengers in the terminal. Cass was dressed in black from head to foot in an Italian-cut trouser suit. Though the pants were frayed at the cuffs, the overall effect was one of "no nonsense." She wore a beret to conceal the graze along the side of her head, but her mother's hug was so strong it knocked the hat to the floor, and as they both bent to pick it up her mother gasped.

"Mom. A cut. It's all right. The hair will grow back." She forced some blond strands to fall over the wound and again fit her head into the cap. She stamped her foot as she did it, trying to stamp back the tears like gnats that plagued the corners of her eyes.

"Cassie. Cassie."

"It's okay, Mom." The last thing she wanted was to be impatient. Mrs. Morgan sensed her mood and launched into her own conversation full tilt, diving into her tales of her clients, her fidgety ingenues and her milk-faced boys who would be better "if they just learn to walk properly."

"You know what I mean, don't you? Without that swish. It's not that they're gay or anything, well, some of them maybe, but it's that spring in their step. I don't mind agility, but it robs the stage of substance. Actors should carry their bodies and use their structures as well as their words and their minds, hum. Their minds."

"Hey, Mom, Olivier was pretty springy in *Hamlet*. Tights and all."

"But oh," she said wistfully, "do you remember how he hung on those stone steps? How heavy he was when confronting his father's ghost!"

Cass was grateful for the darkness of the airport bar, for the red leather chairs that held them nearly concealed from the other drinkers. Blond heads bobbing, sometimes clutching, sometimes laughing, they kept the conversation rolling.

Mrs. Morgan ordered another round.

"Celebration, girls?" the bartender asked.

Cass ignored him. Mrs. Morgan put on a winning smile. "Of sorts, bartender. My baby's home now. Home from the Middle East."

"Not a nice place for a pretty girl like you, Miss." Cass stared at him obliquely. Mrs. Morgan caught Cass's hand. She had curled it into a tight fist against her thigh.

"Baby!"

"So what else is happening, Mom? Who's got better clients, you or McKee?"

"We share. I handle legitimate theater mostly. McKee takes care of the commercials and soap opera clients. It works out. We both trade on industrials. I think we're mature enough not to step on each other's toes."

"Yeah. What about fun?"

"If there wasn't any fun I wouldn't be doing it. McKee's fine. Where could I find a better friend, a better companion, a better soul? Yes, he's fine. My life is full."

"Oh, Mom," she pulled her hand away.

"Cassie, you must be strong now. You must."

"Foster was . . . ."

"I know. I know, baby. It's all right. You can cry now."

But Cass fought it back. "Mom," she said. "I'm not going to let this rest, you know. You've got to take care of some business for me while I'm in Florida. You've got to be in touch with the Syrian Consulate. Open my mail. There might be a letter from Interpol or from the Syrian government or something. I don't want to let—"

"Cass, I'll take care of it. Calm down, now. Quiet down. You're angry, I understand that."

"Mom, that's my flight, I've got to go."

Mrs. Morgan put her hand on Cass' shoulder. "You're home now, you know."

Cass held her for a moment then walked down the mile of linoleum to her plane for Florida, searching in her mind for the words that might get her through the night with Foster's parents. She had never met them before, and now she was bringing their son home in a coffin.

## SEVENTEEN

The iron birds that hung over the orange carpeting of Tampa International Airport were static, vulture-like, frozen in flight. Miriam Foster, her husband, Lawrence Senior, and her second son, James, waited for Cass Morgan's appearance. James spotted her immediately. Their glances crossed.

The Foster family was oppressively black against the flowers and parrots and flamingos that waltzed across the backs of many Floridians. Lawrence Senior was on his feet before his wife could breathe the command. He moved forward toward the girl. He had Foster's build, though age had slowed his pace some. James accompanied his father while Miriam hung back, gripping the security of the plastic chair. She reeled slightly and caught herself as she spied her husband embracing the stranger. James, too.

Flanked by both men, Cass approached Mrs. Foster. The closer she came, the more resolute became the expression on Miriam's face. Cass held out her hand.

"Mrs. Foster."

"Your flight was all right, I trust."

Cass looked back up the tunnel and nodded

dumbly. Lawrence Senior, catching the essence of his wife's bitterness, held the girl's arm. James took the other and they jettisoned Cass out of the airport to the waiting car. The police had been told. The funeral parlor had sent the hearse. Everything was arranged. Miriam Foster paced silently after them into the nighttime heat of Florida. The air blew like car exhaust in Cass' face and smelled slightly of rotten eggs.

The grief that sent them to fitful sleep that night, awakened them the next morning. The Fosters' sorrow played through the day like slow-motion action on a television screen. Their living-room faced out on a garden of prickly plants and orange trees and other lawns, tended mostly by retirees who stood poised over their garden hoses, watching.

Miriam Foster, neatly dressed in a navy skirt and blouse, strode across the room, mouth moving but not uttering a sound, hands never stopping, brow furrowed, eyes pinched, ever in motion.

Cass looked down at her hands. She wanted to put them in her mouth, but there were no finger-nails left to chew. She resigned herself to the cigarette she had tried so hard not to smoke. Mrs. Foster swept the ashtray off the table and marched it into the kitchen. She seemed to be caught up in a kinesis of sorrow, never stopping long enough to really cry, trying to hold it all in. Cass wanted to reach out for her, to stop her motion, but she could not.

Silently, Mr. Foster sat in the chair by the front door, already a stone memorial to his dead son. When Miriam disappeared for a moment to run water into a pot of flowers, he stole a look at Cass as if to say, "It's not your fault, nor my wife's either. Let it play out."

Mrs. Foster whirled into the room, went straight for another bunch of flowers, shoved them around, then pivoted toward the sliding glass doors, took a look outside, saw nothing and swirled back to face Cass, the force of her body making her overstep her mark. She returned to it, and then found a few words.

"How could it happen? How? In his prime. This trip was supposed to be for fun. My God . . ." her sobbing cut through the air like knives and drove Lawrence Senior to her side, and James to his feet.

"I want to know why!" she screamed, like a she-panther pacing her cage, shrieking for the loss of her cub. Her sorrow drew all into its vortex. It burrowed into Cass' brain as she tried to find the words. Lawrence Senior led his wife from the living room. Cass remained, numb on the sofa, and James sat indecisively across from her. Then he grabbed a cigarette and lit it.

Miriam's voice could just be heard, rising and then falling at Lawrence Senior's orders.

"He didn't love her. He was just fascinated by her, and she dragged him into a country where they couldn't possibly cope. Syria, my God! Beirut was bad enough. Terrifying enough for us. He did have a life, my Lawrence, a good life in New York. He was well off. He was . . . he was alive, then she came along with her big ideas and her Goddamned newspapers and. . . ."

Cass strode from the house. The green grass of Florida drove up against her bare feet like spikes. James was fast on her trail.

"Listen, she's grieving. That's all."

"I know. I know."

"She doesn't mean it. She doesn't know what she's saying. It's not your fault. We all know that. Give her some time. She loved Lawrence. It's a mother's grief."

"I loved him. He was it. All of it. He was the best."

"He felt that way about you, too, you know. It's in his letters. It's in the pictures he took of you."

"Christ, it feels so unfair, so much like punishment. Unbearable. We were celebrating. Do you know that? Celebrating the fact that we'd gotten out of Beirut alive, gotten out without tearing each other apart. Foster always said we'd have to go through a crisis and then we'd know if we were really in love. Maybe your Mom was right. Maybe I should never have gone back there. Never should have exposed him—"

"But this was Syria," James cut in.

"Yes, Aleppo. Out of nowhere. So bright out. The desert. No protection. No warning."

"I only know what happened from the official reports. Maybe you can. . . ."

"Official reports, yeah."

"But did my brother have a chance to do anything? Say anything?"

She flashed for a moment on James' face. It was so like Foster's.

"You don't have a lazy eye, do you?"

"No," he smiled.

"Wow, you are so much like him, you know. It's a little scary for me, a little. This ground is moving," she said, "shaking a little."

He said nothing.

"It could have been me, too, that day in Aleppo.

Maybe that would have been better. He saved me,
I think. I think, no, no, I'm sure they were trying to
get both of us. We were coming down the steps of
the citadel. It's like a mountain in the middle of
town, like a huge sand castle. Magnificent, really.
Foster was . . . I'm sorry, I always call your brother
by his last name. Funny, I was always Morgan to
him. Forgive me, but Lawrence. . . ."

"It's okay, go on."

"We were coming down the fortress steps.
There were a bunch of kids playing soccer in the
moat. Way down in the ditch that runs around the
castle only there wasn't any water in it anymore.
Just dust and scruffy little kids and goats. We
were looking down. It was hot. Our shirts were
sticking to us, you know, and our car was down
there. She was all fixed, and we were ready to go
on. Ready to go East. Foster was looking for
nirvana, he said." She trailed off.

"Cass."

"God, he could be so corny." She shook the hair
out of her eyes.

"Please."

"This white Peugeot pulled up to the foot of the
ramp we were coming down. Not parked under
the trees where everyone else was, but really
close. Foster and I had been debating Saladin.
Good man. Bad man. And feeling like infidels ourselves, so white among all those Arabs, but not
badly, you understand, because they can
be . . . and then three men got out of the car. The
first bullet went wild and your brother grabbed
me. We tried to force each other down, you know,
down low like everyone does in combat. You've
got to be part of the fucking ground and he was

crumbled kind of close to the wall and the second bullet hit him in the chest and I could feel it myself. He shuddered. He, he . . . Foster, my God, and the third bullet. Christ, you could hear them and count them." As she was talking her fists were striking out at the air and she was moving, and James could not, would not have approached her now.

"And his face . . . the side of his face was gone. Then another bullet, two or three guns, and Foster fell forward and brought me with him all the way to the ground when the other shots ricocheted and the chips from the stones hit me here. But he, even going down then, was shielding me the whole time. Not knowing what the hell was going on, and he was protecting me from them. And the noise. The car and the spinning tires and all the kids and the soccer . . . it just ended. And they were all running toward us and the blood on the ground was red, only it was like tar. His blood and mine. It was the same color, only his was . . . oh, God." She sobbed and James went for her, but she twisted away.

". . . The same color, you know, running from him. Pumping and his blond hair and his shoulders. Nothing. He was gone, I knew it. I knew it, and there was no river, no water around to wash him, to make him clean."

"Cass. Cass, it's all right. Come here."

"And the ambulance driver took Foster away from me. He spoke some English, you know, but he was crying. Big tears. This poor guy," she laughed, "he was trying. He was mixing up his Arabic and his English and his German and all that he had to say was, 'He's dead.' Oh, God,

James, the ambulance was so hot and they threw a blanket over him, and Foster was so hot." And James hugged her to him then, pulling her hands away from her face and his own tears fell on her hair. He held her head against him, feeling the wound under his fingers, and she shook for a long time and would not be calmed.

The next day, no one spoke in the limousine returning from the funeral home. Mrs. Foster's hands gripped the light blue plush on the interior while Cass and James peered out opposite windows. The hymn "Amazing Grace" repeated itself over and over again in Cass's mind. She hummed a little of it and realized Mr. Foster was doing the same thing as he held his wife's Bible on his lap.

They were all mesmerized by the slow whoosh of the limo as it drifted quietly through the Florida streets. The hot sun that reflected from the hood of the car was dimmed in the tinted glass of the limo windows.

Cass shivered as she reached the air-conditioned confines of the Foster house. Mrs. Foster made for the kitchen, Mr. Foster for the bedroom, James for the den. The four of them split apart like the frayed ends of an unraveling rope.

Louise, the Fosters' dark Bahamian maid, came out of the kitchen wiping her hands on a dish towel. She caught Cass before she disappeared into the bedroom.

"Miss Cassie. New York's been trying to reach you. A Mister McKee."

"Okay, Louise. Thanks," Cass said quietly.

"Louise!"

"Coming, missus." Louise double-timed it back to the kitchen. The doorbell rang; Mrs. Foster burst through the swinging door and nearly collided with her husband.

"It's all right, honey," he said. "I'll get the door." The wake had begun. Cass shut the door to the bedroom. She did not feel like shaking hands with strangers.

Raising the receiver to her ear, Cass dialed her Mother's agency in New York. Adam McKee picked up the phone after one ring.

"Adam."

"Cass?"

"Yes. What's up?"

"Cassie, I've got some bad news for you. There's been an accident."

"Mom?" Bracing now.

"Yes."

"Oh my God, is she all right?"

"She's going to be all right."

"Car?"

"No, no. The hard part, Cassie. An explosion. A letter bomb arrived today. She opened—"

"Christ almighty . . . ." Neither party spoke over the line. Cass held the receiver against her chest for a moment. Her heart thudded.

"Cassie," Adam said.

"Yes."

"The package was addressed to you."

"Mom's face, did it . . . ."

"We don't know yet. The bomb went off as soon she opened it. The police are investigating. They're here now. There's some evidence, some kind of stamp fragments. Arabic. Syrian."

"The package came in the mail?" Cass asked.

"No. Delivered by a messenger service."

"Mom."

"Cassie, she's going to be all right."

"Yeah. I'll meet you at the hospital."

"Roosevelt. Room 1716 West. Cass?"

Cass squeezed her eyes shut. The tears hung at the corner of the lids then rolled down. She brushed them away.

"I'll be on the next plane. Eastern Airlines, I think. I'll get right back to you. I'll go straight to the hospital."

"Cass, she's in good hands."

"I'll be there. I'm coming. Tell her I'm coming. Goodbye." She put the receiver down. James rapped on the door, then entered the bedroom. Cass held him away from her, hand upraised. She picked up the phone to book herself on the Eastern flight to New York that afternoon.

"My mother's been hurt. I can't explain. I'm sorry, James, but could you take me to the airport at, oh, I don't know, in about forty minutes? I'm not quite sure . . . ." She stopped and tugged at the stitches over her ear and caught herself, and cried, and caught herself doing that. By then the doorbell was ringing more and more often. The friends and neighbors were gathering for the wake and above the greetings and the grating of casserole lids and the splash of drinks on ice, James' voice carried over the others, pleading with his Mother.

Mrs. Foster was loath to relinquish her one last son to do an airport errand for "that girl."

"It's your brother's funeral, for God's sake, James."

Lawrence Senior spoke. "Miriam, be still.

Cassie's mother has been hurt. She's had enough sorrow without you making it worse for her. You're being a stupid woman on a day when. . . ."

"I know. I know." Tears brimmed in her voice. "He was my son, that's all. We didn't know her. I'm sorry."

Mr. Foster grabbed her by the shoulders and pulled her toward him. She was limp as a rag doll. She howled against his chest and then stood away.

"I must help her pack," she said, and as if her thoughts were independent of her actions she picked up the ice bucket and went into the living room.

# EIGHTEEN

Adam McKee was waiting in the hospital corridor when Cass arrived. A uniformed police officer stood outside her mother's door.

"Eh," Adam said in a low voice. "She's under now, Cassie. She's not conscious, but she's going to be okay. No, no. Don't look in. She's bandaged and all wired up. Not pretty. Not for you right now. She's out of pain, though."

"The bastards."

"You think it's the same guys?"

"I know it's the same guys." She opened the door and shut it fast. Her mother was unrecognizable.

The doctor came down the hall and told them Mrs. Morgan would be out of anesthesia and able to receive visitors late the next afternoon, but she would not be able to speak. Her jaw was wired shut.

"When that sets a little, when she heals a little," the doctor explained, "there will be plastic surgery. It will be a long process. Her right hand took the worst of it. She's lucky, though. She still has her sight. She's lucky to have survived at all."

Cass stammered something, inaudible. Her face was ashen. McKee took hold of her and led her out

126

of the hospital.

The Morgan & McKee Agency in Manhattan was located thirty floors up; the elevator quietly rocked from side to side as it ascended. Some aging gargoyles peopled the skyscraper next door, and the windows looked up Madison Avenue and out on midtown. The winged griffins, like stone children from a medieval sculptor's bag, held the bomb squad commander's gaze. He had long since turned his back on the newsmen that awaited Cass Morgan's arrival.

She hadn't anticipated them, and when the elevator door opened, the questions and flashing bulbs made her recoil. Then she sprang forward in anger.

"Come on, you guys. Knock it off, will you? Give me a break!"

The *Daily News* man moved in closer and flashed again.

"Asshole. Who let these dogs in here anyway?"

McKee was already in action, running interference for her. Cass resisted the impulse to smash the *News* photographer in the face.

"When'd they take you off matrimonials, anyway?"

Rose cowered behind her switchboard. She must have been blowing her nose and wiping her eyes all day, because her face had broken out in a rash.

"Does your mother have any enemies?" A reporter asked.

"The package was addressed to me," Cass barked.

McKee guided her forward down the hallway, to his office.

"Scumbags, that's what Foster would have called them. Can't wait a moment." She lurched forward as though she was going to shout them down. McKee stood between Cass and the doorway. He leaned against it and it was shut.

For what seemed like the sixteenth time he explained the events of the day, this time halting every so often to make sure Cass was actually listening to him.

There was a lot of camera whirring going on outside, shutters opening and closing, cops powdering and drawing and covering pads of paper with notations. Cass had nothing left inside her but rage. First, Foster, now her mother maimed. The two people who mattered. The only two. There was a curdling going on beneath the plates of her skull.

McKee took a bottle of Irish whiskey from the bottom drawer of his desk. Cass and he drained the first drink and were working on the second when the detective rapped on the door. The sound broke through Cass' concentration and she shook off the intrusion for a moment, getting McKee's last words before she had to confront the mob outside.

She was reacting cooly now and thinking coherently. The reporter's instinct was returning, but this time in a bizarre reversal of her usual role. The letter bomb was a story. It was her mother, but it was also an alarming story for New York. All-News-Radio was headlining it. Business-women and businessmen were already considering what might arrive in the morning mail, and the connection to the murder of Lawrence Foster, an American tourist in Syria, was rattling the brains of those journalists who majored in conspiracies and international intrigue.

Suddenly Cass grew jealous of her own tragedy, jealous of some of the keys she held, the clues that ticked in the back of her mind, and the revenge that was welling inside her.

Gus, one of the network reporters, was leaning against the radiator.

"Cass."

"Hey, Gus."

"I'm sorry, babe, but you can't keep the hounds off this one. Your Mom okay?"

"She'll be okay," she said, turning her back and walking into her mother's office. The cops and reporters backed off. One detective, all business, started a question, but she stopped him. Gus followed.

"Sad, huh? Weird being the story."

"Got no stomach for it, Gus." Gus, with some help from McKee, blocked the door of Mrs. Morgan's office. A couple of F.B.I. men were there. They shut the door on the newspeople as Cass nosed around.

The only signs of the explosion were the rips in the leather desk top, the splinters of glass from the actors' pictures that had been dashed against the wall and to the floor, and the chips out of the paint where the shrapnel had spread. The police had forbidden her to touch anything, but she sat in her mother's chair just the same. She reenacted the morning's events herself as the two men looked on. Her mother's blood was already dry.

As the bomb squad commander entered, the F.B.I. men grew edgy. Locals and feds were a bad mix. Two uniformed cops entered and opened their notebooks in anticipation.

"Miss Morgan?"

"Yes."

"I was wondering if you're ready? We could start now."

She was looking past him, through all of them, and they cast their eyes downward. They wanted to know about the bomb, but first they wanted to know about Foster. They were looking for that elusive "connection."

"Miss Morgan, we're all real sorry about what happened to your mother. These terrorist acts. You can't really prevent them, all we can do is try and catch those responsible. Uh, about Mr. Foster . . . ."

"Foster's dead."

"Yeah, we know, Miss Morgan and we're real sorry about that, too. We sort of want to get filled in, you know, the details, like what you were doing in Syria?"

"Traveling."

"That's a strange place for traveling, isn't it?" one of F.B.I. men asked.

"You mean Hoboken would have been a safer choice?"

"Miss Morgan, I don't mean anything. I know this is hard for you, but don't make it harder on us, okay?" Cass turned her unblinking eyes on him.

The bomb squad commander crashed through the chill.

"Lawrence Foster was stabbed in Latakia first, right, before he was—"

"Yes. Three Arab punks spoiling for—"

"A woman."

"Yes, something like that. Is this all written in your Interpol reports or what?" she said, turning to face the F.B.I. men. "Because if it is I don't see any need to talk about it. My mother is in the hospital because some berserko sent *me* a bomb. Do you want to deal with that?"

"We're looking for a motive, Miss Morgan. It's not every day we get a letter bomb in this city. I mean you gotta know who your enemies are, right?"

Cass stood at the window, tugging on the cord to the venetian blinds.

"Motive, right. Something other than rape." The word tasted terrible in her mouth. "Something else," she whispered.

The bomb squad commander cleared his throat. Cass turned to him.

"I'm thinking," she said. "You got a cigarette?" Three were offered before the commander could shake one out of his pack. Cass took his while the other cops stuck theirs lamely in their mouths.

"They've gone to an awful lot of trouble to get you, Miss Morgan. What did you do to make them so mad? Write a story about someone important? Get something on the Syrian underworld?"

She drew hard on the smoke, letting it sit in her lungs for a moment before she exhaled. "Smart cop," she thought to herself. "Smarter than I am. It's the drugs, isn't it? Mohammed and his little packet of heroin. What else? God, I've been so stupid." She remembered then the glassine packet lying on the sink in the ladies' room at The Blue Beach. Mohammed and his groping fingers and his greedy eyes, blitzed out on alcohol and heroin.

"Oh boy," she thought. "Three boys on a lark

with a big bankroll. Get your hands cut off for that, if you don't watch out, or something worse!"

"Miss Morgan?" The commander was trying to read her agitation.

"You said it yourself, they were hot for a Western woman. Me. Foster got in the way. My mother? I don't know, revenge is pretty strong medicine. Murder isn't a crime in the Middle East, it's a passion. Fun and games. Arab *angst*."

"Did Lawrence Foster throw the first punch that night on the hotel landing in Latakia?"

"He was angry."

"Miss Morgan, did he throw the first punch?"

"What would you do with three guys rushing toward you? And what the hell are you getting at anyway? You think he deserved to be shot and killed? You think my mother deserved . . . God, just like a fucking cop! Yeah, keep writing that in your little scratch pad, too. I've had enough."

"Listen, Miss Morgan." The bomb squad commander rose to his full height, but still seemed shorter than Cass. "Please, we're just trying to piece together the—"

"Yeah, well, piece this. In your little American brains you'll never for a million years understand the mentality over there and how strong it is, and how it could skip right over the Atlantic right into a little bomb factory somewhere in New York. Do something about it!"

"Miss Morgan!"

She stalked past them and threw open the door. Gus was close by.

"You, too, huh? Ear to the fucking door. Jesus Christ." She was flying now, all the pieces to the puzzle were sliding into place, join by join, leaping the synapses in her brain. The drugs, she'd seen the drugs. What else? Moustafa Sheik and his *droogs* had been careless. Now they were trying to protect themselves by nailing her. And Mister Khoury, fine, fat, Mr. Khoury, the city councilman with the gas station and his drug run. She could see it all clearly, and the brother he mentioned, in Brooklyn, right? Import-export business, huh! Antiques, huh!

"Miss Morgan?" The *Daily News* photographer blocked her way and she put her hand over his lens as the flashbulb exploded in light. Then she gave him a solid hipcheck, sending him bang into the *Post* reporter.

"Where are you going now?" a reporter blurted.

"None of your fucking business."

"How does it feel to have your mother . . . ."

"How does it feel? You asshole, how do you think it feels?"

# NINETEEN

A steel-grey Mercedes sped down the Syrian boulevard. A riot of summer flowers adorned the road at curbside. The Mercedes swung into a driveway and up to the front door as wrought-iron security gates clanged shut behind it. A tall man in a pale flannel suit got out of the automobile, carrying a leather envelope under his arm. His shoes grated over the stone steps. A desert wind blowing in from the Euphrates had coated everything with a fine layer of grit.

John Barrows, the Interpol commander, knew he was late as he strode the polished corridors of marble and brass and opened the mahogany doors into the conference room. The conversation halted abruptly. Three men jumped to their feet.

"Morning, sir!"

"Morning, John."

Peter F. Douglas from the American Embassy said nothing as he settled back down into his chair. John Barrows eyed him frostily. Douglas was being churlish, a bad sign in a man who wanted to be a career diplomat . . . if not a career spy.

"Good morning, gentlemen," Barrows said, smiling warmly, then dropping the expression as soon as it had crossed his face. "Where's the girl?"

"In New York, sir. The letter bomb, you know."

"Yes. They've gone to extraordinary lengths this time. A very dirty business." Barrows picked some lint from his trouser leg.

"They don't like that in the states, Barrows. Stirs up a lot of anti-Arab sentiment. We can't afford that these days."

"Anti-Arab sentiment," Barrows laughed. "I'm sure there's plenty of that without Miss Morgan and her lot." He pulled a slim black cigar from his vest pocket, clipped the end and let the flare of his lighter roll evenly over the tobacco, inhaling.

"And the drug connection?" Barrows asked.

"They must have stumbled onto it, sir, but there's been no mention of it. Sets us back a bit. Khoury's a smart man. He'll go underground for awhile and take his Corsican rats with him."

"But as far as the American authorities are concerned?"

"They were unlucky, Barrows. Two naive Americans who ran into a vengeful bunch of Arabs out for some snatch," Douglas interjected.

"Yes, marvelous choice of words, Douglas, always a pleasure to have you around, though I wouldn't call the Morgan girl naive." Barrows turned to young David Greenland.

"Their country, their law, John. That's how it's being read. The idea is to keep the Americans out of this now as much as possible."

"Whose idea?" Barrows snapped.

"Ours," Douglas said.

Barrows put both his hands flat out on the table and turned to the American. "You're new to this part of the world aren't you, Douglas? Where was it before, Panama? You think if you're shy on this one you'll make some points, right, then on down the road you'll singlehandedly woo the Syrians right out of the Soviet sphere. God save us from well-meaning Yanks."

"I am here because Lawrence Foster carried an American passport. I am representing the United States Government and I'll thank you—"

"Yes, yes. You'll get copies of the minutes of this meeting, and any other we call on the subject of Mr. Foster's murder. A little messy for you and your forms in triplicate, isn't it? You might have saved us some time and some energy if you'd traveled back to the United Staes with the Morgan girl. Smart, wasn't she? She made you a mile away. Didn't trust you. You'll have to learn some craft."

Douglas was red to the ears as he rose from the conference table. "If that will be all, Commander Barrows, I'll ask my leave. Any further business, you can reach me in Damascus. Also, please be advised that the F.B.I. is working internally on this case and you must apprise them of your movements."

"Greenland, show Mr. Douglas the door," Barrows said without getting up.

Vortmann, another Interpol agent, spoke up. He had been quiet all this time.

"What about White Light?"

"Still operative," Barrows said and pondered White Light, the code name that still stuck to the agent who worked in Beirut. The code name hailed from the Second World War.

"He hasn't seen action in a while, sir." Greenland said as he resumed his seat. "We have reports he's been hitting the bottle. He is getting on a bit . . . ."

"Getting on a bit?" Barrows said. "We're the same age, Greenland. He's the best agent we have in Beirut and a damn sight closer to the Morgan girl than any of us. I want to find out more about her."

"If she knows about the narcotics, they might try again, sir."

"Yes. Give her some protection in New York. Let me know where she goes, and for Christ's sake keep away from the F.B.I. men. They'll drag the Drug Enforcement Administration into this before we know it. Clumsy lot!"

# TWENTY

Moustafa Sheik sat atop a crate picking his teeth with a piece of baling wire. He watched the running lights on the Turkish fishing vessel as it pulled out of Latakia's industrial harbor, its engine throbbing against the current. Its hold was bulging with heroin packed deep into sacks of spices, wedged tightly between stacks of dried dates. Bittersweet heroin. Sheik could taste the granules sliding down the back of his throat.

"Ya, Moustafa, yalla. Let's go," Nahass called.

Sheik quieted him with a gesture and jerked his head back. Hassan Khoury was lumbering onto the dock, his hands swinging heavily alongside his body.

"Where's Mohammed?" Khoury said.

"Recuperating."

"Fine."

Sheik rubbed his fingers.

Khoury laughed. "You're lucky I'm not paying you with the back of my hand."

Sheik jumped off the crate and stood toe to toe with Khoury.

"You don't frighten me. You're a little brute. Brutes can be smashed, you see, like that." He snapped his fingers just as Sheik whipped out a

138

switchblade. Nahass sprang to Sheik's side but
Khoury remained steady, taunting him with his
eyes. Then it was Sheik's turn to laugh. He folded
the blade down and put it in his pocket and held
out his hand once more.

"Disappear, right?" said Khoury, as he was
handing out the Syrian notes. "I mean vanish for
the next few weeks. There will be no more
shipments until fall. I want you to lie low. I didn't
buy your freedom for nothing, and if I hear of any
more of your games, I will feed you to the
Corsicans. They don't like their supply lines
endangered. Understand?"

"Mohammed understands," Sheik growled. "He
is not so beautiful now. The beard is gone. So is
half his chin."

"I don't want to know the details, Sheik. I'll find
you. You best stay clear of Aleppo for at least a
month or more. The killing was a mistake. The girl
is . . . ."

"Running scared . . . ."

"Perhaps."

"You flatter the woman too much. She is not
important."

"Yes, well, you thought she was pretty important, didn't you? In Latakia, then Aleppo.
You should have killed her then."

"What about you?"

"We failed in New York. A mistake."

"Not to worry."

"If Mohammed hadn't been so stupid with the
heroin, we never . . . ."

"Ma salaam," Shiek said, sprinting off into the
darkness. Nahass followed. Khoury wiped the
sweat from his forehead.

# TWENTY-ONE

It is a hard thing not to shrivel up in sorrow like a flower past its prime. To pull all the petals close. To find solace in a blanket, knees to chin, demons within. To flee the sunlight into dark poetry, sad rhymes. To commiserate with William Blake. Cass Morgan was not as ethereal as all that.

She spent restless nights stalking the rooms of her Mother's Manhattan apartment. Foster's loss, her mother's wounding, kept her always on the balls of her feet. She would go into her father's den and hurl his bedouin dagger again and again into the burlap walls. There was something so satisfying about the sound of the blade as it sank deep into the boards. As it shivered in the light . . . as it shivered in the heart of Moustafa Sheik.

Cass Morgan was feeding on anger and in that process, beating back the guilt of surviving. She honed that guilt as she honed the blade of that little bedouin knife, 'til it was razor sharp, nagging her into action, prodding her into the kill.

Hatred, too, all the suppressed hatred of a woman who spent years in Islamic countries, trying always to be so careful of their sensibilities, so polite, such a hypocrite. Now they had trod on her world, nearly snuffed it out.

She drummed her fingers on the letter she had received that morning from the Syrian Consulate in New York. It was a message from Damascus and it bothered her. It wrapped everything up so neatly, and nothing is ever neat in the Middle East, not even death. The letter said that Moustafa Sheik had been killed after his capture by Syrian authorities. The black-and-white obituary gnawed at her.

A piece of paper wasn't enough. She wanted to see the corpse. She had become used to dancing death figures in Beirut where the militia groups would claim ten dead but only show four bodies in the morgue. What happened to the rest of them? Beirut, Damascus, a criminal's dream. Pay a pound, get killed on paper, change your identity like your dirty shirt.

She wanted to see the corpse.

She picked up the phone and began to dial. The numbers clicked into the computer, another trans-Atlantic call. She was sidestepping the officialdom that so plagued the Middle East. She would deal now with the local warlords in Beirut, where there was no authority to answer to but the leaders who held the most men under arms. She would deal with Ossama.

Ossama was at the Sabra Refugee Camp in southern Beirut when Cass telephoned him. A fan kept the hot air circulating, but the dregs in his coffee cup had solidified. There were no appointments for him that day; he was just juggling around accommodation for several hundred more refugees who refused to return to

southern Lebanon. The Israelis were sending
airstrikes into the Palestinian camps in the south
with renewed vigor. Ossama's job was to see the
survivors settled elsewhere.

He was a Saiqa officer. Saiqa was one of the
several pro-Palestinian guerrilla factions
comprised predominantly of Syrians living in
Lebanon. They were few in number, but well
equipped and disciplined. Ossama's job was
administration. His superiors took care of the
military wing that supported Arafat's PLO.

The Syrian administrator was lean and lanky
with dark hair. Lines traced from his nose to his
thin lips. His eyes were brown and stained the
whites around them. He was sharply featured, but
soft spoken, trained in French schools. He had
been a journalist himself in Egypt, during the
Nasser years, and on that shared experience alone
Cass and he found much to talk about. Ossama
had kept Cass attuned to the general commando
movements when the Israeli invasion hit Southern
Lebanon in March of 1978. He had accepted Foster
as a brash and naive American and had come to
like him very much, despite a few awkward
moments. Foster had compared the Palestinian
camps to Resurrection City. Fourteen children to
a family baffled him, all living on milk rations
from the U.N. or handouts from the PLO as long as
the families supported "the revolution." It had all
baffled him. But Ossama had liked him.

Ossama saw Foster now, as Cass spoke on the
line. Cass was asking the Saiqa officer to use his
contacts in Damascus for some information.

She read him the letter from the Syrian
Consulate in New York, similar to the one that

was already in the hands of Interpol.

> The Syrian Government wishes to inform Miss Cassandra Morgan that the man called Moustafa Sheik was apprehended in Latakia, Syria, on June 22, 1978. The said Moustafa Sheik, age 28, confessed to the killing of Mr. Lawrence Foster, which occurred on June 15, 1978, in Aleppo, Syria.
>
> When remanded to Damascus authorities, the suspect broke free of his security guards and was inadvertently killed in the escape attempt.
>
> We wish to inform you that the Syrian Government, with the aid of the International Criminal Police Organization (Interpol), has an all-points bulletin out for his accomplices and believe that their capture is imminent.
>
> On behalf of the Syrian Government, the Consulate wishes to express again our deepest regrets on this most unfortunate incident. You can be assured the criminals still at large, Mohammed Rawzi and Nahass Ghoudri, will be severely dealt with.
>
> The Interior Minister has ordered a mandatory penalty of death. A tribunal in the case will be convened. You may keep in touch with the developments of the case through Interpol.
>
> Please be advised again that your case and that of the Lawrence Fosters' is number 8697.
>
> Feel free to contact us here in New York if you have any inquiries.

The letter was signed, respectfully, by Sami El-Said Sadri, Syrian Consulate, New York.

Cass read the letter as if she'd been robbed. Ossama noted her intonation and sat silently as she described the letter bomb attack on her Mother. Ossama wrote down the names and underlined them again and again in black lead.

"Just information, Ossama. No hits. I've got to get it all right."

It was a strange request, Ossama thought, coming from this American girl. A specific one: the status of Moustafa Sheik presumed dead. It would be easy to find out. Many Saiqa commandos who had quit the field had become penal guards in Syria, or took part in the police administrations there. They were long on loyalty, discretion, and information to Saiqa.

When Cass rang off, Ossama called for his boys. Two men with Kalashnikov rifles and chest-mounted grenades appeared, and he scribbled a note for them to take to the Damascus runner. At the top: "Priority URGENT."

When Cass rang off, she sat at the phone for a while. She was in her mother's den, or her father's, depending on what objects caught her attention, the old newspaper clippings and press photos, or the posters by Toulouse Lautrec. She looked round at the splashes of color and saw only black and white. She was sitting on the edge of the guerrilla movements now, on the outlaws' fringe.

She stood up, the little dagger loose in her grip. She did not like the terrorist tactics that Saiqa and the Palestinian commandos used against the Israelis, but she had begun to taste their desperation, their suicidal war of attrition to regain a homeland that would never again be theirs.

It was a deviation from everything she had been before. Fear clutched at her heart. A fine sweat broke out over her body. She spun on her heel and hurled the dagger again into the wall, but this time her aim was off. The knife blade shattered the glass of her press club award. The frame dropped to the ground in a shower of splinters.

She got down on her hands and knees, cursing herself, and dumped the whole thing into the garbage, scooping up the glass with her fingers.

"Busywork, keep me occupied," she thought. "The bomb. The letter bomb. The Syrian government has disavowed any knowledge of the explosives. The package was delivered locally. Locally."

Again the crab of fear pinched at her. "Khoury. Khoury's brother and his little antique shop. Got to track it down before the cops do. Or should I . . . ."

She shoved the trashcan out of her way and hauled out the telephone books. Of the sixteen Khourys listed, seven lived in Brooklyn.

She yanked the phone cord and caught the phone as it fell off the desk. Then she began dialing.

"Hello. Is this Mr. Khoury? Yes . . . good. This is Miss Simpson from Borough Hall? We're doing a survey of Arab/Americans? It's part of our voter registration drive. I wonder, if you don't mind, could I ask you a few general questions? Thank you. You came from what country? When? Uh huh, and how long have you been living in the United States? Are you a citizen? Thank you very much, Mr. Khoury." Her voice was low, even, businesslike. She checked off the names as she followed down the column in the phone book.

She struck paydirt on the fourth call. A Mrs. Amar Khoury answered the phone. Yes, her husband had been born in Latakia, Syria, and yes, he was a naturalized citizen. He was not home just then because he was working at the antiques store. Yes, he still had relations in Syria, a brother who was a councilman.

Cass swallowed and went out with her interrogation, glad to have found a talkative wife. No, he hadn't voted in any U.S. election, but after the phone call from Borough Hall, Mrs. Khoury promised that he would. The antiques store?

Why, yes, of course she could have the address.

Cass wrote it down, folded the paper and put it in her pocket. She tied the laces on her sneakers, tucked the workshirt into her jeans, and hit the streets soon after.

She was undecided about her direction, whether she should go directly to the hospital or down to the gun shop on Houston Street. Maybe something light . . . low on splatter. She changed direction.

It was not out of character for Cass Morgan to stride six blocks one way, then switch direction on a whim, weighing the walking against the subwaying, or the bus against the taxi cab. It was all in the motion. Continuous flow, Morgan's way of riding the city's energy. Something was slowing her down, though. She had a present for her mother in her camera bag, a bottle, and it thumped against her hip bone.

She switched direction again, abruptly, and noticed a man in a blue denim jacket, dark hair, sturdy build, roving eyes.

She turned again, east toward the river and the 59th Street bridge, sauntering along the sidewalk, then did an about-face. She caught her tail off guard. The man in blue denim slipped awkwardly into a doorway. She marched toward him, arms swinging.

"You're not being very bright about this, rookie," she said and took off at a sprint, down one flight of subway stairs, up another.

She took the B.M.T. to Houston Street and emerged in the late afternoon sun striding toward the gun shop. A man, the color of the sidewalk, lay slumped in a doorway. She hesitated. He moved. She walked on.

Squad cars were parked at the curb at odd angles, lights flashing. Cass stood her distance. There had been an armed robbery at the liquor store that abutted the gun shop. She listened intently to the chatter of the crowd and heard the police talk over the short wave radio.

"Damn," she said. "Too damn crowded." She looked around her with some frustration. The Brooklyn connection would have to wait. She turned on her heel, flagged down a cab and made straight for the hospital.

Visiting hours were nearly over now. Cass stood at the nurses' station and thumbed through the clipboard containing information on her mother's condition. She had been taken off the intravenous and could now take a liquid diet. Cass hung up the clipboard and padded down the hallway to her mother's room, stopping just short of the door. Opening it a crack, she saw McKee sitting on the radiator. Three of her mother's young actors were performing a scene from *Lady Windermere's Fan*, but there were no women, so a pale boy in a red wig was playing the Lillie Langtry part. Mrs. Morgan did not have the luxury of expression. There weren't any tubes sticking out of her any

more, but she was still entrapped beneath her
bandages.

Cass didn't feel much like applauding, and she
didn't want to get trapped by actors hungry for
the human response. Too close, better in a
darkened theater than in that bright, artificially
lighted hospital room. She shut the door and stood
outside for awhile, then slid down the wall to a
squatting position in the hospital corridor. She
could think better that way. She hung her head
between her knees, resting, like an Arab beside the
road.

A cart wobbled by on rubber wheels. An intern
in a light green suit, his mask pushed down
around his neck, strode by without remark. Cass
fingered the stitches over her right ear.

"Those look about ready to come out," a young
nurse said, standing over her.

Cass looked up and the nurse gave her a hand.

"Where?"

"Emergency room. They'll do it for you now,
probably, if you like. The rush hasn't started yet."

"Your cap's falling off."

"Oh, thanks." She jabbed at it with a bobby pin.

The elevator was as wide as it was high, with
yellow walls and stainless steel buttons. She rode
down to the basement and poked her head in a few
doors. A doctor with a beard was reading a paper-
back book and sitting on the examining table.

" 'Scuse me," she said.

"Yeah? What can I do for you?"

"Think you could take these out for me?"

He beckoned her closer, ran his fingers over the
spidery black stitches. His sleeves were shiny with
starch.

"Done all the paperwork at the front desk?"

"Nope," she said, "snuck in the back way. No medical insurance, you know. Thought if you weren't doing anything. . . ." She looked at the book in his hands.

"Harold Robbins," he said. "I'm a sucker for sex and violence. Sure, sit down here. What's your name?"

"Cass Morgan."

"Oh yeah? Any relation to Helen Morgan on the seventh floor?"

"Um."

"Hum. Yep, all healed." He patted the white coverlet on the examining table and said, "Hop up. I'll get to it now."

He walked over to the steel tray and pulled out some scissors. He was silent, but not voluntarily so. Cass could see the curiosity running across his features. He wanted to ask a lot of questions, but he didn't. Cass was grateful for that.

A nurse peered in.

"It's all right, Newberg, everything under control here." She nodded and disappeared in a blur of white.

"That's quite a nasty graze you've got there."

"Don't even notice it. You know anything about plastic surgery?"

"Some."

"You now my Mom's case?"

"Heard about it. We've all heard about it. Isn't often we get a letter bomb injury. Knifings, car crashes, bullet wounds, beat-'em-ups, drug overdoses. All that stuff."

"She going to be all right?"

He looked down into her earnest eyes. She

looked young and untried in her sneakers and
rock 'n' roll tee shirt.

"You got any brothers and sisters?"

"Nope." She swung her legs and then jumped off
the table.

"My Mom going to be all right, or what?"

He tossed the scissors into another tray, daubed
at her head with alcohol and said, "I don't know.
I'm not her doctor. I wasn't here when they
brought your Mom in."

"See ya," Cass said with a toss of her head.
"Thanks."

She headed toward the elevator.

The applause had just subsided in Mrs.
Morgan's hospital room. A gunnery sergeant of a
nurse, Nurse Brophy, stood at the door looking
very sincere. She had her large arms folded across
her ample chest and was giving McKee what-for
for too many visitors. Cass stuck her nose in.
McKee spotted her and leapt from the radiator,
ignoring the nurse.

"Cassie," he said.

"Oh, McKee, just a minute. Forgot something."
She jogged down the hospital corridor and
skidded into the nurses' pantry, scooped some ice
out of the freezer compartment into a cocktail
shaker, stirred it gently then jogged back to the
room and burst through the door as the nurse's
jaw fell open.

"It's okay," she assured the nurse. "One of the
family. No problem No problem. We'll be out of
here soon enough." She patted her on the shoulder
and led her out. "See you soon." The actors gave
Cass a round of applause.

"Thank you, thank you," she said bowing low,

"Thus be the end to petty tyrants. Sorry I missed your performance, but . . . some pressing business here." She unveiled the cocktail shaker and a couple of glasses. She pulled a jar of olives from her camera bag and then rummaged around in the chest by the bed and found some paper cups.

"Mom. To your speedy recovery." She poured out a martini, plunked an olive in it and then a hospital straw. "Think you can manage?" Her mother's eyes were cheerful. She raised her good left hand and gave the okay sign.

"She's sick to death of soup," McKee said. "I think you've got something there, but I'm not sure about the olive."

"Just for effect," one of the actors said.

Mrs. Morgan grabbed Cass by the hand, took a sip, then closed her eyes.

"All right," McKee said, rubbing his hands. "No need to be stingy. Got any more in there for us?"

"Sure do," Cass said. She poured some more in glasses, then pulled the bottle of vodka from her bag and poured a round in paper cups, stealing ice from the water jug that stood sweating on Helen Morgan's bedside table. They all raised their drinks in a toast to Mrs. Morgan.

"To Helen," the pale-faced boy said, "Speedy recovery. We need you. *Salut!*"

Nurse Brophy stuck her head in the door and cleared her throat like socks on a washboard.

"Right," Cass said, knocking her drink back. "We're on the way out." McKee stood at attention. Two of the actors marched out first, then McKee and the pale boy, arm in arm. They shook the nurse's hand with great reverence. Cass put the martini glass on the bedside table and left the shaker.

"There's a dividend in there, Nurse, if you'd like?" Cass bent down to her mother's ear and said, "I love you." Her mother caught her lightly. Cass kissed her hair and curtsied to the nurse on the way out.

# TWENTY-TWO

New York's finest were canvassing every Syrian/American neighborhood in New York and not being very subtle about it. The cops were in her way, but maybe, maybe, she thought, they'd actually catch Khoury's brother. In her eagerness to get back to the Middle East, she left it to them.

From Cass' airplane window, Beirut glittered like a pearl on the Mediterranean, but as the jet banked and landed on the tarmac the ravages of war were apparent. Slowly, slowly Beirut was trying to throw off the butchers who had turned the cultural and cosmopolitan center of the Middle East into a slaughterhouse. The jet taxied to a halt and Cass disembarked in the sunshine.

Scanning the landing strip east to west, Cass spotted the camouflaged troop carriers parked at the end of the runway. Several U.N. convoys were lining up for their trip to the south. Lebanese security guards rushed her through customs. As they searched her bags for guns, Cass' mind was turning over the information she'd gotten from Harry the Joint.

"Pass!" the customs official said. He banged her baggage shut. She lifted the suitcases off the conveyor and made her way out to hail a cab. A

Moslem boy rushed to help her, but she waved him away. He looked as though he wanted to kick her, his face all pinched up with anger, so she relented. For the equivalent of a quarter he not only took her bags but also got her a cab.

"Much obliged," she said in Arabic. He gave her a sharp salute as the driver pulled away.

The cab screeched around the curves and leveled out coming through the bends in the coastal road. Cass sat in the back seat flipping through her notes on her phone conversation with Harry the Joint. It was all still full of holes.

Harry the Joint was a Maronite Christian by birth. A hash dealer by trade; to most outside eyes, a silk trader. He loved lavish colors and smooth textures. His taste in hashish was unsurpassed. He dealt drugs to the Europeans, to the Americans, Syrians, Egyptians, all of them. He sent the oily resin by the ton in sealed trucks overland to Europe and by shipload to Egypt, where *el primo* of Lebanese gold was snatched up. There were even still some caravan runs through the Sinai into the back streets of Butlea, the hash district of Cairo just north of the city of the dead. Heavy baksheesh ensured that the cargo found its way into the proper hands.

Harry had just returned from Afghanistan when Cass came to his door in Beirut. She had already checked into the Commodore Hotel and rented a car, a sleek little blue two seater Mercedes. Guy, Harry's lover, asked who it was before he slid back the bolt.

"*Ma petite*," he said with tears in his eyes. "Look, look, Harold, Cass has returned." He gave her a fleeting hug, then danced away from her.

The grapevine had informed Harry and Guy of the death of Foster in Syria. The letter bomb attack on her mother came as a shock. Guy inhaled, puffed out his cheeks as the French have a way of doing, and clutched her hand. His own felt like a bird trembling in her grip. Guy was tall and dark. His skin was transparent, consumptive, too many drugs. He had the look of a hemophiliac with penetrating blue eyes.

Harry was just the opposite, roly-poly about the face and hands. Guy was a head taller than he. They had met in Paris when Harry was on the run from the civil war. Guy had returned to Beirut with him when the situation had calmed down.

Harry prepared a narghile, a water pipe, and loaded it with the tarry hash he had brought back from the Mazar 'I Sharif region of northern Afghanistan. The pipe was cut glass with three stems wrapped in black velvet. Sequins dangled from the tubes; the mouthpieces were made of hollowed stone. Harry threw off his green silk cloak and took embers from a brass brazier that sat in the middle of the living room. He stoked the mixture of hashish and black Turkish tobacco, adding a pinch of sugarcane. The three of them sat crosslegged, propped against pillows embroidered in dark wools.

Out the open window imperial palms lined the Mediterranean bay, but the trees had gone bald from the pecking of snipers. The Holiday Inn towered over the skyline several blocks away like a huge pitted shoebox. Further to the south, the Saint George Hotel had lost its front teeth. The latticework sign on that international haunt read "Gorge." Its stately entrance had collapsed like a mineshaft during one of the firefights.

Guy gurgled loudly on the pipe and settled back with smoke in his lungs. Both he and Harry were wearing Afghan pants that bloomed from a silken sash at the waist and bloused down to a gathering at the ankles. Harry looked like a pasha.

He spoke softly. "You have fallen in with a crowd that even I don't like to deal with. The heroin trade in Syria is big business, but it is tightly controlled by very few men. I can get you the information you need, but what are you going to do with it? Write an expose that will stand as a posthumous reminder of your folly. You are a marked woman. They may be following you now, here."

"I won't be writing any more stories for a while, Harry. I just need the information."

"Hire a few guns, hum? Vigilante. They won't come cheap for a contract in Syria and tangling with the Ouzais . . . . I don't think so."

"I'll worry about that later. What I don't understand is what Sheik and his boys were doing with the dope. They're not users themselves. I saw no tracks on their arms."

"Runners, probably, skimming a little off the top. Their superiors won't like that. In fact, the three of them may be dead right now."

"I'm finding that out, too," she said.

"You're pigheaded, Cass. If I didn't know you better I'd swear you were Lebanese."

"Go on, Harry. I'm listening."

"The Corsicans are using Middle Eastern chemists, now. They've got to. Too much heat on the European labs, so they go closer to the fields and further from the Drug Enforcement

Administration. The Ouzais in Syria do a lot of business for them, take care of it within their borders, then ship it out refined. Much easier to smuggle it then, and with war on the doorstep nobody bothers to look. I don't know the setup, it's not my poison, but I'd venture to guess there's a lab in Latakia. Filter it down then ship it out. I can find that out for you next week.

"The Turks send their opium, raw, overland into Syria, nearest place. Sometimes the black jelly has been partially refined to morphine, about a tenth of its original weight. Easier to carry. Easier to store. It has no odor then. But the last process from morphine to grade four heroin is a long and complicated one. I wouldn't mess with it. It must be done under intensely controlled conditions."

"It requires a master chemist," Guy said. "There are quite a few in Syria. Some trained in France. Others in the States. Some even in the Soviet Union." He took another pull on the pipe. The open window dissipated the smoke.

"You are only concerned with a small part of the dragon, Cass," Harry resumed, "the tail end. But if you burn the tail, the dragon will turn. For your own protection and ours, you shouldn't come here anymore. Let me find you."

"All right," she said. "I'm sorry to get you into all this. I don't really know who else I can go to. You're my local drug expert."

"There's nothing local about me," Harry said. "You are dealing with a man of the world." He breathed out a smoke ring and poked at it with his finger, laughing. "Nice stuff, huh?"

Cass nodded.

"Don't worry," Harry said. "I'll find out what

you want. Foster was my friend, too. He was a beautiful man, and the first, Cassie, who ever held you in tow."

Cass rose from the pillows. "He's still got me in tow, Harry. You can reach me at the hotel. Just leave a message if I'm not in. I may spend some time up north with Chuck Vazcatchian and his wife. They want me to stay on their farm for awhile." She let the pipe stem drop and said, "Tell me something, Harry, do you ever have any dealings with that Latakia crowd?"

"I sell them hashish, sometimes. That keeps their suppliers happy. Nothing better than a stoned Turk padding around his poppy fields. Keeps 'em giggling, you know. The Turks can't grow their own without facing jail, but opium . . . well, all Anatolia's in bloom, legally, these days. The Syrians are the middle men. Boring, really, quite straight most of them. They get the gravy from both sides."

"Don't burn your fingers," Cass said.

"Have I ever?" Harry answered, picking at the coals in the bowl of the waterpipe.

"Okay then, leave a message at the Commodore or at Vazcatchian's in Becharre."

"I wish you luck, Cassie, but I don't envy you right now. You have tangled with the worst." Both he and Guy escorted her to the door. Guy brushed her forehead with a kiss.

"Take care, petite."

Cass got into her rented Mercedes and eased back against the leather as the engine growled into life. She pulled into the street and began putting the car through its paces. Double clutching on a tight corner, she swerved slightly on sand, then

snapped the Mercedes back under her will. The
car throbbed as she pulled it back down to city
speed, stop and go. The streets of Beirut were
calm. Soldiers sat perched on their sandbags
dressed in olive green fatigues and black boots.
Surrounded by sprigs of barbed wire, they spewed
their sexuality down the muzzles of their guns.
The checkpoints were fluid, vanishing as the
political situation changed, only to germinate
anew in other neighborhoods, on other hatreds.

Cass Morgan passed through four of them
without incident.

"Sahafiyeh, journalist."

Two American marines were jogging along the
corniche in their sweat pants, passing a frisbee
between them. Cass swung the car away from the
sea and pulled up to the front door of the
Commodore, motioning to one of the bellboys as
she did so. He parked the car down the block for
her.

Cass hadn't seen anyone in town except Harry
and Guy since Foster was killed. She felt very
much alone now. Her fists were curled deeply into
the pockets of her khaki jacket. Her blue jeans and
halter were faded and bunched in at the waist with
a length of rope. Her father's beduoin dagger was
tucked in one of her back pockets, affording her a
curious sense of security.

Air conditioning shivered through her as she
made her way down the lobby. The men behind the
desk nodded to her.

The Commodore was reputed by many to be the
greatest journalists' hotel in the world. A lot of
whiskey was drunk there. Many guns changed
hands. Countless deadlines were digested. Editors

were lambasted at one bar stool while assassinations were plotted at another, and it was sometimes difficult to discern who spoke with more venom.

A grey parrot with powdery white wingtips held court from his huge wire cage in front of the bar. The BBC correspondent had adopted him. The bird's favorite tune was Beethoven's *Fifth Symphony* and he could hum the first four notes with alarming clarity.

Cass rounded the corner, head down, seeing the white tile of the lobby give way to the red carpeting of the bar. She wasn't the kind of woman who made entrances. She just got there. She spied Kodak loafing over his mug of beer at the other end of the bar and crept up on him.

"Hey, Pox-face!"

He swivelled toward her and grinned. "Hullo, you tart!"

He bundled her up in his arms. She resisted momentarily, and then surrendered to his warmth. The tears that she fought burned in her eyes.

"It's all right, baby. Got two shoulders here, both reasonably dry." He paused. "Chuck Vazcatchian was here a moment ago. He told me about your Mom. My God, little girl! And Lawrence. You have had a time of it. What brings you back to this snake pit, anyway?" He looked directly into her eyes.

"Just keeping busy," she said. "Working up some magazine pieces. May even be doing a documentary."

"Oh yeah," he said suspiciously. "And who's your cameraman?"

She gazed around her and studied some faces at the bar, then turned her eyes full on Kodak.

"Ho, no, babe. ABC. They've got me now, lock stock 'n' expense account."

"Oh yeah?" she said. "Company man, huh? Grand champeen of mileage and meal allowances."

"I'm working to get myself out of this rattrap, you know."

"What about Sally? Where is she?"

"She's flying, probably in Riyadh by now. I'll be seeing her on the weekend in Athens. I think she's got her heart set on sweeping some oil sheik off his feet. So far she's been doing most of the sweeping . . . ."

"Kodak!"

He shrugged. "And what fly-by-night organization is paying your way this time, my sweet?"

"I'll let you know later, but they're keeping me well heeled." She turned to Habib, the bartender, who had been awaiting her order.

"Scotch and a splash for me and one more for the gent."

"Oh, come on," Kodak said and shoved the money back at her. "You can have the next round. I'm surprised you're back, Cassie. Thought the Arabs might have left a bad taste in your mouth."

"Yeah, well," she said as the scotch went down, "the whole world tastes the same."

"Your Mom. How's she doing?"

Cass brushed away an invisible fly. "When was the last time you took a flak jacket out and shot holes in it?"

"Last week. Knocked off a few tin cans as well.

You interested in a little plinking?"

"What are you shooting these days?"

"Cowboy issue .45. Hey, when did you start getting interested in guns?"

"Too much caliber," she said, avoiding his question.

"My dear, this is Beirut. You can find anything your little heart desires. What are you looking for? A little pocket protection, perhaps? A derringer to slip into your long johns? Jesus, Cass, do you ever wear skirts?"

"Only under duress," she said. "All those prim girls' schools. They never do teach you how to sit properly in front of men. I'm looking for an automatic, light and lethal. Easy for me to handle."

He chewed on that for a moment. "Well, it's been quiet here for a few days. Downright drag if you ask me."

"Wait five minutes."

"Yeah, but if it holds we can go out shooting tomorrow afternoon."

"A deal," she said and ordered the next round just as Chuck Vazcatchian entered the bar area. He looked like an Armenian Jimmy Breslin in his ill-fitting dark suit with a suspicion of pin stripes. Vaz clapped his arms around Cass and Kodak.

"Children," he intoned, "you are looking at a happy man. Five races today. Five winners."

"And five whiskeys," Kodak said, pulling away from Vaz' embrace.

"Maybe six," Vaz winked. "Cassie." He seemed to focus on her for the first time.

"Don't get sloppy now, Vaz. You're getting misty around the eyes there." She slipped her arms around his neck and gave him a kiss. "We'll talk tomorrow, huh? Lunch at the Austrian's. How about it?"

"Yes, yes," Vaz said, "but how about one for the road?"

Cass began to slide off the bar stool, but Kodak caught her hand.

"We've got some catching up to do, eh?"

Cass looked at him directly, and he returned her glance without guile.

"Yeh, okay. But Vaz," she said, turning, "we'll see you get home safely, eh?"

"Okay."

They raised their hands in unison.

# TWENTY-THREE

Vaz finished his steak tartare and pushed the plate away, wiped his lips then tossed his napkin on the table.

"You're an amateur, Cass. You've got no business thinking this way."

"I won't be an amateur for long, Vaz." She sipped her second cup of black coffee. Vaz ordered a bromo seltzer and a brandy.

"You ever fire a weapon before?.. Ever kill—"

"I've been shooting a few times," Cass cut in. "I was an expert shot at camp. Prepubescent and paper targets. The talent's there, Vaz."

"And the will?"

"You know it is."

He pondered that. He saw in her something of himself three years before, when his sister had been killed by a sniper. He had gone on a rampage like a rogue bull. Many people fell under his gun before he pulled himself out of it and observed the ruination of his sister's children. They had been sent to Athens after the worst of it. They cowered even now at the slam of a door, quaking with fear.

He saw that Cass was no rogue. Somehow that worried him. His own passion had spent itself, but Cass was being cool, calculating, immoveable.

"You'll never cross the border," Vaz said finally.

"It's not like you to say never, Vaz. I will cross the border and I'll show you how." She began sketching her plan in a notebook, blocking out the route.

"You and Ingrid could do me the biggest favor of all, Vaz. It might not be half bad."

"Go on," Vaz said, leaning closer to her.

"I'd like a horse. I'd like you to buy me a fine saddle horse at Mohammed El-Masri's Stable. A mare, maybe, or a small gelding. Short-gaited and strong, spunky enough not to need any coaxing. The horse should not cost less than six hundred dollars nor more than eight." She counted out a thousand dollars American and gave it to Vaz. He pocketed the money without comment.

"The animal's got to have a lot of heart."

"And so do you. I know what you're saying, and I know what you want to do. It's bold. It may work." Vaz thought for a moment, then nodded. "It will be a pleasure to deal with that pirate El-Masri again. You'll have a fine horse."

"Nothing too leggy, Vaz. Don't get carried away, okay? Stamina's the thing."

"Yes, yes," he put his hands up in protest.

"But that's not all."

"More?" he said. "This could cost you."

"Don't I know it," she said. "Listen, get out that old Leica of yours. Dust off your lenses. Get a flash if you have to, and take some pictures for me. There are some places in Aleppo. Some nightclubs . . ."

"I know a couple."

"Specifically, the Aleppo Nightclub and the

discotheque, The Blow Up."

"How do you know about these places?"

"Moustafa Sheik mentioned them that night in Latakia. The night he tried to . . . the fucker!" She slammed the table and the glassware shook. Vaz caught her wrists and brought both her hands down against the table.

"Be a tourist," she went on, calm now, "but let me know where the holes are. The exits. Any high walls and empty lots. Stands of trees."

The waiter came by and poured another cup of coffee, then moved away from the table.

Andrew Pym sat about twenty feet away from them, his vision obscured by a partition of banister railing overhung with plants. He was watching the two of them together with some interest. He wondered what they were talking about.

"The horse—that will be easy. I relish it. Masri, that old Bedouin bandit, I've known him for years. Met him at the track a couple of times. It will be a natural for me, traveling to Aleppo for good Arab stock to replenish my stable. Ingrid will love the outing."

Cass nodded gratefully and promised to watch over the farm at the end of the month, when Vaz planned to make the journey. In the meantime, she had a little over three weeks to prepare and to let things cool down in Syria.

"Shweya, shweya, slowly, slowly."

"That's the only way, Cass," he agreed. "If you go through with this, you'll be tangling with an Arab tribe that has roots in the field, but bears fruit in the Parliament houses and at the bank. If Foster . . . ."

She grabbed his wrist and squeezed it hard.

driving back the image of Foster being pulled
from her arms by the Syrian ambulance
attendant. She saw a falcon as the carrier of
Foster's spirit. The bird soared in her mind, high
over the minarets, and was gone, slicing the sun in
two with the majesty of his wings.

"Exits, Vaz. Just find me some outs."

Vaz sighed and finished his bromo. The effer-
vescence had died.

Andrew Pym came over, drink in hand, and
plunked himself down at their table.

"Hello, Andrew."

"Hello, my love. I heard about—"

Cass put her finger to his lips. She tore a page
from the notebook. Vaz folded it and put it in his
pocket, then slapped Andrew on the shoulder.

"Had five winners yesterday, you know."

Andrew groaned. "Next time you're going, take
me along, will you? I could use some luck. Mine's
been rotten lately."

Pym patted Cass' hand. He was somewhere
between 45 and 70. His cheeks were like dried
apricots, and his rheumy blue eyes often fought
for sight through wisps of white hair that fell
foreward over his face. A few liver spots marred
his long-fingered hands that were always busy,
sheafing through papers or lighting yet another of
his nonfilter cigarettes. The fingers of his right
hand had gone yellow with tar.

Pym had that type of withering figure that
seemed to be part of the British tradition of
growing old. He was small boned, with spindly
legs, but paunchy in the girth as if to announce,
quite without words, I may be old, but I live well.

"Well, sorry to call you up short, Pym, but

Ingrid is waiting. Cassie, you'll be hearing from me."

"Goodbye, Vaz. Andrew, I'm sorry, too, but I've got some work to do. I'll catch you later." Pym caught her hand and squeezed it without a word. She smiled at him and left the table.

Pym had taught Arabic for some years at Chemlain, nicknamed the British spy school, formed when the League of Nations did its minuet through the Middle East carving out territories with the flourish of a French pen.

Journalism and Arabic tutoring had kept him going when he lost the government job. He might have held onto that if he hadn't written so many scathing articles about Britain's broken promises to the Arabs. If he had been born thirty years sooner he would have ridden camelback through the desert with T.E. Lawrence. Lebanon was his home now.

He sat still for a time, then, peering at the floor, he spotted a wadded-up piece of notebook paper. He picked it up, flattened out the creases and tried to decipher some of the scribblings. Nothing. Some of Cass' doodles. A picture of a horse. He tossed it away.

# TWENTY-FOUR

The struggle to get into a commando cell was tougher than she thought. Of the thirty odd militia groups operating in the Beirut area, only a few really had precision-trained guerrillas, and only a few were willing to talk to an American woman. She ruled out the Tigers, Chamoun's men, as too fanatical, too elite. She ruled out the Phalangists because they knew her too well and were inclined to be indiscreet. Mourabytoun? No, the Nasserite cowboys in that ragtag bunch were reckless and sloppy. They might cost her her life before she even reached the Syrian border. Fatah? No way. Too much ego to deal with.

She toyed with her Saiqa connection, but discarded the idea. She'd already called in her favors and did not want to press her luck. Ossama had come through. He winnowed through the ratshit of penal workers and paid performers of the public good and provided the information that Moustafa Sheik had not been killed by security that day in Damascus, as written by the Syrian Consulate, but had been released for two thousand Syrian pounds, hardly more than five hundred dollars. He was back in Aleppo running errands for Khoury and the Ouzais. An orphan,

but son of an Ouzai wife, the clan quickly
reclaimed him. Oh, how Allah loves the orphan.
Blessed be the orphan and the wayfarer. Foster
was a wayfarer. Bastards.

Moustafa Sheik was now serving the Ouzai from
Baalbak to Aleppo and sometimes making the
Turkish run to Mersin or Gazientep.

Ossama explained that Moustafa had made
himself valuable to the Ouzais, valuable enough
for someone in the government to pull strings for
his release.

"The money came from Latakia," Ossama had
said, "from some very clean fingers."

She ran down the checklist of commando
groups again and always came up with the same
red star, the same positive slash.

The PFLP. She had set up three meetings before
she got to the top. Three meetings with the
physical, before she could approach the cerebral.
Somewhere atop that teetering mass of Marxist
ideologues and walking cannon fodder, somewhere beyond the closemouthed lieutenants, she
got to B. They had met before in grim circumstances during the war.

She was playing his game now, not challenging
his reasoning. She drew on every instinct, plucked
on every string, delving down into her reptilian
brain to try and convince the PFLP she wasn't a
spy, nor a volunteer for Palestine. She just wanted
training. She had no arms nor radio transmitters,
and she was not an undercover agent for Israeli
intelligence.

"Hell," she remarked to B. "I'd train on that
side of the fence if I could, but it's a closed shop.
Seems they have a better survival rate," she

added.

B. let that one pass. The two fingers of his right hand tapped on his desk.

The Marxist Popular Front for the Liberation of Palestine was the torchbearer of international terrorism. B. was third man in line, chief polemicist and strategist. George Habash was his immediate superior. The number one man was allegedly dead and buried in Baghdad, but no one could swear that he would not rise from the grave, least of all the Israelis.

B. was a soft-spoken intellectual with a spine like steel. Half his face had been blown away by a parcel bomb. The Israeli who sent it had a sense of humor. The explosive came bound in a book called *The Art of Guerrilla Warfare*, by Che Guevara, required reading for any Marxist guerrilla.

"You are spooky, you know, Cass."

"Come on, B., I'm not C.I.A. I'm not a flag waver. This is something personal."

"The PFLP is not personal. We don't set up the camps for summer games."

"How many times do I have to tell you, to convince you, this is not a game. Your face. My mother looks the same now because of some scum in Syria. I'm prepared to eradicate him, but I need the skill. You don't have to know the details. Just be assured I'm not on some kind of undercover mission to destroy the PFLP."

"You couldn't."

"Wouldn't. I don't even want to talk to your commandos. I saw enough of them in the orange groves this past spring. I simply want to learn to kill and survive."

"The killing is easy, but survival is a promise a

Palestinian never makes." His eyes blazed beyond the immediate visage.

She sipped her coffee and traveled over the posters on the wall, pictures of the so-called martyrs of the revolution and one photograph of the desert airstrip where the commandos had blown up three Lufthansa jets. Was there anything human flying out of the cockpit, there?

"You've never killed before. What makes you think you can kill now? What makes you think you can change all your attitudes now? Wasn't it you who argued against the use of violence? Wasn't it you who looked upon the PFLP as a bunch of savage animals? Bah! You're an American woman, not a Palestinian. You are used to silk shirts and fine food and polite conversation. You cannot change. It is insane even to think about this training."

"I can change. I have already changed a great deal."

"You are naive."

"Determined."

"Yes. You seem steady now, but what happens when you must pull the trigger and watch the bullet fly through flesh and gristle and bone? What happens if you hesitate? Boom, you are gone, just another pile of guts, just another—"

"You don't have to describe mortality to me, B. I've seen it. The dismembered bodies. The overturned cribs. The indignity of the polyethylene shroud . . . ."

"But can you really be responsible for that kind of carnage?"

"You seem to find some nobility in it, some sense of purpose, some sense of justice, eh? For something that happened thirty years ago."

"Something that continues," he said. "Don't get carried away here. You Americans have never called it justice. It's always been terrorism. Don't confuse yourself, or are you really changing your mind now?"

"I'm not confused. I know who my targets are. Not a busload of innocent children, but four men. Surgical."

"We always try to be surgical, but no one is innocent. The operating theatre tends to expand with the circumstances. Don't be so assured you won't hit someone else, and then what? A woman full of remorse. A pitiful thing, the luxury of guilt, the gravest mistake you'll make before you die."

"There's nothing innocent about the men I'm after. They are no better than cockroaches."

"Can you kill a cockroach without being squeamish, a big fat cockroach?"

"These cockroaches." But she laughed nervously.

"Why waste your time?"

"That's a strange question coming from you."

"I'll think about it," he said, pulling her up short. She left without a goodbye. Four days she waited. Then a runner from the PFLP summoned her back to headquarters. B. was standing at the window as she entered. He told her to sit down. She did so quietly and waited, like a defendant in the dock.

He turned and looked at her. "There will be no other women in this cell, Cass."

She leaned forward. "How many?"

"Five."

"That small?"

"What about your Arabic?"

"I can get along pretty well with it now. I don't intend to talk much anyway. Maybe this will take care of a few questions." She fingered the slug-colored scar over her right ear. "Recruits, you say?"

"Yes."

"I've got ten years on them. It won't be hard."

"Maybe. Maybe. The master of this particular cell has taken on the friendly alias of Baba, but that's as far as the warmth will go. He doesn't like the idea of a foreign woman in his cell. A young Palestinian girl, that would be different. You are already made. The raw male recruits have a tough time, and he doesn't want to pander. You may find yourself isolated. Bab will eat you without salt if you try anything. If you understand too much, if you ask too many questions or break any of the codes that will run your life for the next two weeks . . . or if even a spoonful of that misplaced American humanity is passed on to one of the boys, you are finished. You're not my affair anymore. You're his meat."

"Two weeks."

"That's all you get, Cass. I'm already breaking too many Goddamn rules for an American imperialist weapons supplier of the Zionist enemy." Half his face smiled.

"I'm a quick study," she said.

"You'd better be."

## TWENTY-FIVE

Three days later, at midnight, they came and called her from the hotel room. The blindfold was wrapped over her eyes at the city limit. She had bolted her crash course in Arabic at Chemlain like castor oil thrown back in her throat. The British government had allowed her in as a courtesy to the international press corps. They had tried to drive the Egyptian intonation out of her speech. When she wasn't at Chemlain bent over the books and listening to the rasp of her instructor's voice, she was at Kitchener's Pub picking up colloquial Arabic from Andrew Pym. The British Arabist had a quirk to his speech that left off R's and replaced them with W's. A speech impediment of her own might help on the road when she was dealing with the Arabs in the field. A stutter maybe, some slight idiocy that would get her over the rough spots. Pym's lessons always finished with a Sadat joke or a dirty anecdote about King Farouk. Beirut even had Pym on edge at this point. It seemed everyone was saying goodbye to the city and all its holes. The smell of the civil war was returning, like an overturned compost of corpses and vitriol.

She had dressed in her workshirt and jeans, a pack of cigarettes in her pocket and about fifty bucks worth of Lebanese money. No hash this go-around. Her papers and documents had been entrusted to Kodak. He had gone to Athens to visit Sally, so she had been saved the explanation of her two weeks' absence.

The car door closed against the butt of the bodyguard's sidearm. And then she felt the engine of the Mercedes wind up and they squealed away from Beirut. Her shoulders barely touched the men on either side of her. It had been underlined. This is special. Hands off.

Two weeks was all she had. B. said that's all the cell could manage seeing as how she wasn't to be used in any action. The only thing in return for the free training was a little English language for the recruits and some long conversations with B. on her return. She had gotten a last promise from him.

"No Cubans, right, B.? I don't want to have to write a story about this."

"No Cubans. Just five Palestinians who may hate you after two weeks. It's a long time to get acquainted."

"Not time enough to be indoctrinated."

He nodded slowly.

The Mercedes traveled for about two hours down the coastal road. Cass could hear the baaing of newborn lambs along the way, the soft thud and ring of cowbells, and the car horns past Sidon, then a sharp left close to the area the Israelis had won for a time in their March invasion. Maybe they would cut north to Nabateah, skirting Christian territory, maybe south toward Bint Jbeil, through the Christian lines somehow. The U.N. troops certainly wouldn't let a car pass

through with one passenger blindfolded in the
back. Before further speculation the Mercedes
bumped to a halt, grinding over a rock that might
have scarred the undercarriage. A security check.
The jumble of Arabic. The car started again.

"Cigarette?"

She lifted the proffered cigarette to her lips,
heard the flare of the match and took in a lung full
of sulfur and tobacco, a balm to her insides. A
window opened. It was dawn air, clean and grey
feeling. The ruts were interminable, each thump a
little torture throwing her against her unyielding
companions. The sour-faced veterans didn't know
her and didn't ask questions. She was traveling
into a reality hard-edged as a guillotine, off in
some grove somewhere in Fatahland.

Before they took the blindfold off she was
struck in the stomach with a bundle of clothes.
Her new uniform.

"Made," a voice said," . . . made by the sons and
daughters of the martyrs. Wear them."

"Oh Christ," she thought, "I hope there's no
pledge of allegiance."

The first blur coming into her eyes was the face
of the bearded man in front of her. Shredded
wheat on his chin, brown eyes over furrows like
well-worn farmland, iron grey streaks in his hair,
and sweat stains the only thing decorating his
uniform. A chain hung around his neck, but
whatever medal hung from it was buried in chest
hair. His raisin-dried eyes locked on hers. He was
built big and squat, barrel chested, and she was to
call him Baba, simply "old man" or "respected
father."

Cass had kept Ossama in the dark about her

whereabouts. She did not want anyone in Saiqa messing with anyone in the PFLP. The jealousies between the Palestinian factions sprang from old forges. She needed that Syrian connection, but little did she realize how clumsy his men had been in their inquiries. She just followed her straight lines, never letting them diverge or overlap each other.

The commando camp was a grim little community, a pocket of malcontents without electricity and scarce water. There was one roof in the compound, of corrugated tin, over the master's office. Baba's hut contained a small desk, a cabinet with rifles chained to the wall, and a kerosene lamp and flashlights. The terrain was brutal and simple. There were plenty of rocks, an occasional scrub pine that a squirrel would find uncomfortable, thistle and Spanish bayonet. Two thorn trees stood at either end of the camp. A shrike with dull plumage would impale her catch on those barbs. There was not a friendly blade of grass or a dandelion anywhere. The lizards were the only signs of life.

The dirt was red and the stones were grist colored, but knuckled like rock candy. The road that had brought her was no road at all, just a half-mile track through territory that only a shepherd might cross, in hopes of finding something green on the other side. No shepherds here. The warning had gone round.

Cass felt exposed. The femininity in her collapsed inside her rib cage. She lifted the sleeping bag out of the car, but Baba took it and tossed it back inside.

"You'll sleep in this, and dry your face in this,

and bind your wounds in this if you're unlucky."
He thrust out a towel, an army issue blanket and a
checkered keffeyeh.

A blush spilled through her cheeks. She stared
at the ground. He handed her a pair of shears and
grunted at her hair. The blades were sharp and her
hair fell in a golden pile to the ground, last
vestiges of her vanity. The haircut bared the bullet
scar over her ear, an unspoken testament to her
experience. She had lost ten pounds since Foster
died and her broad shoulders had become a bony
yoke to hold up her shirt. Her breasts had
flattened. Her nipples grew stiff now under the
rough washed shirt of drab green. Fear maybe.
The reluctant cadet.

Baba looked her over. Her eyes were clear,
green-grey like the sky before a summer rain. The
short hair gave more prominence to her patrician
nose. It was a hard sculpted nose with a severity
that was betrayed by her small mouth and the
dimple that played havoc with any attempt at
ferocity.

They welcomed her in peace because of Allah.
They welcomed her in victory because they were
Palestinians. They hurled their Arabic at her and
she spat it back, first embarrassed, then . . .
grammar be hanged. Her sentences were short
and clipped, mostly in the present tense. She
refused to give more. Anything past was her affair.
The scar threw them off.

Woman or no, it made no difference to them.
She was a commando in training as they were. She
had to do what they did and rub gun bluing out of
the pores of her skin and not pale at the weight of
a grenade in her hand. She kept her ears pricked

like a rabbit far from his warren. She did not like to be touched and touched she was, pounded and pulled and wrestled and thrown to the ground, and she had to return and fight and spin and swear by God to kill. The master preached a martial art that was half Arab desperation, half Oriental restraint, graceful and deadly and sometimes savagely economical.

Cigarettes were allowed. They were shared, the only sharing but for the sweat that rolled between their legs and gummed their features.

She exhaled and pondered the men around her. There had been no tyrannies in her childhood, in the Eisenhower years. America had been at peace under a general. There had been no soldiers in the streets. No broken, desperate men peopled her dreams, as they did the restless nights of the Palestinian children, when Israeli jets screamed overhead, dropping their payloads in attempts to root out commando nests.

There had been the occasional bloody noses of youth and the disappointment of being a girl in a neighborhood full of boys, but when her strength and her swiftness failed her, her wits took over. It was her woods where the tire swing was, her tree where her father had built her a fortress of boughs. He conspired with her and gave her baseball mitts instead of dolls, hiking boots instead of dresses and a confidence in her body that matched the confidence of her mind. When he took his women out to dinner in New York, every ounce the ladies, the waiters fawned and her father's eyes shone with pride.

When he began to die . . . his own coordination flagged in the ravages of cancer. Cobalt treatments whittled him away. He would have bounded for the door of death once, knowing that it would not be shut until he was on the other side, but the disease crept slowly. He saw the wasting of it reflected in his daughter's eyes. In the end, by some merciful stroke, he was gone before all dignity failed him, but Cass felt cheated. Her friend and colleague had been stolen away from her. Too soon.

Cass felt his energy now, his genes working in accordance with her own. The companionship of his spirit warmed her as if he sat perched on her shoulder, never letting her fall too far. On the other side, she was bolstered by her memories of Foster. His spirit too would come, whispering jokes, reminding her of the absurdities of life, and she was capable then of welcoming death, even if it came without her invitation.

The day began before sun up when the red veins pulsated in the sky, when the air was wet and clean. She crawled over the rock ledges, learning bruise by bruise to keep stones from tumbling down and giving away her position. This was hardly the kind of fighting that she would expect in Aleppo, but the demolition training was fitting right into her scheme. Latakis, she figured, the sumptuous Mr. Hassan Khoury, would be a piece of cake. The training she was getting now was belly-down silence, lone commando warfare, creeping under barbed wire and past invisible sentries, all business. She learned time detonators, tailpipe bombs, explosives wrapped in paper packages.

There were no friends here. Each commando

was an armed suicide unit loaded up with
Kalashnikov rifle or sidearm, not both, RPG's on
special occasions, clips of ammunition, four
grenades, a packet of explosive of varying
mixtures, a knife, fuse wires and nylon cord. In a
hazy kind of make-believe, some would be asked to
carry messages to units working within the Israeli
borders. Others would take transmitters or make
contact to complete the cycle that would set the
works in motion for another terrorist act. Their
batting average was pitifully low and their
mortality rate, appallingly high. They did not trust
her at first with live grenades, so weights were
clipped to her chest straps. Whatever breasts she
had left were periodically crushed by these things.
Grenades wouldn't be a bad idea on her own
mission if things got beyond her.

They were all malleable under the master. His
control classes on hand-to-hand combat were
things that Cass would never like to go through
again, like a bad dream on West 98th Street with
three against one. They fought sometimes bare-
fisted and unarmed. Cass became especially good
at dodging and weaving then using her feet instead
of her hands. She had a tendency to protect her
head, which the master called cowardice.

She chipped her front teeth and nearly got her
jaw cracked when she and Hamdy fought rifle
against rifle. They banged barrels like pugil sticks,
as if their weapons had been emptied in battle,
and this their last chance to get the enemy. The
broken teeth had made her angry. She ducked,
then swung the gun with all her weight, letting the
butt sink like a depth charge into her opponent's
stomach. She spat out a piece of tooth, but the

master didn't give her time to nurse the jaw. He had her in a hold she could not break.

"This is death," he said. "This quick. Get used to it, and learn to get out of the hold." Then he made to fling her on the ground and brought her up with a shake to balance her, then propelled her to her own corner of the compound.

And she must not cry. That's what she told herself now in front of the mirror, a piece of a mirror hung on a nail in the plank that stuck up from the ground. She felt ugly and lean. Foster would loathe her like this. He always brought out the femininity in her. Their warmth together brought out an easy definition of their sexes. Now she had no one to bounce her signals off. She looked haggard. The simple fare, the commando special of foul beans and pita bread, had given her dysentery, so more pounds had gone. The sunburn had long since peeled, and the tan went deep against her nose and cheeks. Dark shadows underscored her eyes and her mouth had become very hard. She made a smile; the dimple appeared faintly. She was sexless now, a sexless thing. She was turning into the killer she wanted to be. Syria. It was an acid bath for her brain.

She ran her fingers through her short hair. They had played such a rough game with her that day. Steal the bacon, only the bacon was the radio pack she had strapped to her back. Hamdy had gone through it two days before and hadn't said a word since a trip-wire laid him flat. The dummy transmitter had shattered under his weight. He had been mortified.

Her tongue surveyed the sharp edges of her teeth. Didn't show much. No nerve damage.

She had carried the pack from point A to point B, but in reality would have been full of holes on delivery.

"You don't do Palestine any . . . ."

She shut him up with a wave of her hand. His own lashed out.

"It is Palestine. That is all!" he screamed.

She could not react to the rallying cry. It was not her war.

She had chilled them then. They no longer spoke with her.

Her routines became fiercer. The following day she had her initiation to the dance of death.

"Okay, listen, you guys. Fun's fun, but could we forego the provo shuffle today." The gunman motioned her out of line and directed her to the foreground, a clearing girdled with thorn trees.

"Oh yeah, right, keep moving or lose your kneecaps . . ." she ranted.

The first bullet hit two inches in front of her . . . splattering dust over the toes of her boots. She was in motion before the second one left the chamber. She was feeling silly and scared shitless at the same time. Even when the bursts of fire stopped, she kept moving.

"Nerves of steel," she said, her fingers shaking as she accepted a cigarette. The gunman shouldered his rifle.

Baba's voice brought them to attention. "Here," he said gruffly and tossed a metal object to the nearest guerrilla. "For you, and you." More objects. The men turned them over and over.

"We are burglars now, eh?" said one of the men as he held up a padlock in the sunlight. Baba had his back to him, handed another lock to Cass and said, evenly, "You may have to get into a magistrate's house, a dormitory locker, the dining hall of a kibbutz. It would be nice if you could do it without making a noise. Here." He threw a bundle of tools to the ground, slim as wires, but crooked at the ends. "Play with those for awhile." He strode away from them, his meaty hands swinging in time to his pace, his grey hair catching the sun, his shoulders thrown back as if he constantly carried a pack.

Cass looked down at the mechanism in her hand and saw the faces of the other commandos mirrored in the metal. She looked on them dispassionately. They would probably never make it. Israeli intelligence, the Mossad, would make mincemeat out of them before they ever reached the barbed wire. If they chanced to find a hole in Israeli security they would blow themselves to bits before capture, taking with them any innocent Israelis who had the misfortune to cross their crazed paths.

Cass knew, too, she could never return to Tel Aviv now. The Israelis were thorough. She would be branded a Palestinian sympathizer, if not one of their agents. She laughed at herself then, at the idea she might survive to visit the holy land again.

Sympathy? She had little for either side. To the Israelis and Palestinians, compassion for their enemies was sin, not virtue. Both nationalities viewed men, women, children, parents, all as soldiers. There were no innocents. They were all combatants. When they looked to the future, if ever, the picture was charred at the edges by the cruelties of the past. To the Israelis it was centuries of brutality and senseless slaughter of those of the Jewish faith. To the Palestinians it was the seizure of their homeland and the branding of them as refugees. Defeat was a word neither side ever used.

The lock sprung open in her hand.

"Jesus," she said, pleased with herself. Hamdy looked up with some disdain, then redoubled his efforts. She tried to look serious as he worked, then his own lock sprung open.

"W'Allahi," he said, "by God." They nodded at each other in recognition. Baba dismissed them with a gesture from his watching place some distance away.

Hamdy and Cass rose and walked from the circle of commandos, not talking, just walking. Their hands were deep in their pockets. Their thoughts on the trials yet to come.

It was graduation time for Cass. Her two weeks were nearly up. the twenty-four-hour undercover would be her last lesson. She was not allowed to talk, to eat or to share a cigarette with anyone for several hours before her departure. Then, when darkness fell, Baba sent her out. For twenty-four hours she must not be found. Then she must return to camp voluntarily, past the sentry, avoiding capture by those guerrillas sent out to find her.

She could smell the night closing over her, sense the subtle crack of twigs in the underbrush, feel the prickle of fear creep over her body. At times she remained deathly still, then dashed for trees and gullies that provided cover. Her stomach growled and she gnawed at her knuckles as one of the guerrillas neared, but at the end of it Cass came through at the top of her class, ruthlessly binding the comrade who tried to capture her, stuffing a gag in his mouth and nearly suffocating him under the banana leaves that had kept her shelter in a grove three miles from camp.

At sentry's call, she had sprung from the rocky escarpment, disarming him, but he did not go down. In a frenzy he rushed toward her, angry and still off balance from her attack. She used her forward momentum and clapped his two wrists together, spun and brutally cantilevered him over her body. She lifted the sentry's rifle ready to bash his brains in. Her look warned him if he made a move or cried out she would shoot him.

Cass turned in at midnight. She had not spoken to the master nor Hamdy or the others. They were there, celebrating some bomb explosion in a Netanya vegetable market. Her two weeks were finished at dawn. Her ears still buzzed from the small arms practice that evening. She was a good steady shot twenty meters or less. Far better practice for her than the rifle nonsense. There would be no room for a long barrel in Syria. Close range, clean and final.

But a sixth commando, an interloper, did not let her have her last night's sleep in peace. Her body had surrendered to slumber, a wave rushing over her and rolling her under. She never made a sound in her sleep, an observation of the master.

Suddenly she was jerked up, out from under the blanket to a standing position a little taller than her height could bear. A forearm held her up by her chin, a knife was trained at the corner of her eye.

She did not move. She wanted to tear him apart. She could not move. She dug her fingers into his arm, but it remained pressing against her windpipe.

"Where are you from?" he said.

Silence.

The knife flicked at her cheek. A drop of blood.
"What is your name?"

Silence. The forearm squeezed tight against her
throat and she released herself to the loss of
breath. She choked, then sent her right arm
skyward, knocking the knife up and away from
them. With the same arm she drove into his
stomach, but he twisted and swung her so she
nearly fell. He raised a hand over her neck but she
tackled him . . . low, very low, and sent her fist
hard into his groin. He crumbled as if his legs
were made of plaster, but he still gripped her and
pulled her down on top of him in a distortion of
the sexual act. She could not get up and away from
his hands, so she threw all her weight into him. He
tore the front of her shirt and she struck him in
the face, then struggled away from him. She was
panting. The whipcrack of her first reaction had
echoed out through her system until every nerve
was electrified.

She scrambled away, and pulled her small
bedouin dagger from its shelter, but he was on her
again, his own knife upraised over her chest.

"This is from Moustafa Sheik," he hissed, and
began to plunge the blade downward. She thrust
her own knife into his side and he looked at her as
if he had been insulted. The report of a small
pistol split the night. The downward motion of his
dagger glanced off her shoulder without harm, but
his blood poured over her as if from a pitcher. She
rolled out from beneath him, feeling the scream
welling within her.

Her master's voice was steady. "If that upsets
you, you have already failed to understand
anything we have taught you."

"Baba," she said. Hamdy stood behind him.

Baba stilled her with a gesture of his hand. He checked the clip and the bore of the gun he had just fired, rammed the clip home, turned it butt side round and handed it to her. He turned the corpse over and examined the pockets, the markings on the uniform.

"Saiqa," he said, without surprise. "You have ruffled some Syrian feathers, eh?" She switched the gun from right to left, then back to right.

"Oh, that . . . the deadly widow, I call it. Small grip. Made for a woman," he said. She held it firmly in her hand, pointed at the ground.

"Corsair Unique. French made. .22 automatic. It's yours. Don't thank me for this. Any intruder into this camp would have been shot. The gun—it is a loan. The leadership said you had a mission. The deadly widow may keep you alive long enough to complete it. If I don't receive the gun back, I'll know you are dead."

He rolled the body over again.

"Yours?" he said, pulling the small dagger from the side of the corpse.

Cass looked up at him. Baba nodded. "A little small perhaps, but the wound is good." He ran his thumb down the blade and then wiped the blood across her forehead. He handed the knife to her then, hilt side first, and strode away.

Hamdy waited until the master had returned to his hut, then brought Cass a jerry can of water. He slopped some into her hands, then put the can beside her and walked away.

At dawn she left without a goodbye, blindfolded again. When they took the blindfold off, the Mercedes had swung round on the coastal road. It was heading toward a Syrian checkpoint at the western side of Beirut.

# TWENTY-SIX

Within a few days she had gathered her wits and her strength. The dysentery that had weakened her during training was vanquished with a diet of yogurt and rice. She had meals in her room. She had told the management not to say she was back, and with a ten dollar bill to each of the boys, her whereabouts remained unknown until she was ready to emerge. She was kill-ready. But "shweya, shweya, slowly, slowly." The knife scratch at her cheek was no more than a bad insect bite, but she fumed at the mirror. She rubbed some rouge on her cheeks, but furiously wiped it off with the end of the wet towel wrapped around her head.

She sat on the bed still dripping from the shower. Someone knocked at the door and she slipped into a white terry cloth robe, pulling the gun from its holster on the bureau. She stood squarely in front of the door, her feet spread apart. She held the pistol against her cheek, resting the crook of her elbow in the palm of her left hand, her left arm crossing her waist. The knock came again, faster this time. More urgent.

"Who's there?"

"Harry," he said. "Let me in for Christ's sake!"

"Okay, okay, simmer down. Just a moment."

She put the gun on safety and slipped it into her pocket.

She swung the door wide open and Harry stood nervously in front of her, decked out in knee-high boots, blue silk pants, a swordsman's shirt and a blue felt hat with a long feather sticking out of it.

"Well, if it isn't the Scarlet Pimpernel. Come on in."

"Cassie." He looked around him and Cass motioned for him to sit on the bed.

"What is it, Harry? More news?"

"Cassie, there's a death warrant out for you. You've got to get out of here." He removed his hat and with a flourish pitched it across the room to the chair. It flopped on the ground. He shrugged. Cass sat beside him.

"Slow down, Harry. Let's hear all of it."

"They're gunning for you."

"Who's they?"

"Khoury paid the contract. Apparently he's hired a couple of guerrillas from Saiqa. Old favors."

"Yeah, well, one of 'em's dead."

"Cassie," he looked appalled. He took the corner of the towel and wiped his face. She gave it to him and tugged at her damp hair.

"You're looking positively boyish, these days," Harry said.

"Yes. The Peter Pan in me."

"This is no time to joke. I'm telling you, they're out for blood. Yours."

"I'm flattered. They're going to an awful lot of trouble, don't you think? What's the story, anyway?"

"That night you were in Latakia, a big score was

going down. Khoury and his boys. Your friends, Moustafa Sheik and all, were delivering goods to the Corsicans, or already had by the sound of it. Lots of money in their pockets."

"Yeah, so?"

"Khoury's been taking a lot of flak lately for late deliveries, for lack of discretion, you know, boasting about the wad he was getting. Flashing it around. The Corsicans were getting pretty pissed off about it. They're cornered. They've got to buy his refined stuff because of the shutdown of the European labs. But they don't like him. They like to keep things neat . . . a tight lid, security and all that. When Khoury's bravos got sloppy and let you see the stuff, your fate was sealed. Khoury heard about it, apparently knocked Rawzi around.

"They're gunning for you now. Journalist, you know, think you'll blab about it to the Drug Enforcement folks. Interpol."

"Oh, yeah, the angels in rumpled trench coats."

"The narcs have been trying to bust up the Corsican/Syrian connection for the past two years. They always get skunked by Syrian cops on the take."

"But I haven't told anyone about it. I'm being a pretty nice kid, in fact."

"They're going to make sure that you don't. You're an added insult. A woman. They've got a lot of money riding on this venture, and they don't want any fool-headed American woman getting in the way. They're liable to throw you down a well if they get hold of you."

She went into the bathroom, shed the robe and put on a shirt and jeans. She tucked the shirt in as she came out. Harry was sitting dejectedly on the bed.

"Here, I stopped at the optometrist's for you."

She took the contact lenses, looked them over and tossed them on the bureau.

"Listen, Cassie, get out of here. You're in over your head. I don't want to see you get smashed up. Nobody around here does. You've got some fool idea that you're Superman or something, but they'll get you."

"Want a drink?"

"Yeah, sure. I guess so." She dialed room service.

"Scotch okay?"

"Sure," he said twirling his braided belt, "Chivas." His face was white; he hadn't been out in the sun in a while. But his eyes were clear. He hadn't been smoking.

"Yeah," Cass said into the phone. "And could you ask Omar to come up here if he's around? Thanks."

The waiter appeared with the drinks, followed by Omar El Gamazi, son of the owner of the hotel.

"What can I do for you, Miss Morgan?" He was always polite, immaculately turned out in a tailored suit. His shoes were polished and a ring gleamed on the small finger of his left hand. That one fingernail was an inch long. He carried a revolver in a shoulder holster.

"Omar, have you still got people watching my car?"

"Yes," he said, "as you requested."

"Anyone looking for me, at the front desk? Any inquiries?

"A couple of people. One we know to be your friend, Mr. Andrew Pym. The other—well, we weren't sure. We said you had not returned." He held his hands up together in front of him and eyed Harry's getup with some distaste.

"Okay, just checking. Harry here seems to think it's a matter of life and death."

"It always is," Omar said, smiling with even white teeth.

"Let me give you this, anyway. Pass it on to your boys. I don't want anyone to outbid me." She handed him a sheaf of twenties.

"It's not necessary, Miss Morgan. Don't we always take good care of you?"

"Just making sure, Omar."

"It will be billed under special services on the final tally for your stay. Would that be satisfactory?"

"That's fine. Just try and keep the hounds from my door, eh?"

"It's a pleasure," he said. "Will that be all?"

"Yes, thanks a lot.' He bowed to both Cass and Harry. As the door closed behind him, Harry mixed himself a drink.

"You're kidding yourself, Cassie." He untied the silk scarf at his throat, then retied it again at the mirror, so the knot was to the side, the scarlet ends flaring out.

"Harry, thanks for the warning. I hope I know what I'm doing. Here's to . . . I don't know, here's to what?"

"Here's to a bountiful hash harvest." Harry grinned.

## TWENTY-SEVEN

"What the hell have you done to your hair?" Kodak said as she entered Kitchener's Pub, but it wasn't the hair so much as the chiaroscuro of her face that shocked him.

"I've taken the veil," she said with downcast eyes, "and I thought I'd have a last drunk with the boys before prostrating myself before Our Lady of Lebanon."

"Good God, get this girl a sandwich!" Andrew Pym demanded, lurching from his bar stool.

"Just a little stomach trouble," she said. "Happens to the best of us, Andrew. Don't worry. A Scotch and soda will suffice."

"Where have you been?" Kodak growled, pulling her toward him.

"Researching the documentary. I've been down south with a Lebanese family. Their hospitality was wonderful. Their food . . ." She opened her arms. Pym spotted the bulge of the gun at her right hip.

"Come here, you bag of bones. You look bloody awful with that hair, you know. What happened? Case of nits?"

"Arghhhhh! It's cooler this way."

"Joe Taylor's been looking for you. He's sent

several telexes. Seems to think you might want to work for the *Herald* again."

"Through A.P.?"

"Yeh."

"Tell him I'll be out of pocket for awhile. Going up to Vazcatchian's farm. Pym, why don't you fill in?"

"The *Herald*'s never particularly liked my style," Pym confessed. "Too bleeding-heart liberal. So really tell me about this documentary," he said switching to Arabic, insisting on speaking it with her.

"Did you see any ships in the harbor?"

"At Sidon?" She had to cover herself now.

"At Sidon."

"A few. One Turkish. Two Lebanese. Fishing vessels. They were dynamiting their catch."

"Very sporting of them."

"You can't eat sport," she said, responding quickly in the Palestinian way. Pym's eyes brightened. He had caught her inflection, she saw it. Pym was a master of Arab dialects. He had served in Palestine with the British Army during and after the Second World War and had studied the language. He could switch at will from the soft "hut" of the Marsh Arab to the gutteral hard "G's" of the Egyptians of Aswan.

"Would you stop speaking that bloody language?" Kodak broke in.

"Christ," she said, "You'd think you'd learn it after three years in this Godforsaken hell hole. The most you can say is 'bastard' and 'whore' and 'shit.'"

"That's all a cameraman needs to say, thank you very much."

"Well, children, excuse me, but I've got to make a stop at the White House."

Pym didn't go to the bathroom, though. He went to the phone, making sure he was out of earshot.

On the third ring he heard the click at the other end.

"She's back," Pym said. "Tough as hell, I'd say." He waited for the Interpol Commander to respond.

"Yes. Pea shooter. Maybe a .22 or a .25. A defense weapon, maybe." He held the phone away.

"Yes, I will, but so far I can't get a thing out of her. She's reacting like a professional now, but that could slack off. She's only just come back. I'll watch her as best I can, but she's no dummy." In a few moments he said, "Right." Then he rang off.

The Interpol Commander leaned back in his chair. He slapped a folder of papers on the desk in front of him, picked it up again and let it fall. His charge d'affaires waited.

"She's valuable," he said. "She's managed to give us the slip twice. Pym seems to think she's been trained. Palestinian maybe. What has she got in mind?"

"Maybe she just wants to defend herself," Greenland said.

"Maybe, maybe." He gnawed at the end of the pencil. "What I don't understand is why the C.I.A. didn't tap her long ago in Cairo. Her knowledge of the language. Her contacts."

"They did, sir," the aide said and turning to a paragraph in the dossier on his lap, "They approached her twice, and she told them to go to hell. Journalistic integrity and all that."

The Interpol Commander smiled. "Well, we

might have to recruit her ourselves."

"She wouldn't stand for it, sir."

"She doesn't have to know about it. Save us the trouble of paying her. Just keep her alive. I don't see how we can stop her if she's determined about this." He pressed the intercom and told his secretary to reach a number in Damascus.

## TWENTY-EIGHT

The two-seater Mercedes clung to the coastal road at seventy miles an hour as Cass headed north. She reached L'Aiglon, the Vazcatchian farm, by midafternoon. Ingrid came out on the porch to greet her, and they embraced stiffly.

"You know," Cass said.

"Yes," Ingrid said, stepping back. "I'm not supposed to talk about it. Vaz' orders. Ever the obedient wife."

Cass smiled.

"But it frightens me, not just for you, but for him, too. You have awakened something in him. He wants to come with you. He wants that . . . ."

"I thought you weren't supposed to talk about it," Cass said soberly. "Besides which, he's not coming. He knows that. If you both want to help me with preparations, that's fine. If there's going to be an argument—if this is going to drive a shaft between—"

"All right," Ingrid said. "You make me feel weak." She took a deep breath and stood at her full height, about four inches taller than Cass.

"Listen," Cass said. "Don't bully me, just because you're bigger than I am. Wouldn't do you any good anyway."

199

"Oh, yes," Ingrid said, taking Cass by the scruff of the neck and leading her indoors. Cass could feel the pressure of her fingers like an unspoken command, but she broke free goodnaturedly. To much sentiment. There was no time for weakness now. Ingrid watched in silence as Cass strode from one end of the livingroom to the other, like a green horse, but there were no ticks or kinks. The gait was firm, resolute and controlled. Nothing excessive.

"You'd better go outside. You'll wear through my floorboards if you keep that up."

"Makes me calm," Cass said. "Just roaming around. But you're right. Am I driving you nuts?" she said turning abruptly and halting midstride.

"Come on," Ingrid said. "I could stretch my legs myself."

They strode out into the sunshine, taking a right turn at the paddock and climbing the hill. Vaz was just coming in from the vegetable garden with an armful of lettuce and radishes.

"Hello, ladies."

They both waved. "How would you like to be chef tonight?" Ingrid called.

"Fine," Vaz said. "The meal will be underway by sunset. Don't stray far."

"Badein, then, later," they called and disappeared over the headland. Neither spoke again. They just climbed, through the line of cedars into the open spaces of table rock and rubble and the distant cry of birds. They climbed higher and let the cool mountain air fill their lungs, and the view, of Becharre and the Mediterranean Sea beyond, fill their eyes.

Vaz was hard at work below, dressing the lamb

and stoking the wood-burning stove. The salad greens were washed and hung up to dry in wire mesh baskets over the sink. The first floor of the Vazcatchian farm was one large room with a stone fireplace at each end. Great glass windows anchored in heavy wooden frames looked up the mountain on one side and down the mountain on the other.

Vaz stood at the up-mountain window watching for some sign of them. He sipped uneasily at his cognac, listening. Varmint was quiet in the paddock. The birds were just beginning their last choruses before sunset when he heard the women coming through the door.

"Good appetite, eh?" he said as they walked in.

"I'll say."

"We've been long, no?"

"All the more glad to see you, my pretty wife."

The dinner began deliciously. The roast lamb was served on a bed of fresh mint. The table was covered with a white damask cloth, Ingrid's embroidery decorating the edges. Two candles burned in silver holders at either end of the table. The salad, the new potatoes, the wine—everything had been just right. Except that an argument had begun. Vaz was challenging Cass' defenses, seeing that the confidence of daylight had given way to doubts.

Cass abruptly stood up from the table.

"I think the Palestinians know something about assassination," she barked.

"I think they know something about suicide," Vaz said. "You think you're prepared for this. For this journey. You've got some cowboy logic working in that brain of yours; the Syrians will tear you to bits."

"So . . . what?" she shouted. "Give it up? when all I can see is Foster's face? My mother's? Should I leave it to the authorities? Moustafa Sheik isn't dead. You think they're going to arrest Khoury, even question him? A councilman!" She struggled to control her emotions, succeeded.

"Why would the Syrian police become involved with this? You don't give them much credit."

"I'm not blaming them," she said quite calmly. "They had a body. It was identified as Moustafa Sheik by an elder from the Ouzai tribe. The confession, the story about his death when attempting to escape, was something to please their own superiors. You don't think plenty of money crosses hands when heroin's involved?"

"But they can't know that's what is involved. They wouldn't stand for it. Hashish, maybe they allow that, but they wouldn't allow their own Syrian youth, their own children, to engage in the shooting of heroin into their veins. They want soldiers, not junkies."

"Vaz, it's not a Syrian problem. This stuff goes out, internationally. Some of it reaches New York. A lot of it, Paris. You think the French like their kids teetering around in a rehearsal for death?"

"You should leave it to the authorities," Vaz said stubbornly. "Give them the information you know. Let them handle it. You're a young girl. You've never been married, had children."

"Do you think that's even a consideration for me?" She looked at Ingrid. "Lawrence Foster would have been my husband. He would have been the father of my children. And they cut him down, because of me. Because of this," she pulled at her blond hair, "because I'm a woman that they wanted. The bastards! And they were so stupid as to allow me to see their drugs, their dirty narcotics, their dirty hides. God!"

"All right. All right, but I wish I could send someone along with you. An experienced gunmine."

"No. I can't have that right now. Don't you think I'd welcome some aid? It's going to be difficult enough for me to move freely. I can't even cross the border at the normal checkpoint, my name's so hot. Oh sure, I could get the proper papers. They've already been ordered, but what then, rent a car, travel by foot. The horse is the key. You find me that key, Vaz."

"But you've still got to travel by train," Ingrid said. "You can't cover so many miles on horseback. You'll have to deal with too many people."

"I'm not worried about that," she said. "Andrew has been working with me, drumming Arabic into my brain. Look here," she said, pulling a map from the knapsack that lay on the couch. "Here, the train route from Tall Kalakh to Tartous, then a livery truck. Here, six miles from the abattoir to Khoury's and all along the way. The only great distance I have to cover will be from Latakia to Jisr Esh Shugur, and the only way to cover it safely will be on horseback. The authorities won't be searching for a simple farm boy. It's the only way I can fade into the scenery undetected."

"You'll have a horse then," said Vaz, "and you'll get some training from me. The Palestinians." He spat. "They are a race of angry children. No technique. No finesse."

"Who else knows about your plans?" Ingrid asked.

"No one. You and Vaz. Harry has some idea, but he'll close his mind to it. By your Armenian blood, Vaz, I'm asking you to forget anything I've told you."

"We would not be friends if we didn't try and talk you out of it."

"You can't."

# TWENTY-NINE

Vaz and Ingrid left to Aleppo the next day. Cass took them to the service-taxi station in Tripoli and from there they went to the railway depot in the Syrian town of Tall Kalakh. While awaiting the train to Homs and Aleppo, Vaz was to take pictures of the railway depot and the shops and stalls in the area. Ingrid, in a sunbonnet, would be speaking in Arabic to the villagers, asking prices for baskets and weavings and picking up information on the rail spur that would soon carry Cass halfway to Latakia. They had asked a neighboring farm owners, Selim, to meet them at the Syrian/Lebanese border in five days with a horse trailer.

Cass was left alone in the farmhouse. She took to the chores with a vengeance, filling her hours with milking the cow, carting the manure to the garden, and running the stallion in the main paddock. Varmint was a backyard-bred horse, half Arab and half English cavalry mount. He was eleven years old, with long hairs prickling from his chin. In his prime.

Cass grew accustomed to Varmint, to his habits, but taking him over the border would be a mistake. She knew it. Stallions were too

unpredictable, too noisy. They could nicker at a
passing wind, a mare in heat, a bird in flight. Too
jittery. The Arab chieftains always rode mares.
They were quieter, more dependable, not so
prancy as a proud stallion.

Varmint helped her get her legs back in shape
for the long ride. He was good training. She rode
him bareback, using a halter and two ropes as
reins. She took the kinks out of him, driving him
up over the headland along the rocky trail and to
the clearing above, where she could survey
L'Aiglon. In a clip-on leather holster at her right
hip she wore the Corsair Unique.

The late afternoon heat baked in to the stallion's
hide. She brushed him down, pulled his mane and
then gave him a swat on the rump and sent him
flying across the paddock. She took the gun from
the holster and walked up the headland again,
carrying with her a tin bucket which she hung on a
cedar branch about the height of a man's chest.
She backed off to twenty meters and fired, moving
closer to the target as she found the .22 lacked
penetration. She would have preferred a bigger
caliber gun, but she did not want the added weight
and length of a silencer. After she had run through
four clips, the bucket looked like wormwood.

She lay at the window that night watching for
headlights, differentiating between the sounds of
the stable and the sounds of her own fear. Moonlight played in the warp of Ingrid's loom and
through the gauzy curtains that hung at the
windows. She felt trapped inside the house,
trapped in her waiting for the puzzle to fit together. Slowly, slowly.

She flipped on the radio and listened to the

World Service of the BBC, then Radio Damascus
with its martial music signaling the next news-
cast. She repeated the Arabic words as they came
over the air. The Palestinians had fired on the
French United Nations troops charged with
keeping Israelis and Palestinians apart. A French
colonel was badly wounded. A French soldier was
dead.

In front of her, spread out on the bed, was the
map of Latakia that Harry the Joint had given her.
The heroin processing lab was marked, about a
quarter of a mile south down the coast road from
Hassan Khoury's gas station, on his property.

The lab produced heroin that was 80 to 90
percent pure, but now, in midsummer, there
would be a lull in the manufacture. The lab would
be running full tilt by November when the first
harvest of Turkish poppies would be brought
down for processing. The summer lull gladdened
her. She did not want to tackle syndicate
protection at the lab site. Harry had figured that
morphine from last year's crops might be under-
going processing to keep the locals satisfied and to
have samples on hand should any new buyers
come through, but no particular precautions
would be in force. No big guns.

She had packed and repacked the saddlebags,
weighing each item and its importance. Five
pounds of gelignite, three percussion caps, fuse
lines, six clips of ammunition for her .22, and a
timing device. She had a suit of men's clothes,
French cut to accentuate her broad shoulders and
to flatten her chest, a long, nightshirt-like
gelebeya, a cloak, two extra shirts, a compass, her
satchel of maps, a roll of bandages, alcohol and a

few tins of canned meat. With a wry smile she had
included a bottle of vodka.

She ran through the Arabic book again, studying
the characters and feeling the pronunciations
slip over her lips. Andrew Pym had been a good
teacher. He had warned her to get the Egyptian
out of her dialect and replace it with the more
common pronunciation of the Arab levant. Mix it
up, he told her, and you'll get along anywhere.
What had he known, she wondered. She thought
kindly of Pym then, Pym who was aging with the
Middle East. The political turmoil there was
written in the bend of his spine and the frown
lines that ran longitudinally down his thin face.
His eyes were bright blue, tinted with yellow from
his many bouts with hepatitis, but he figured if the
guns of the civil war didn't get him, neither would
a failing liver. She caught him sometimes holding
long conversations with himself over what was
just and right. His love for the Palestinians was
marked with extreme hatred at times, but he never
wavered from their cause. He had served in
Palestine as a British Army officer. His own father
had been an army chaplain. He remembered the
explosion at the King David Hotel, picking
through the pieces of his own comrades. He never
forgave the Israelis, the Irgun, the Stern Gang.

He stood with Israeli troops in 1948 at the
Allenby bridge when Palestinians by the
thousands crossed over to Jordan. Some swam in
their panic, never to return again. He followed
them but he did not weep for them. He sang the
songs of the Palestinian heroes. The same heroes
that produced a hail of long range artillery into
their camps, where U.N. issue pajamas hung

limply on the clothes lines.

She saw the drab green, then, and the Kalashnikov rifles chasing through the orange groves of southern Lebanon. She had done the killing dance with them, but cheated them of her ultimate purpose. She had no cause with the Israelis, but she had been trained by their enemies, engulfing their intensity and melding it with her own struggle to resolve her own question of justice. Her resolve did not waver, though the woman's fear, the fear of the empty womb, of being alone, clutched at her.

She felt the floor creak under her bare feet, saw the fire licking at the grate. She poked the wood and had turned toward the door, heading for the stable, when the phone rang.

It was Henry the Joint. The package that she had ordered would arrive by runner the following morning. She would have four glassine bags of heroin in her hands by noon. When she rang off she felt the loneliness again. The eaves of L'Aiglon cried in the nightwind. She went to the stable, her hand never far from the gun.

She buried her face in Varmint's neck and ran her hands down his mane, over and over, feeling his warmth, his steamy breath on hers. He was quiet. The cow was lying on her bed of straw, chestnut colored in the lamp light, a brighter red by day. Cass found a blanket and spent the night on the stable floor. She showered at sun-up, outside, in the wet morning air; the mountain chill was just giving way to the summer's warmth. The runner arrived with his sealed package and was gone with an extra ten Lebanese pounds in his pocket. She stashed the dope and went out of the house.

The stiffness in her limbs from the barn floor loosened with the pace. The sweat began to run on her third mile; she was counting every other stride, methodically driving her body on. She sprinted, then jogged, then sprinted, and leapt over the rocks in her path, grabbing a fence post and vaulting over the low wires into the grassy fields, watching for rabbit holes and listening to the sound of her own breathing.

Her long legs pumped. The beads of sweat were a glaze over her body. When she thought she could run no more, she ran all the harder, exulting in the pain hammering in her lungs, inside her calves. At last she turned and headed back. At the barn she slumped to the earth and waited for her throttling heart to still. She threw clods of dirt at Varmint as he trotted in the paddock, then gathered eggs from the chicken house for her breakfast.

Once fed she sat down to the telephone. It was early morning in the United States, before dawn, when she roused a night intern at Roosevelt Hospital.

"I'm calling from Lebanon," she said. "Please, can you tell me how Helen Morgan is doing?"

"Yes, of course," he said wearily and walked away from the phone. Cass heard the rustle of papers as he sat back down.

"She's in good hands, Miss Morgan. She's doing very well," he said. "The doctors have taken some skin from your mother's thighs to begin the surgical reparation of her face. The jawbone is setting properly and her face will appear normal, though slightly rough in texture. Most of the stitches will be lost in her hairline, but . . ." he paused.

"Go on, please."

"She will lose some of the expressiveness, some of the muscle tone that normally punctuates the human face. The lines that come with smiles and frowns. Do you know what I mean?"

"It's very clear," Cass said. "Could you tell her, please, that I called and send her my love? I'm taking a trip for awhile and won't be near a phone."

"All right, Miss Morgan. I'll tell her. Is there . . ."

"Thank you. Good-bye." Cass put the phone down and made for the headland again. More target practice.

She turned and fired, knocking the eye out of a tree. The branches quivered and she shot again, lower, harder, firmer this time, grasping the gun with both hands, steadying her aim, easing the trigger back. She returned to the house through the mountain stream, her boots slung over her shoulder, her socks drying as they hung from her belt. The icy water ran shivers up through her body and turned to steam at her pumping heart. Foster's heart. She felt him near her then, just beside her. Then she saw him go down as the slugs hit his body. Saw his own flesh against the stones of Aleppo.

Cass was sauntering up from the creek toward the house as she heard the honk of a horn. The trailer had arrived. Selim jumped out from the driver's seat, and Vaz and Ingrid opened the door on the other side. Selim clapped his hands and rubbed them on his pants, slapping them free of sweat, chuckling to himself, waiting to show off the prize in the back of the van.

"Well," said Cass, "welcome home. Let's see what we've got here."

Vaz raised both hands, a gesture of wait, wait. He was dressed like a baronial Arab in the long white thwab of Arabia with a black kaftan thrown over his shoulders. The keffeyeh had fallen down from his head and now circled his throat. His well fed belly protruded from the folds. Ingrid joined him, dressed in a black desert dress embroidered with red flowers. Her own hair was trained back from her bright and open face, and she smiled. They each took a trailer door and swung it open.

"Nice haunches. So far so good," Cass said. "Ho, girl. A mare. Perfect. Nice. Strong. Ho, ho, give us your head."

"You'll have to speak to her in Arabic," Ingrid said.

"Taban, of course." Cass ran her right hand up over the haunch to the backbone, well covered. She eased along the left side of the horse, untying the halter rope, then backing her down the ramp.

"Good and sound," said Vaz. "Not too ostentatious. Not a crowd gatherer, but a pure-bred Arab just the same. Look at her lines."

"A beauty. Young, though. She been schooled?"

"She's two and a half," Ingrid said, "saddle broken. Done some jumping, but she has a tendency to throw her head, throw herself off balance. I've got an old martingale in the barn though. We should be able to correct that. Otherwise she's got a tender mouth and even, short gaits. We'll have her in shape in no time."

"Expensive?" Cass asked.

"My dear," Vaz sighed, "A Syrian horsetrader never lived who could better this Armenian. We can dress her up in silver shoes and still have some for champagne and beefsteaks."

"Champagne and steak it is, then," said Cass. "Has she got a name?"

"The stablehands called her Mabruka, 'Congratulations.' Apparently the mare who bore her had a hard time with the birth."

"Mabruka, huh? That's fine. Ingrid, you feeling like a ride? Varmint's ready. I'll get the other saddle."

Ingrid changed clothes and dug right in. Her blue workshirt was tied at her waist, above the leather belt that cinched up a pair of Vaz's baggy blue jeans. She had pulled her hair up under a red bandanna. They set up cavalettes to train Mabruka to jump properly, pace herself before the fence. The mare proved an apt but unwilling pupil, driving against the martingale that held her head at an even level with her chest.

On her third refusal of the fence, she reared, then threw her weight to the right, dislodging Cass from the saddle. Cass, angry with herself as well as the mare, mounted again, drawing her horse under her, collecting her, keeping in constant contact with the horse's mouth. When the canter was even, she took her to the fence again, this time not moving her legs at all, just squeezing, her heels silent against Mabruka's flanks. The mare took the fence big, clearing it with two feet of height to spare, bucking on the other side, throwing her Arab tail high.

Ingrid cheered. Vaz watched from the sidelines, smoking a pipe, and calling out whenever he saw

Cass using her English riding aids.

"Longer stirrups! Keep your feet forward! Ride loosely like the Bedouins, not so stiff and military. This isn't a dressage lesson! If you want to slip through Syria undetected, you must ride like an Arab."

"Christ!" Cass called out, "My old riding instructor is probably turning over in his grave. He'd crack me with a crop for riding like this."

Ingrid and Cass both flourished in the sunshine of the next few weeks, working their horses. Ingrid worked Varmint mercilessly on Cass' inspiration. Soundness came back into his legs, and the future stud in him was apparent. The woman's blond hair lightened, while their fingernails grew dark with hoof blacking. Ingrid mixed up a batch of olive oil and iodine to darken Cass' skin still further.

They mucked the stable together and both found solace in the soft muzzles of their horses. Varmint was looking younger than ever, pleased with his stablemate. Cass warned Vaz again and again to keep Mabruka and Varmint apart; she did not want to ride a horse in foal over the Syrian border. Vaz gave in, but reluctantly. The dream of building his stable had been growing as he watched Ingrid and Cass gallop in tandem over the fields.

One evening while Vaz and Cass sat by the fire working out each step of the journey and cleaning their guns after target practice, Ingrid climbed the stairs to the loft. Cass listened as Ingrid sat down to her loom. The thud of the crossbar drove another strand of Mabruka's tail into the saddle blanket. Ingrid had been quiet the past few days.

Cass listened as the bars of the loom shifted back and forth, warp and woof. She excused herself and Vaz nodded as Cass mounted the stairs.

"Ingrid."

"Yes, Cass," she said turning slowly toward the girl who stood on the top stair. Cass was lean, her figure cut from moonbeams. Her skin took on its illumination and her eyes were dark.

"Some brandy?"

"Yes, please."

Cass walked towards her with the bottle and two glasses. She pulled up a three-legged stool and sat beside Ingrid, lower, smaller on the stool like a child. Ingrid turned the flame of the kerosene lamp higher and laid out the blanket.

"Talismans," she said pointing out two eaglets she had embroidered in the blanket. "If all else fails, they may get you through with a prayer."

"A prayer to whom?"

"I don't know. I suppose to whatever is firm beneath your feet and clear in your head." She heard Vaz stirring downstairs.

"He wants to come with you," Ingrid said. "I can see it in the way he's handling that gun again. In the way he moves, as he did during the civil war. He's shooting at phantoms when he hits a treetrunk. He's protecting L'Aiglon. You and me. You mustn't let him. There's no war here."

"Ingrid. We've already discussed it. There's no way he can come. He's only trying to teach me his knowledge, his feel for . . . the kill."

"I don't like this. I don't like what you're doing. Foster wouldn't like it, Cass."

Cass shut her eyes. "If it had been me, he would

have gone back. Is it any different?"

"Yes."

"No," Cass said. She reached into her pocket and pulled out a cigarette. The flare of the match brought Ingrid's features into focus, the light freckling of her nose and cheeks and her blond lashes. She wore a soft cotton shirt, faded from many washings. The collar lay back under the weight of her hair.

"You can dye wool," said Cass looking at the saddle blanket, "Can you dye this?" She ran her fingers through her short cropped hair.

"Black?"

"Yes."

"Now?"

"Yes."

Cass watched as Ingrid went to one of the tall wicker baskets that stood by the window, tearing out rags and swatches of cloth. Skeins of wool and balls of string hung from the hooks on the wall in a confusion of colors. She found the package she wanted and went to the bathroom for a basin of hot water. As Ingrid's fingers worked the dye out of the package and the water turned black, Cass went downstairs for vinegar.

"Too dark, do you think?" Cass said later, standing before the mirror and wiping the rinse water from her neck with a towel.

"Yes, too dark, but the sun will lighten it soon enough."

Cass cocked her head, moved it from side to side and pushed the wet hair this way and that, checking her fingers to see if any of the color came off.

"It will stay," Ingrid said from the bathroom,

dumping the basin of water, "until it grows out. How soon do you go?"

"Within the next few days. Vaz and I are still studying the pictures you took in Aleppo and working out just what I should carry."

Ingrid poured herself another brandy, offered more to Cass, who declined, and sat back down at her loom. Cass came close and gave her a kiss on the temple.

"I'll be sleeping outside from now on. Close to Marbruka" Ingrid held her lightly by the shoulder then released her. She was beginning a new weaving; Cass left her to it.

The next morning Cass was running through the northern pasture when Andrew Pym and Kodak arrived. Vaz stood on the porch and waved them in, offered them a cool drink and called Ingrid from the barn.

"All right, where is she?" Kodak said.

"Taking a walk. She'll be back soon."

"Quite a place you've got here," Andrew said stalking the length of the living room, admiring the rifles that hung from the far wall.

"A long way from Beirut," Vaz said.

"Don't you miss it sometimes?"

"Never. I get down for the races, you know, and to see family, but the city itself sickens me. The magic's all gone. Smells like a rotting carcass."

"Yes, it's heating up again," Andrew said. "I'm thinking about pulling out myself."

"Back to England?"

"No," he laughed. "You can never go back. Well, for a visit perhaps, but this is my home now. How has Cass been? She was acting rather strangely in Beirut."

"She's fine, just trying to get over Foster's death. She's got a horse now. A fine mare. We may breed her."

"You've sort of adopted Cass, then, have you?" He spotted the bluing rags that lay in a basket by the fire place. "Been shooting?"

"A little tin can practice in the hills. Cass is quite a good shot. She nailed a rat by the barn at a dead run yesterday. Quite a shot."

"Get a cat," Pym said. "Far less noise."

"Good idea," Vaz chuckled.

"What's she thinking about? This documentary, has she spoken more about it?"

"Give her time. She's worried about her mother, worried about herself. The farm's been doing her good."

"I'm sure it has," Andrew said. They both looked out toward the barn where Kodak and Ingrid stood by the paddock. Varmint and Mabruka were nuzzling over the dividing fence.

As Cass loped around the far stand of trees she saw the car in the driveway and stopped short. She pulled a kerchief from her pocket and covered her head with it, readjusted the blousing of her full shirt and walked toward them.

"Hullo, Kodak," she yelled.

"Hey you," he said. "A.P.'s been trying to find you. Seems your resident correspondent, Cochran, has split town for Iran. The *Herald* wants you to fill in. Got a pocketful of telexes here, including a few from the Australian company. Everyone wants you back at work. Isn't it nice to know you're loved?"

"Yeah, well, tell them to forget it," she said, "I'm a country girl now."

"Come off it," he said, "once a newshound always a newshound. You said you wanted to be busy, keep your mind off . . . things."

"I've got other things to think about," she said, crawling through the fence. "Here you go, girl. Have some sugar. What's a few cavities between friends?"

"She's a beaut all right," Kodak said. Ingrid left them alone.

"Want a ride?"

"Well, I'm not exactly an equestrian, you know. She gentle? Does she buck or anything?"

"Naw," she said, "just like a puppy dog."

"Well, I don't know. Andrew's here."

"Andrew?"

"Yep. Old home week."

"To what do I owe this pleasure?"

"We were kind of worried about you. Just wondered what you were up to. Besides which, we could make some money together if you got back in harness."

Cass springed up the front stairs and pulled Vaz aside, scowling.

"I invited them, Cassie. One last dose of reality."

"Yeah, and put yourself in danger. No one was supposed to know I was here."

"They'll be quiet about it."

"You're crazy," she said.

"My dear," Vaz said, soberly. "No one passes this threshold without an invitation from me."

"Vaz," she said, plaintively.

"Just one last attempt to make you see reason."

"Well, what about it, Cassie?" Kodak called. "You with us or not?"

"Nope, not this time," she called back. "Not hot

enough for me. You can go fool around with the Palestinians and the U.N. troops, but I'm not going to get myself shot up like a sieve just to get a byline on page 17. There are plenty of other things to get shot up for."

"Yeah, like page one," said Andrew, Vaz and Kodak in unision.

"You guys!" She chuckled. "The news can wait."

Andrew and Kodak returned to Beirut that evening. Cass threw off the scarf that had concealed her black hair and made ready to go. Mabruka was groomed and fed. She herself ate little for fear the kitchen noise would awaken Vaz and Ingrid. She did not want to say goodbye.

# THIRTY

The morning came brisk and clean off the sea. Cass was a day's ride from L'Aiglon and a day's ride from the Syrian border. She had spent the night under the shelter of the stars and even now was loath to see them fade in the dawn sky.

The fire was long out and scattered after the morning coffee. The saddle of handspun wool, stretched on a frame of leather and wood, lay ready to be slung over the mare's back.

Mabruka stood still in the cool morning air. With each stroke of the brush on her flanks the horse gave back some pressure in response. Their movements obeyed the twist of a single key. Horse to rider, clear channel transmission, two way, rider to horse.

Girth tightened, stirrups lowered, Cass swung into the saddle. She turned Mabruka slowly away from the sea.

The border crossing she had chosen was about halfway between the coastal Lebanese town of Arida and the wheat fields of Dabbussiyeh, a stretch of some fifteen miles; not even the Syrians had enough soldiers or barbed wire to cover that stretch of terrain.

They were thorough, though. The Syrian military's chief concerns were for the main roads, the coastal route from Beirut to Tartous and up to

Latakia, and the inland highway that stretched east toward Homs and south toward Jordan. The Syrians were always looking for guns, for mortars, for booby traps, Palestinian or Christian. Near the Golan . . . Israeli.

Mabruka had fallen into a comfortable trot. The rhythm changed only with the terrain, when she picked her way through orange groves, or along high-ridged irrigation ditches. She jumped a stream in elephant grass tall as her withers.

The sun began to bake into the wool of Cass' vest. She shed it and tied it to the back of the saddle with a leather thong, dropped the reins on Bruk's neck, and let the horse find her own pace.

When the slowness of it gave way to drowsiness in the sun, Cass would collect the reins of her mount and spur her on. When the farmer's road stretched wide and long ahead of them . . . they were off, galloping past the women in the fields.

To all eyes she was a farmer's son, quite wealthy probably. She held herself tall in the saddle, her face wrapped in a checkered keffeyeh, her strong legs covered by the black mutton leg trousers of the Maronite Christian. A loose white cotton shirt with billowing sleeves was held tight at her waist by a woven woolen belt in reds and blues.

She neared Dabussiyeh. The old paths of the drug smugglers could still be found winding in and out of the rocks. For centuries the hashish of Lebanon had been carried by horseback to the sultans of the Ottoman Empire.

There were many blind spots. A lot of cover some hundred meters from the strands of barbed wire that marked the Syrian border. Cass and Mabruka found protection in the rocks. They had left the treeline long ago.

From the crest of a hill, Cass scanned the area looking for a soft spot in the fence. She needed a clearing, some room to ride, to gain momentum. Mabruka struck the ground with her right front hoof. Cass stilled her, waiting moments . . . then quarter hours. She'd found her spot. All was clear. Away from the curious eyes of the farmers and out of the sights of a Syrian soldier's AK-47, she rode to the fence, dismounted and pulled the white rags from her saddle bags.

She let Mabruka's reins slip to the ground and the horse stood quietly while Cass tied each of the four rags along the top wire of the fence. Her horse would see exactly what to jump. The rags hung down about a foot touching the next strand of barbed wire. They made a white picket effect in the otherwise brown and yellow landscape.

Up in the saddle again, Cass reined her horse away from the fence and circled her, kicking her, kicking up puffs of dust and insects in the brown grass, then rode up the hill once more. A stride before the barbed wire, Cass was up halfway out of the saddle and her movement was shadowed by the upward curve of her mount. For a split second, like Zeno's arrow, they were motionless in the air, aloft above the fence, forelegs to Syria, hind legs to Lebanon, and then Mabruka's hooves gouged into the earth on the other side. Cass settled back slowly in the saddle, running her left hand down her mare's neck, bringing her to a halt. Cass cut the rags from the fence and stashed them behind the saddle.

They cantered north toward Tall Kalakh. The railway depot.

She rode down from the mountain ridges, threading her way through broken tables of lava, heading west toward the sea and toward the valley town.

When green grass and young thorn bush presented themselves along the way she allowed Mabruka to stop and crop. The mare had a small breakfast of barley, but not enough to silence an occasional rumble of hunger. Stones slid out from under her hooves and rattled down the hill path they followed to the market.

The sun was high and just beginning to break sweat across the mare's flanks. Tiger flies buzzed at her ears, but she plodded on. Cass was again wearing the brown contact lenses that would mean less suspicion for her in the bazaar.

A checkered red and white keffeyeh was wrapped around her chin, revealing only those brown eyes. The cloth hooded her features. Her face and arms were dark from the sun.

Tall Kalakh was a drowsy one-street town. Workers slapped whitewash on the walls of the village mosque between sips of tea and an occasional swipe at a passing fly. The railway station stood to the east; haphazard carpentry shored up sagging beams that supported the roof. The walls were a scabrous yellow. A portrait of Syrian President Hafez El-Assad, painted in greenish hues, hung over the main gate with sketchy strokes of troops marching behind him. Signs were written in Arabic script, French and English.

Cass turned and looked far down the track. The train had not arrived. Behind her, livestock were being driven from the holding pens. She skirted

the herd and asked one of the farmers for the
nearest granary. He motioned with his stick
toward the end of a row of shops made of
mudbrick and corrugated tin. Mabruka eyed the
woebegone cattle and goats as Cass spurred her
on.

There were several horsemen kicking up dust on
the street. Young boys with their cotton robes
hitched up to their thighs worked in their shops,
sweeping, piling, packing, pounding on metal.
There were a few cars, some Russian built, an
occasional sunscorched Mercedes, and bicycles
that looked like messenger vehicles from World
War II.

A few women hovered like dark birds about the
public water pump at the northern end of town. As
Cass rode up to them, they cast their eyes downward, holding the black cloth of their veils
between their teeth. Cass motioned to her empty
waterskin and smiled. A young woman with a bold
look took the skin and filled it with four dippers
from the well. Cass wheeled again, trotted back to
the granary and dismounted where an old man
squatted before his burlap sacks filled with
barley, oats, dried fodder and heaps of the Arab
clover known as berseem. White English biscuits
were stacked to overflowing in a battered tin, and
to the left of the feed and bread grains were bags
of raisins, dates, cashews, peanuts and pumpkin
seeds. Further down the line Cass spotted a crate
full of apricots, the first she had seen in a long
time. She loaded the scales with as many of the
fruits as she could hold in both hands.

The shopkeeper peered at her languidly from
the shade.

She helped herself to a full kilo of grain for Mabruka, using a third to fill the canvas feedbag that slipped over her muzzle. Then she weighed out three sheaves of berseem and threw them over the saddle pommel. As she did, she noticed a brown hand on the mare's right foreleg.

"Eh da," she said, "What's going on?"

"Peace be with you," said a voice from the other side of her horse. Cass swung under the feedbag and waited for more from the stranger. She did not return his greeting but looked closely at his face. He was thin, well hewn, a desert-etched man of about forty with a hawk's nose and brightly lit brown eyes. A mischief-maker.

"Fine horse you have there, boy."

"My father's pride," replied Cass and turned to adjust the feedbag.

"Though she isn't sound," he clucked as he ran another long-fingered hand down her left foreleg."

"She's not for sale, friend, so don't start."

He stroked the mare's neck and examined with his eyes what might be beneath the wool of the saddle bags.

"Hey," she said sharply and pulled her face down and close to her chest to motion him away from her mount. He responded with a bow.

"Fine horse," he said again. "She looks as if she's been dipped in ink . . . so black at the face and so white at the tail. As if you pulled her from the fire." Mabruka threw her head toward him. He laughed.

Cass asked the shopkeeper for the tally for her goods. She split an apricot in half, ate the side without the pit, then pulled the stone from the fruit and offered it to the stranger. She split another and shared the fruit between shopkeeper and Mabruka, sliding the feedbag off the horse's nose.

She took the proper coins from a leather pouch at her waist and gave them to the old man.

"Better grain than gasoline, eh?" he offered. "Good journey and God be with you. The train will be slow in places. They are making repairs to the rails further north, but you should have no trouble reaching Tartous in a couple of hours."

"I want to go on to Latakia."

"It's a long ride by horse, but you can take one of the livery trucks."

"Don't let them cheat you," the stranger said. "You must bargain for your fare. They are all scoundrels." He hitched his dark cloak behind him and gave her a leg up into the saddle. She took the favor and mounted.

"Thank you, friend, and God be with you."

"Fine horse," he said again and gave the mare a slap on the rump just as Cass was securing the fodder to the saddle.

She laughed and spun her horse around toward the railway station.

She found the station master and booked her passage in the livery car to the rear. Better to ride with her horse than chance an encounter with army officers who rode closer to the locomotive. She led Mabruka down the line of cars and stopped at the loading ramp. Three young farmers leaned in the doorway. One, the same one who had given her directions to the granary shop earlier, leapt to the ground to help her load her horse.

"Fine animal," he said slapping some dust from Mabruka's right flank. "Steady. Strong."

Cass thrust her chin up in agreement. "Chukruhn," she said, "Thank you," and led her horse to the rear of the car. The loading ramp was hoisted inside.

The engine bucked and lurched and the livery car clanked against the coupling, hung back, then responded as the train pulled out of the station. The wooden floor was littered with straw and dried offal. Mabruka steadied herself against the car's inertia and stood quietly, content to digest the food in her belly. The car reeked of sheep and goats. Small breezes found their way through the slatted doors of the freight car and the air was heavy with dust and flies.

The farmers tried to cajole the horseman into their card game, a loud, thigh-slapping amusement called Bosra, but she refused, closing her eyes against the heat and the smells and falling into the rhythm of steel wheel on roadbed. They let her be. Two hours passed.

At Tartous they slowed, then halted; a swarm of railway workers were carrying loads of stone away from the tracks in baskets, their bandy legs bare to the sun and the shirts on their backs stuck to them like second skins.

One of the farmers fired up a small kerosene stove and made glasses of sweet tea. She accepted hers with spoken thanks to God for his foresight in offering the refreshment. Her words heartened the young farmer to ask questions, but she pled fatigue after a long night's journey.

"All out. All out," yelled the station master.

After a few moments rest beside the tracks Cass walked Mabruka to the truck depot, joining one of her train companions and his cattle on the way.

There six flatbeds with plank sides, each bearing inscriptions from the Koran, stood ready. The burly Syrian driver was a gruff and grizzled Arab in western clothes. He had a rag over his ears to wipe the sweat away and to keep the dust devils at bay. He welcomed them, heartily, and led the farmer's cattle up the ramp of his leviathan. Cass let the farmer bargain; they found a fair price and the driver got into the cab. The driver motioned Cass up front, but she said she preferred to remain in the back with her horse.

"You're a crazy one," the driver snorted, and mounted to the cab of his rig.

Cass stood for the next two hours, bracing herself against the walls of the truck and looking out at the sea that rolled away west of them.

The driver tried to talk to her, twisting around in his seat, thumping the wheel after every clattering jolt, but she yelled she couldn't hear him. The farmer turned up the radio, rocking back and forth to the music, and they bounced onward. As darkness they were passing through Latakia's outer limits.

As they neared the port area of the city, the concrete buildings and the dredging barges, Cass rapped her fist on the roof of the cab. She motioned him to a halt at the side of the road.

"I'll get off here, please!"

"Sure," the driver said, jumping from his cab. Mabruka was skiddish, unnerved by his abruptness; her nostrils flared. Cass held her tightly by the halter. The ramp slid out and thudded to the ground and with some insistence she led her horse, clomping down to the road.

A flame burned a halo in the night sky above the

oil refinery, but all else was diesel black. She
adjusted the girth and mounted, wishing the
drover good prices in the slaughterhouse. Then
she was gone, heading south, skirting the
industrial center of the city along the Mediterranean Sea. Her stomach growled and she
ate another apricot, then trotted toward a row of
bare light bulbs above a small store, one in a
cluster of tiny establishments. She bought cheese
and olives and a bottle of wine. The proprietor and
his companions were talking about politics. Their
supper of bread and tahine lay untouched before
them in the heat of the argument. The owner
looked up at the dark-faced rider, as if waiting for
the rider's support, but Cass shook her head and
rode on. She had six miles to to before reaching
Hassan Khoury's gas station.

As Cass remounted, the mare was prancing, glad
to be rid of the tumble and roll of the truck. Her
hoofbeats were muffled in the sand alongside the
road, and they cut down toward the sea.

About two hundred yards from Khoury's warehouse, they found shelter low down on the bank.
When Mabruka was tethered, Cass stole up the
ridge. There were no windows on the warehouse
except those panes at the doors. She scratched the
glass; they were painted from the inside.

Crickets and lizards scuttled along through the
grass. The sea was behind her. She adjusted the
gun at her side as she crouched down behind an oil
drum. She could just make out the silhouette of
Khoury's gas station, the pump lights ablaze, just
off the coastal highway. The station was two black
boxes joined together, the larger housing the
garage and lifts, the smaller housing Khoury's

office and cans of oil and gasoline additives, fan belts and tires.

She crept toward it, feeling the earth ooze beneath her, seeping with spilled oil. She rounded the rubbish pile of tin cans and worn auto parts, passed the crude privy and reached his office window, where a dim light made the curtains glow blue. Through the mesh she saw Khoury's heavy shoulders and fleshy neck. He was leaning forward over his desk speaking with someone, but she could not catch the words.

She sat under the window sill with her back against the wall and breathed quietly, pacing off the station yard with her eyes, measuring the distance to the warehouse and back to the sheltered ridge that concealed her horse and the explosives. Khoury's proximity resounded like the first rumblings of a volcano in her body. The smell of the gas, the oil stuck to the soles of her shoes, made her feel entrapped in mechanical filth. Khoury's filth. For a moment she saw Foster standing over her, offering her a hand up from where she sat hunched in the blackness.

She crawled to the side, away from Khoury's window, and crept back to Mabruka, whispering the name of her dead lover, feeling his agile feet brushing the grass behind her, his spirit keeping her company. She looked around once, and decided it was wrong to wait for the following night. She was ready, now. There were two and a half hours until midnight, by which time the bomb would be laid, and the charges set around the warehouse.

Back at camp she brewed herself strong coffee. Mabruka struck the sand with her hooves and was hushed. Cass unrolled the plastic sheath that held the gelignite, blasting caps and gun cotton. She pondered the yellow roll of fuse wire, bared both ends with her knife and cut two lengths. The rest she tied to her belt. She measured out three pounds of the plastic explosive, then another two pounds of gun cotton. These were for Khoury. She packed the gelatin, the cellulose nitrate, fuse wires an detonator caps into a linen sack with a shoulder strap, then worked out what was required for the warehouse, again weighing in her hand and her mind just how much of a blast she would be able to pull off. She should have carried more in her saddle bags, for the remainder would do little more than blow the steel doors off the warehouse building. That might be enough.

She eyed the dark sea, swallowed the first cup of coffee then stripped down for a plunge. Mabruka strained to follow, but it was no time for fun. It was time to arouse all her senses, her tactile responses to the terrain. In the murky water a fish brushed by her leg and she nearly leapt out of her skin.

Then, dressed in her black shirt and trousers, she slung the bag over her shoulder and gave Mabruka one last word, trying to impress upon the mare that she must not shy during what was to follow. Then she scrambled up and over the ridge like a retreating spider, into the long grass, and made her way to the warehouse. She laid the charges around the doorway. She checked her watch: eleven o'clock. The three-quarter moon was rising, casting shadows in motion across the turf. At the warehouse she left her only timing device. She did not set the charges, but they were

primed and ready at each hinge. They would wait.
She must hurry now. Khoury would leave the gas
station at midnight, it was his routine. She hoped
that his companion would be gone. Khoury was
the only man she wanted in Latakia.

On hands and knees, she crawled to the edge of
the greasy tarmac where Khoury's Buick was
parked along the grass border. She looked around
for the boy who pumped gas, but his motorbike
was gone. There was a second car on the lot, a
swift little Fiat. Khoury's companion was still
with him.

She removed the sack from her shoulder and
slid it beside her as she eased under the Buick's
carriage, on her back. She said a prayer of thanks
to Detroit for building their cars so high off the
ground. It gave her room to work.

Her small hands moved up under the engine,
finding the ignition, the electric starter that would
set off the detonator. She adjusted the small
flashlight to give her more light. She trailed the
fuse wire down to the wad of gelignite that she
jammed up above the bell housing, planting the
blasting cap deep in its putty-like consistency. The
engine was cool. She was thankful for that. Then
she began to spin wire round the explosive so that
it would not fall to the ground when Khoury's
bulk hit the driver's seat.

A beam of light scanned across her, blinding her
like a laser. She shied away from it as if burned
and the flashlight clicked off. The door of the
office swung the rest of the way, and Khoury and
his companion walked outside. The companion,
speaking a lilting kind of Arabic as if it were not
his native language, returned the package that

Khoury had just handed to him.

"Tomorrow, then," said Khoury. "There will be more, but not much more. You will have to wait for the season."

The other man proceeded to his car, not ten feet from where Cass was lying dead still. She held the fuse wire above her head, away from her face, as the other car started, then pulled away. She felt the hot air of its exhaust.

Khoury strode back toward the office, but changed his mind, swinging the brown paper parcel in his right hand. He opened the door of the Buick and sat down, with one leg on the ground. The Corsair Unique was already in Cass' hand. If he turned on the ignition at that moment, they both would have been blown sky high.

She heard a key turn, but it opened the glove compartment. Khoury shut it with a bang, slammed the door and walked back into the office. Cass wiped the sting of perspiration from her eyes, adjusted the fuse wire, and slid out to the passenger side of the car, opening the door as she lay on the ground. From her tools she extracted the steel stiletto with the crooked tooth, got into the car, and jimmied the lock. Inside the glove compartment she found a pistol and the brown paper package. She unwrapped it; a kilo of refined heroin lay in her lap. She flipped it over and over, a fortune in her hands, glancing always at the office door. She grabbed a half brick from the edge of the tarmac, wrapped it up in the brown paper and put it inside the compartment. She slipped the heroin into her sack.

She shut the car door quietly behind her, and jammed gun cotton up the exhaust pipe for good

measure. Ten minutes to midnight. She depended
on his punctuality. She slunk away to a position
about a hundred yards from the pumps, still two
hundred yards from the warehouse. She heard the
shudder of the screen door bouncing against its
frame, then saw Khoury's broad figure making his
way to the car. Khoury, the mastermind of
Foster's death, the patron of the Saiqa guerrilla
who tried to slash Cass' throat in the Palestinian
camp. He walked on toward the Buick. She
crawled further back, behind a hillock of grass
and stones.

The car door slammed. And in the eternity of a
second he switched on the ignition. The explosion
made her leap to her feet. Only the car roof was
visible above the fireball as the blast sent it fifty
feet in the air. Bumpers and shards of steel
clanged against the pavement and rang in her ears.
The flames coiled out of the car's frame and
followed the route of oil to the pumps. They too
exploded in towers of fire. She bolted toward the
warehouse, the second of the white wall of flame
behind her pressing her onward. She crouched
down by the timing device, flicked the lever, and
raced for the ridge, but not fast enough. She had
not obeyed her own rule, "slowly, slowly." In
throwing the lever so abruptly, she had offset the
timer. Shrapnel flew from the blasted doors,
chemicals inside burst into flame. Gases expanded
and blew the lids off oil drums. She fell, then ran,
then threw herself on the ground once more as
things whistled over her head. Something like a
lash crossed over her left arm; smouldering hunks
of metal thudded around her in the undergrowth,
pounding into the earth, bouncing off rocks. Then

there was only the spit and fizzle as fire raced across the wooden support beams and blistered the paint on the warehouse walls.

The blaze lighted her way back to Mabruka. Cass held her left arm steady against her ribs, not daring yet to look at the damage. She was angry at herself for being caught by her own bomb, but jubilant in the very power of it. Khoury dead, incinerated, gone. There was no remorse.

The mare pivoted back and forth, jerking the tether that restrained her.

"Easy, easy, girl," Cass said. "It's all right." She saw the foam on Mabruka's lips and whispered more urgently, low and sweet to her horse. She held out a hand. The mare calmed. Cass picked the tether out of the air as Mabruka turned and she brought her close. The animal's eyes reflected the fire behind her.

"Easy, easy, girl."

The mare was packed and saddled. Cass did not waste time removing the halter rope. She brought it up with one of the reins, put her left foot in the stirrup and swung up just as Mabruka reared. She caught hold and drove her own weight down into the saddle, bringing the mare back to earth, under her, between her knees. She found she could not grasp the reins with her left hand, so switched to right and dashed along the sand in a gallop of old bones, bottle caps and broken shells. They reached the pathway to the highway where the ridge leveled out, and, seeing headlights, plunged down again until the danger passed. They darted across the road, east, away from the highway and away from the red flares that defined where Hassan Khoury's gas station once stood.

# THIRTY-ONE

They cantered when they could, trotted when the dirt road broke down in a confusion of paths, and then walked through the crevices in the foothills about fifteen miles from Latakia. It had been a grueling three hours. Cass would have liked them to be further away, but the going was treacherous and the moon, an untrustworthy companion. She knew that the highway swung low and away about two miles south of them, giving them some margin of safety.

The jagged rocks, the striated cliffs and scrub pines were harsh comfort to her now as she steadied her horse and dismounted, near a stand of trees. She poured water into a tin cup, gulped it down, then refilled it for Mabruka. Only then did she look beneath the wet and ragged sleeve that hung on her left arm.

A piece of shrapnel had sheared off the skin on her upper arm. The wound was like a band of red about two inches wide and three inches long. The blood still ran freely, down between her sticky fingers. She put her right hand to her mouth to clear the fingertips of salt and then she felt around for any bits of metal. She felt faint, but caught herself. Nothing. No sharp bits. A clean wound for

now, but one that would stiffen her movements
later. No muscles had been harmed. The cold fear
of infection was as strong as the pain. She felt like
dropping to the ground, knotting herself up, but
there was still work to do.

She raised herself up, unlatched the girth and
dropped the saddle to the ground. She unhitched a
bundle of the clover she had bought in Tell Kalakh
and placed it under Mabruka's forelegs. Then she
rummaged through the saddle bags for the
rudimentary first aid kit she had packed at
L'Aiglon. Bandages and alcohol. She lit a cigarette,
then holding it clenched between her teeth, she
opened the bottle of alcohol and let it run searing
into the wound. Tears splashed down her cheeks
involuntarily. She flinched, stopped the treatment
long enough to wriggle out of her black shirt,
fearing its color might run into the wound. Then
she poured more. The pain of it penetrated her
brain like slivers of glass. She saved half the
alcohol for the morning, then wrapped a bandage
round the wound until the cloth itself lent support
to her upper arm. She tied it off, using her right
hand and her teeth, then found another shirt to
cover her body from the night flies.

She held the ember of her cigarette close to her
watch and saw that it was after three o'clock in
the morning. They were too close to Latakia. She
planned to sleep until sun up, then ride further
until she found a stream where she might water
her horse and bathe the wound. Only the
throbbing of her left arm kept her eyes from
closing, then that too, dulled with exhaustion.

She awoke shivering, her body piled against the
stones and the bandages on her left arm cracking

as she moved. Mabruka stood docile and expectant, tossing her head up and down at her mistress.

"Morning," Cass said thickly. She felt swollen and sore as the rising sun flowed into the capillaries of the sky, filling its dark sack with a pink and sickening light. Cass felt that her left arm had turned to wood. She flexed it achingly and moved her fingers.

"Well, it still works," she said aloud to her mare, "but barely. God damn it. God damn it." She raised herself up on wobbly legs and tried to focus on her surroundings. She was safer than she had dared hoped. They were past the first fringe of jagged hills that concealed traffic on the coast. She could no longer see the Mediterranean. Only shepherds and vagabonds would roam here: the terrain was inhospitable at best.

She stretched herself, but nearly fell as the dizziness carbonated behind her eyes. She grabbed the mare's back for support; Mabruka stood like warm stone. Standing there for some moments she collected her thoughts in the scent of her horse and the strength of the mare's body. She had a fever; she could not go on. Not yet.

"No good," she said, "no good." There was no energy in her to build a small fire for coffee, so she did the next best thing and opened the red wine she had purchased the night before, wedging the bottle between her legs as her left arm hung useless by her side. At the first draught, she vomited, violently, and in anger smashed the glass against a tree.

She curled up into herself with tremors running through her body. Asleep, she tossed with feverish

dreams. Palm fronds rattled against the walls of
her imagination, outside a chapel where the con-
gregation was mumbling incoherently, deep and
low. She sat in the fourth pew and when the
reverend's eyes were not rivetted on her she
looked round and found her father sitting further
back, staring straight ahead of him. One of the
ushers padded down the aisle and turned to her.
Lawrence Foster was dressed in a black suit and
tie, his brown hands extending from sleeves that
were too short. She made to rise and go to him, but
found she was planted in her seat. She watched his
mercurial face change from smile to frown and
turn away.

Then the sound of wheels behind her. The coffin
with silver handles was hoisted off a hospital
stretcher upon the shoulders of six faceless men.
Whose body?

The reverend stretched taller as if he were made
of elastic, and began the funeral oratory. Images
blurred. Smoke blew through the open windows
and a ghostly choir began to sing. The altar was
draped in black and white, like the cowl of a nun's
habit, but those colors gave way to an opulent
crimson that unfurled in velvet swatches along the
pews and up either side of the nave.

She felt sweat between her fingers, between her
breasts, congealing at the backs of her knees as
the coffin came closer to the altar. Her mother
was in the choir, her eyes turned away, her face
concealed in the collar of her robe. Then her
father came forward, carrying with him cool air
that soon dissolved in the furnace-like heat
blowing from the windows. The hot breeze tore at
Cass' hat and whipped it from her head. She

chased it, running as it twisted and bobbed toward
the coffin when the bell choir sounded. Low bells,
then tinkling bells, a carillon of mourning.

The coffin rolled on a ramp toward a white light
that burned behind the minister's head. She could
not get to it. She was vaulting over kneeling
people. The bell, the bell, she must get there.
Foster extended his hand to her and she felt his
fingers upon her left arm, singeing it, and she
broke free. Her father reached out, too, but the
hat, she mustn't let the hat burn. It was careening
along the main aisle, bouncing off the feet of the
pall bearers. One looked up. It was Khoury
grinning at her, reaching for the hat . . . and the
bell.

She jerked awake, wet with sweat. East of her a
large goat cropped at the rough grass. The bell
around his neck rang back and forth against his
chest. Other goats followed and spread out to their
pasturage. Then came their shepherd, a young
boy, perhaps fourteen years old.

He stopped in the shade of an upended boulder
and peered at her.

"Hey," she said. "Welcome. Please come closer,
I want to speak with you." He hesitated.

"I won't hurt you," she said. "Christ, I can't even
move," she added to herself, unbending her limbs,
letting the blood flow through her veins and
sending it once again to the wound. Mabruka
snorted and struck the earth with her hoof.

"Well, if you won't come to me, boy, I'll come to
you." The keffeyeh had long ago fallen from her
head and the short cropped black hair stood at
odds with gravity. She combed it back with her
fingers and made her way toward him, working

her jaw open and shut to get the stiffness out of it.
She hiked up her pants and tightened the belt.

"Friend, I am very thirsty. Have you got any
water with you?" He smiled and pointed down the
slope to the north. Then he outlined the track of a
river with his gestures. He pointed at his mouth
and shook his head. His ears were concealed
under a mat of dark hair. His body was splotchy
with dirt.

"A river," she said. "Is it far?"

He held up one finger and a little bit. About a
kilometer and then some. A kid bounded before
him, chased by a nanny goat. He grabbed the she-
goat and beckoned Cass forward. He motioned
toward her udders, which were protected from the
mouths of the hungry kids by a green sack.

She smiled at him and brought her hands
together, closing her eyes as if saying Thanks to
God.

He untied the green sack and produced a tin
cylinder from his belt. The squirt of the milk rang
against its sides. Cass sipped at the warm froth.
Her body rebelled, but she drained the cup and
kept it down. She did not want a second. He
shrugged and tied the goat's udder back into the
cloth protection.

Cass fished around in her pockets and found a
coin, but he refused and brought two fingers to his
lips, then puffed at an invisible cigarette. She gave
him two, and a pack of matches. He lit one at once
then pointed again toward the river.

"A thousand thanks and peace be with you," she
said. She cinched the saddle tight against
Mabruka's belly and mounted the horse carefully.
She adjusted the keffeyeh over her head once

more and trotted through a small ravine, then down toward the sweet water that bubbled clean from a mountain stream.

It was two and a half days ride to Jisr Esh Shugur, then 75 miles by train to Aleppo. She and Mabruka followed the goat paths through the Syrian mountains, once in awhile running alongside the main roadway ànd dropping into the tamarisk and olive trees to rest in the heat of the day. Military convoys rolled West toward the coastal highway, new men, new weapons for the peacekeeping forces in Lebanon. The only people who waved at her were farmers, but they said nothing as she passed.

She had tinned meat enough to sustain herself, but she had little appetite. The fever came and went as the wound on her arm suppurated. The alcohol was long gone and she had taken to soaking the bandage in thimblefuls of vodka, the only wistful addition to her survival kit. Mabruka went steadily onward, never jarring her rider, never throwing her head, nor breaking at strange noises. They found plenty of water in the mountains and good pasturage along the way. Once they came upon the camouflage hangar for fighter-bombers and veered from their course to avoid any military eyes. The planes were scattered as part of the desert deployment to make air reconnaissance all the more difficult and to spread their planes apart so that a single bombing run would not take out the bulk of the Syrian Air force.

The pain weakened Cass and sent electrical charges throughout her body, making her start as she dozed in the saddle. When all else failed to

numb the pain, she unfolded an envelope of heroin
and snorted it up each nostril, feeling the narcotic
take gentle hold of her brain and of her limbs,
dulling the throb in her left arm.

Jisr Esh Shugur was a desert town. The few
modern municipal buildings by the main highway,
built of red stone and glass, did not disturb the
overriding desert hues of browns and golds.
Gnarled olive trees lined the streets, and palm ribs
were woven into thatch for the roofs. The train
station was to the south of the city, near the
military base where drab green jeeps and drab
green men raced back and forth sending up
showers of sand to fall on all that stood too close.
The women were draped in black, their faces
unveiled and their skin date brown in the
sunshine, their bodies nondescript under the
folds.

Near the government buildings, people walked
the sidewalks in western garb, but away from the
streets, where the desert was reclaiming the
asphalt, lean dark figures stood like pencil
drawings on a field of yellow paper desert. The
older men wore dark sports jackets over their
Arab robes, and had white or checkered keffeyehs
anchored on their heads with black lambs' wool
coils.

Mabruka had proved her stamina in the hills,
but now she needed rest. Cass dismounted stiffly
and pulled the cloak over her left shoulder. The
wound was seeping through her shirt. She felt, as
she touched ground, that she had just
disembarked from a ship long at sea. Her legs
were weak and spongy. The narcotic made her
drowsy but unworried.

At the flyblown market she purchased a kilo of sugar and some dates. She rode half a mile out into the sand, and beneath the spines of Spanish bayonet and devil's backbone she dumped out the bag of sugar and refilled it with the heroin. As she departed, a battalion of ants were making short work of the sugar spilled on the ground.

She rode into the southern sector of the town where children the color of earth were playing games with stones. Poverty hung like the burlap curtains at the windows and in the guileless eyes of the womenfolk.

Cass was entering a daguerreotype, passing through a time warp. The brown lenses over her irises gave everything around her a sepia tint. Desert eyes.

At the railway station she dipped her keffeyeh in well water and again wrapped it around her face; it roused her some from her somnolence. Mabruka drank from a trough along with a mare and a stallion belonging to two other riders. The chestnut mare had red wool braided into her tail and ribbons tied in her mane.

Cass strode round the mare, her right hand on the horse's rump.

"You going to sell her?"

"Sell her?" the taller of the boys laughed.

"I just bought her," the younger one said. "A beauty, hum?"

Cass looked appraisingly at the chestnut then back at her own grey mare.

The younger rider nodded. "Yes, she is a nice one, too. Do you travel far?"

"Aleppo," she said turning away.

"That is very near my home," he said eagerly.

"Just six miles further on toward the Euphrates. My town is Nayrab. Have you been there?"

Cass smiled and turned away.

"Where are you from?" The other rider asked. "What's your name?"

She didn't answer. She walked back to Mabruka and lifted one of her hooves.

"Will you be staying long in Aleppo? You must be very rich?"

"Can't you hear?" The taller boy said.

Cass moved to the other side of her horse. The younger rider wrapped his striped cloak around his gangling body and strode up to her.

"My name's Tallal. What's yours?"

Cass turned a weary eye to him and bent again to her task, checking Mabruka's hooves for any stones.

"Boy, can you hear?"

She waved him away and he appeared startled at her rudeness, then strode back to his companion.

"Saudi," the taller one said and laughed.

"No, no," Tallal responded with vehemence. "Lebanese. Not very kind."

"Well, you'll have the whole train ride to talk to him. Maybe he's sick."

"Bah," Tallal said and cuffed the taller boy on the shoulder.

Cass led Mabruka away to the far end of the trough, then sat down beside it. She rested her head on her knees and listened to the two boys. Their speech ranged three octaves, modulating with good humor. They pushed at each other and tussled in the dust. Cass closed her eyes.

At four that afternoon the hiss of the locomotive

shook Cass from her sleep. Mabruka's head was above her and she held onto the halter rope for support.

"Hey, hurry up, boy," Tallal yelled. "They won't be holding the train for you!" He stood back inside the livery car as Mabruka's hooves thudded up the wooden ramp. Tallal clapped Cass on the shoulder and she spun toward him like a snarling dog.

"I don't know you, boy. And I would rather you didn't touch me as a friend. We have a long ride ahead of us and I am feeling like tar. Please, leave me alone." She slid down the far wall of the train car. "By God," she said. "The world is hot."

Mabruka was tied, but not very happily, near a load of steers. Cass threw bits of dung at her to get her attention. Tallal moved his mount closer to Mabruka and secured the rope, running his eyes over the mare.

"You are Lebanese," he said more a statement than a question.

She assented with a nod, studying her own mutton leg trousers and the blousing under her cloak. She should be wearing the gelebeya now. Two other men squatted at the far end of the car. They were the drovers for the cattle. They paid no attention to the two young boys and their horses.

"I am Tallal Ibn Abu Sayed. I am the oldest son of a Bedu chief, though our feet have found roots in the earth. We left the nomad's life some years ago before I was born. I am charged with bringing home the brood mare for our stable. This is my first journey of so many miles and, by God, it has been a good journey." Cass stared at him, then dropped her eyelids and leaned into her saddle pommel for some rest.

"We're moving," he said. "Ah ha, we are moving." He knelt down beside her, puffing up his chest. Cass did her utmost to ignore him.

"See this," he said, holding a string of beads, "for my mother. And these, for my sisters." He ran more glass beads through his long brown fingers. "And for my father, Helwa, the beautiful mare. She is a proven breeder, you know. Two fine foals from the stables of Abdul El Mahabi and now she is of the stable of Abu Sayed. Our stable is very famous in Tell El Nayrab."

Cass closed her eyes again and he was quiet for a time, fidgeting with the beads when wrapping them up once more in tissue paper, tucking them carefully back into the bag that never left his side.

Cass watched his pleasant face through her lashes, then drifted off to the rhythm of the rails, never quite sleeping, but never quite awake. The narcotic was wearing off and left her with a headache. She awaited her chance. At last Tallal strode off to the corner of the car to piss out the back of the train. She pulled the heroin from her vest pocket and put a few granules on her fingertips. She sniffed at them, and wiped the bitter powder from her lips. A swallow of water followed. She offered Tallal a sip before putting the skin away.

The cattle thumped against each other and lowed. One kicked the side of the car and a drover moved up on him and whacked him soundly on the rump.

Mabruka and Tallal's chestnut mare whinnied to each other, snorted resumed their own rest in the late afternoon heat. The temperature had dropped some, but the car still held its occupants in a miasma of animal vapors and motes of dust. Bits of straw swirled gently across the floor and dung, dried light as ping pong balls, rolled to and fro. The track wound north to Aleppo, the city of the citadel.

The smell of spiced coffee fought its way through the cattle car and up into Cass' mind. Her eyes fluttered open for a moment and Tallal sprang for her attention slapping her good-naturedly on the arm. She let out a screech before she could catch herself, and Tallal recoiled as if the agony had stung him as well.

"I'm sorry, so sorry. I didn't mean to hurt. . . ."

"Eh, what's the trouble? What's the problem?" the drovers said, starting toward the boys.

Cass opened her cloak and rolled up her sleeve. The scab had again broken and fluids flowed pinkish white.

"A fall. I had a fall from my horse," she said. "I cut it on the rocks. It is nothing. A trifle. Ma'alesh."

"But it is not all right," Tallal said, bringing his nose close to the bandage. "Well, it is not so bad either."

She herself sniffed; there was no putrefaction. The wound simply would not heal, and the white blood cells were racing down her arm to beat off infection. He helped her unwind the soiled bandage and the drovers clucked and shook their heads.

"It must dry," one of them said pursing his lips.

"I have some of these," Cass responded and found the first aid kit. She unrolled more gauze and then brought forth the bottle of vodka.

"Here you do it."

Tallal looked at the bottle. "Do you drink this?"

"Sometimes," she responded ruefully, "but it is just as good medicine outside as inside."

"You are Christian?" Tallal was puzzled.

"Yes."

"I am Moslem," he said pounding his chest.

"Yes, I know, but it doesn't bother me. You are welcome to share these fine accommodations with me."

He laughed at that, as did the drovers, and Tallal bent to the bandage. The tears rolled down Cass' cheeks. The drovers turned away at this show of weakness.

She said, "I cannot help it. It's not my doing. It stings so it smarts my eyes. Have you got some coffee?" The fingers of her right hand had curled around her holster.

"Of course, and you are very welcome."

One of the drovers crabwalked across the floor toward his coffee pot. The train had begun to rock back and forth on the road bed. The couplings creaked and the chains rattled at either end of the car. A whistle sounded once, then again as the train sped past a herd of camels. Lime green bushes grew close to the ground, the only vegetation on the desert floor. The plants were tough as sea coral but the camels masticated the branches between their teeth and regurgitated, then swallowed the slime again.

The younger of the drovers returned, clinking his tiny china cups, deftly pouring out two swallows of coffee for each person. When they were drained they shook them with their fingers and again the coffee pot went round.

"Hawayeech. Yemini coffee. The magic is in the

spices," he said proudly, slurping the bittersweet flavor.

"Very good indeed, by God," Cass responded and offered them cigarettes.

By the time they reached Aleppo the fever was again upon her. At the station, she started to get up and felt herself falling back. Tallal helped her to her feet.

"Listen friend, you must come with me. What business you have here can wait until you are well. It is a short train ride from here to Nayrab. You are a traveler and in the eyes of God you are my responsibility. My guest."

"Tallal, there's an inn near here, near El-Masri's stable...."

"That old donkey dealer! That insect of the dungheap...."

"Tallal."

"You are coming with me. It has been decided."

She protested, but feebly, and followed him off the livery ramp and onto another train traveling east. They reached his village just after nightfall. He galloped ahead toward the glow of oil lamps, slung outside the main house. He called for his father, announcing his return, warning that he had brought company from Lebanon, alerting them to open the doors of their hospitality.

Dogs barked, children rushed forth, horses came to the wire fence to see what the commotion was about. The oldest daughter, dressed in a pink silk tunic over dark cotton pants, ran barefoot to Tallal's horse, holding the bridle while he dismounted. He stood nearly a head taller then she, though the family resemblance was apparent in the lamplight, a soft circle of illumination outside the front door of the house. It was not a door at all, but a curtain of green canvas.

Tallal patted his sister on the shoulders and whipped his hand inside his blouse, bringing forth a string of beads.

Cass was still mounted, with her hands crossed over her reins above the saddle. Mabruka was snuffling at the dogs.

"Magda," Tallal said, "second oldest. Nadia," he opened his arms to the little girl who ran toward him, "third oldest. And. And," he looked around him, then grinned, "Hamdy, my brother. The youngest." Little Hamdy stumbled, fell to the dirt, righted himself and wobbled toward his brother. Tallal's mother stood in the doorway, leaning heavily into her seventh or eighth month of pregnancy. She appeared about the same age as Cass, with a soft unlined face and large brown eyes.

"Welcome," she said to the horsemen. "Welcome to our house and thanks be to God that the journey went well for you. Look, look, Yuessef. Tallal has brought us a mare."

Her eyes strayed to the strange rider who still sat upon her horse.

"Magda, his reins!" Magda handed the reins of the chestnut mare to Tallal and walked toward the rider. Her eyes were cast shyly to the ground and she held the bridle without looking at the visitor. It was improper for a young Arab girl to meet the eyes of a strange man.

Cass slid to the ground, thanked her with her eyes, too, looking earthward. Talla's father, Yuessef, appeared at the door. He was not as tall as his son, but compactly built on a light frame.

Though in his mid-forties, his face was wizened as an old man's from the sun. His right eye was tightly shut. As he came closer Cass noticed the scar tissue puckered around it. His good eye roamed back and forth, between his son and Cass. His gait was graceful and feline.

Yuessef did Cass welcome, and then went straight for the new mare. Tallal removed the saddle and trotted her back and forth before him. Yuessef rubbed his bare chin, then took the reins himself, stopped her short and picked up each hoof in turn, feeling her bones and her hide, touching the muscles of her neck with approval. Tallal grew taller even as his Father examined the mare.

"We shall see better by daylight, son."

When the horses were bedded down in the near paddock, ringed by olive and tamarisk trees, they all went inside.

Cass was immediately assaulted by the aroma of roast mutton. The greasy smell crept into her nostrils and made her gag. She held it back and forced herself to become accustomed to it. It pervaded the inner chamber, along with boiled onions, garlic and beans. Her head was spinning and she could not swallow.

"Excuse me, Tallal, for a moment. I've forgotten something." She returned to the paddock where Mabruka was scattering her dried fodder. She sensed Tallal behind her and said, "I think it's the arm. It's making me a little feverish."

"But you must eat," he said. "It will give you strength. My mother has prepared the best of meals for us. Come. There's bread and tahine, babaghonouch from the aubergines of our garden."

Cass studied the sky, searching for the polar star and her sense of direction. Aleppo was seven miles to the west. Yes, she must eat, fight back the illness. She rallied.

"Mother," Tallal called.

"It's all right, Tallal. You troubled too much." But his mother came just the same and led her to the shed under a bright light where she could examine the arm. She sent Tallal to the kitchen for hot water, then she reached up on the shelf and brought down a tube of salve and a box of powder. She pondered the two and put the salve back.

"This will dry it out."

"I suppose if it's good enough for horses, it's good enough for me."

"People, too," she said, her eyes brightening with mirth. "It won't hurt. It just brings out the poison." The powder quickly coagulated the moisture that oozed from Cass' arm. She sprinkled more until the wound was completely covered, then she turned the arm back and forth in the light. Cass watched her.

"You have blond hair on your arms," she said.

"Some European blood in the family, some time back," Cass replied pulling the arm away. Tallal's mother looked closer into her face, not at the eyes but at the cheeks and chin.

"How old are you?"

"Nineteen," Cass said.

"And not a whisker? You are making some deception, I believe. By God, you are a wom . . ."

Cass hushed her, but not soon enough. Yuessef had come to the entrance of the shed.

"What's this?" He said. Neither woman spoke.

"Come, woman, bring our guest. We are all hungry, especially Tallal."

"A moment, husband. We will be there." She wrapped the wound lightly with two layers of bandage. Cass grasped her hand and whispered, "I will tell you all soon enough. Please, but not yet."

Tallal's mother made no response, but her eyes were troubled.

Cass played with her food, but ate nothing. When the dishes were empty at the other places and the fat from their fingers wiped clean on a communal towel, Cass leaned forward from her seat of pillows and received the host's permission to speak. She conjured up some magic. She put her fingers to her eyes and lifted the contact lenses from her pupils. The kerosene flame reflected from her grey eyes into those of the family around her.

"Eiyee," Yuessef said, "What costume is this you wear over the eyes God gave you? You are a Christian no doubt, but this disguise—it does not become an honorable man."

Cass glanced at Tallal's mother, peering intently into her wide eyes. The mother rose, picked up the baby and grabbed the hand of her youngest daughter.

"Come, Nadia. Come, Magda. It is getting late." They followed as if in a dream.

"I am not an honorable man," Cass said soberly. "I am an honorable woman."

Tallal sprang to his feet as if a snake had wriggled into their midst. He beat his hand against his temple.

"It's not your fault, Talla. I did not want you to know. A woman traveling alone in Syria. It is safer for me to travel as a man."

"Why have you come?" Yuessef asked. "Where are your father and your brothers?"

"My . . . brother was killed here in Aleppo just over two months ago. I have come to find his murderers."

"It is not a woman's work," Yuessef said. Tallal had his back to them, but spun once more into the lamplight and sat down, this time further away from his guest, but craning closer to hear her words. His fingers clicked along a strand of prayer beads, counting each one over and over.

"I cannot believe it," Tallal said. "You ride and talk like a man. You smoke cigarettes. You stare boldly. You travel and joke, you. . . ."

"I must," she said. "Three men of your faith—I'm sorry," she added, "—shot down my brother at the citadel. I believe they would like to kill me, too."

"He was not your brother," Yuessef said. "He was an American. We all heard about it. It was in the papers. You are not even Arab."

"That, too, is true. As I reveal all this to you, you may want to turn me out. I will understand. I am American, but I have spent some years in your part of the world. Long enough to get to know a little of your people. I have not come to do you harm. I would have refused this invitation if it had not been for this." She lifted her left arm. "I did not mean to deceive your son, nor have I lied to him."

"What about the police? Have you gone to them?"

"In the beginning, but I do not trust them, now."

"But how can you trust us? We may turn you

over to these same authorities." Tallal seemed startled by his father's remark, but he said nothing.

"You know better than I what they would do to me. I am armed. I have no papers."

"Your real father. Your real family. Where are they?" Yuessef calmly reached in back of him for the narghileh and folded himself once more cross-legged on the cushions. The dirt floor was packed down hard as iron.

"My real father died some years ago of a wasting disease. He was strong like you."

"By God," Yuessef said softly.

"By God," Cass responded. "I have no brothers or sisters. My mother lives in New York, but the same people that killed . . . my intended . . . my dearest friend . . . sent a bomb to me in the mail. My mother opened it and . . . she is still alive."

Tallal struck the ground hard with his hand.

"Who are these villains, these criminals who set upon you?"

"Three men. I know their faces and names. They thought they might have a western woman one night, but they didn't reckon on my companion. They were angry. They shot him in anger. They would like to shoot me, too, because I know about this." She dropped the envelopes of heroin on the ground.

"Drugs," Yuessef said, "the scourge, the Turkish plague from the north. They said nothing about this in the papers."

"No. They wouldn't. The corruption goes deep."

"Eiyee. I believe that's true. We do not trust the law here in Nayrab. Only the old Bedouin law and the laws of the Koran."

"But I'm surprised that you know of this."

"We have all been to school. Even my daughters will go in their time to learn to read and write and think about places other than Syria. We are not all small minded, not all illiterate nor uncomplaining. Even now, in Damascus, they talk about Iraq as if she were our friend. The Russians with their heavy hearts and Godless souls come here to foul our minds. We are fortunate. We are simple folk. They leave well enough alone. The horses have brought us much luck and prosperity, though one vixen of a mare took the sight of one of my eyes. I had just given her a new pair of shoes. She was very ungrateful."

He sucked at the water pipe and continued. "It was not so long ago that my grandfather's family roamed the desert along the Euphrates River, bringing camels and sheep to the market in Aleppo. My father's father met there a city girl, a merchant's daughter, well endowed and landed. She would have no part of the nomad's life, but he desired her. He counted his money and paid the bride's price in many sheep. He settled here. This is the house he built on the foundations of hard work and faith in Allah.

"We bid you welcome to our ancestral home, but wonder at your mission. You are American. To us, you have come from another planet."

"Do you know where they are? Where they hide themselves?" Tallal asked.

"I don't think they hide at all," she said, then imagined them going underground following the blast in Latakia. "Maybe they do, but I think they are cruel and stupid men. They will come out, if only to do their dirty business."

Yuessef took a pouch from his vest pocket and refilled the narghileh with black tobacco. Tallal brought embers from the brazier and applied them to the tobacco as his Father inhaled on the pipe.

"Tallal. Go get Nasir. Send him to Khidri's farm and bring back Samir." Tallal disappeared through the doorway without a word. Cass was alarmed.

"No, don't worry," Yuessef said. "Samir knows much about the drug trade, but his loyalty is to the tribe of Abu Sayed. He does not waver."

"This is not your fight," said Cass.

"No. It is a blood feud, your own battle. But you are a guest in my house. As a guest we must help you and keep you from harm."

She laughed at that, but Yuessef did not smile. He hesitated, then handed her one of the pipes that trailed from his narghileh.

"It is an honor," Cass said and drew a long and hard on the pipe, holding the smoke for awhile in her lungs, then sending it skyward.

"Yes, an honor reserved only for the most venerable of women . . . or the most worldly. My wife would not touch it. Americans. You have strange customs. They do not mix well here in the Middle East, like oil and water. The sunlight burns you where it gives us strength. The politics confuse you where they fall in the natural division here of black and white, good and bad, the confounding of traditions. God never blinks in the desert, and the desert does not think twice about the weak and the strong. It takes the weak and challenges the strong, but we bow to the will of Allah."

"Allah be praised," his wife said from the shadows.

"Allah be praised," he repeated and beckoned his wife into the circle of light.

Samir, Yuessef's neighbor and friend proved an apt informant, circulating through the souks in Aleppo. He had leathery skin stretched tightly over his bones, and his face was like a weasel's, winking and darting with sagacity. He knew the perimeters of the heroin networks dealing in Aleppo, although hashish, and its delivery through the postal service, was his main accomplishment, favors done for farmers with less clout at the customs offices. The officials he knew grew fat on baksheesh. With money for bribes provided by Cass, he made sure a package, weighing approximately one kilo, would reach its destination in Brooklyn. It was addressed to Mr. Amar Khoury, Antiques Dealer, brother of the slain Khoury of Latakia. Cass believed that the letter bomb that maimed her mother came from Brooklyn.

She wrote a separate letter to the Drug Enforcement Administration informing them that narcotics were about to be received by a Syrian/American. Even if the snare failed to ensure an arrest, she knew the feds wouldn't allow Khoury to stray from their surveillance.

Once done, package and letter posted, and Samir cackling over his coffee in Yuessef's main salon, she put full energy into the tracking of Moustafa Sheik and his comrades.

She and Tallal exercised their horses on the old Baghdad caravan route to the outskirts of Aleppo. Once she ventured in by day to the Telecommuni-

cations Center. There Cass put a call through to
the United States. A nurse in Room 301 was
brought to interpret for Cass' mother. There were
long pauses while Mrs. Morgan scribbled down
notes for the nurse to read to Cass over the long-
distance line. Her own voice echoed back at her,
reeling off the satellite, reverberating through the
cosmos. Cass told her mother she was still in
Lebanon, that she was stalling the newspaper
request while she got her thoughts together on her
friend's farm.

Yes, she was riding a good deal, the horse fever
of her youth had returned, and she was caring for
the tomato patch behind Vaz' house.

"I love you," her mother tried to say through the
wires in her jaw. Cass got the message and came
out of the booth shaken. The dimple that once
appeared in her cheek was now a hollow, mirrored
on either side of her face. The skin of her nose was
taut against the bone. There was no excess flesh
on any part of her body; her wrist bones were
large, and her spine had scant padding now.

To all eyes she was an Arab youth. To Tallal, she
was an enigma, burying the usual signals of her
sex in an overlay of masculinity. The boy found it
difficult to throw off the traditional manners he
afforded women, but he knew he must or his
companion could not travel without suspicion by
his side. He spoke to her in the masculine gender.
They had rehearsed some scenes in case curious
minds sought to pry into their relationship, but
they dropped the pretense when they returned to
Yuessef's farm.

The Abu Sayed household went about its tasks
as if Cass had always been there. She lent a hand

with the horses and did imitations of her own severe and exacting riding instructor, a Prussian. She sometimes had Tallal rolling with laughter as he slumped in the saddle, then fell to the ground. The family welcomed the extraordinary as if it were routine. It was all God's will.

In the evenings Cass' presence opened their minds to other things. She was an alien, and her foreignness brought questions long before any discourse on religions. Both Cass and Yuessef battled with their preconceived notions and spent themselves in eager debates, under the billows of black tobacco smoke.

Yuessef saw the danger in her, the threat to his son's stability, but he weighed that against what he viewed as the greater danger, that his son might never know anything but the stables and the mud-slapped domes of Nayrab. It was a hard time for Tallal. He was to be drafted into the Syrian Army. The papers had already been sent.

He was to go to cadet school in Aleppo not far from home, but Yuessef was bitter about relinquishing his first-born son to the military machine. He felt no national pride in the Syrian flag. He scoffed at its saber rattling. He loathed the rigidity of the Syrian generals, the state of constant confrontation with Israel. The fight that had droned on for 30 years seemed to pull Aleppo southward against its traditional independence as a city state, renowned for its trade on the great caravan routes, for its art and its literature. The Golan Heights might as well have been in Alaska for all Yuessef cared. He had no patience with the Palestinians, because the only strength he recognized was that of the individual man.

His vigorous mind sometimes overstepped the bounds of the Islamic faith, astonishing Cass. Deep rooted in his Bedouin background was a boldness that set the struggle of his life not between Yuessef and other men, for he was not cunning, but between Yuessef and the white heat of his God. Shackled to his faith, he looked outward, believing in God, yet believing in his own determination as well.

Samir had come and gone that evening full of stories from the souks. He had spoken with many men in the bazaar, talking of the Latakia explosion, how it had been rumored that the contract on Hassan Khoury was paid for by the Corsicans. He helped flame the rumors himself, he said. He had delighted in the hush that fell over the crowd round the backgammon tables in Souk El Hal. He whispered of subterfuge, of the greed of those Syrians who dealt along the coast, a different breed of Arabs, who out of stupidity had allowed some dissatisfied foreigners to engineer their demise.

A brash thug from the farthest table shouted him down, saying Samir was talking like a frightened old lady, a cow with nothing between her shrivelled ears. Samir held himself in check as this Latakia youth of the Ouzai tribe defended his brethren. The youth picked up his stool and set it down with such force he knocked over a backgammon board and scattered its players. He moved closer to the old man so his breath played in Samir's ear and his words struck into Samir's brain like an etching needle, scratching the pattern of drug dealing from Aleppo to the coast. The Corsicans had denied the Khoury killing.

Samir bowed to the youth's intelligence and awaited more wisdom, but another man came and the youth became silent. They left the gaming house together.

When the full moon was on the rise behind them over the eastern desert, Tallal and Cass rode into Aleppo along the airport road. They cantered south past the crumbling walls of antiquity and rounded the citadel moat. The view held Cass in thrall only for a blinding moment when she saw Foster crash again and again onto its stone steps. She wiped the vision from her eyes and cast her gaze ahead toward the nightclub district. There she hoped to find Moustafa Sheik and his companions.

Both Tallal and Cass were dressed in western clothes. Hers were the black jacket and tie of a schooled Arab; his were the blue jeans and long-sleeved shirt of a city youth, with his father's sports coat draped over his slim shoulders. Tallal's mother had brushed a kohl paste into Cass' hair. It was swept back in greased strands flat against her head, and her eyebrows and lashes had been darkened.

It had been agreed that Tallal would take no part in any firefight that might erupt. His father had refused to arm him with anything but a curved dagger. Tallal had bowed reluctantly to his father's wishes, choking back the slight to his pride. Cass had smoothed it over as best she could, outlining the unwritten law of the blood feud, that no other should take part lest the blood taint innocent families, lest her own battles spill over into the Abu Sayed clan that had offered her hospitality and protection. Her age—she was more than ten years Tallal's senior—added authority to her orders, but her sex rankled him.

They had reached the Aleppo nightclub. She left him with the horses and vanished inside. Through the stone-cut arabesques of the wall that separated the bar from the tables she could see dancers on the patio floor. The patio was ringed by palm trees, illuminated by green and yellow lights. The music was a mixture of Arabic, Italian and American, some disco, but mostly French and Italian crooning. Men and some women, milled about the periphery in tight-knit clusters of three and four. The girls, most twenty or older, were dressed in Parisian fashions with spangles on their arms and gold earrings dangling. Their dark hair was curled or swept up. They giggled and spoke in low tones, and when the slow dances came they drifted, lightly touching their partners' arms, with modest grace.

Above the tables cigarette smoke was tangible in the soft night air, hovering momentarily above the faces animated in conversation, the gesturing hands demonstrating the force of an argument. Pieces of conversation fell upon Cass' eardrums and were ignored.

Cass felt set apart from the others. She was a lone wolf that night, prowling in a solitude that was suspect to the Arabs. It was a western invention, this inability to get close to people. In Syria, in all the Levant, people hung close together. Boys held boys, girls held girls, and on the dance floor the sexes mixed, but she stood apart, and in so doing she aroused their attentions momentarily.

She moved in toward the bar which offered fruit

juices and whiskey. She ordered her Scotch neat,
but after the first swallow she asked for ice cubes.
It was the first alcohol she had taken in several
days, and though she longed for its relaxation, she
could not afford to lose her alertness.

Over the bar were posters of Mick Jagger,
Jefferson Airplane, The Beatles and one or two
Arab groups she did not recognize. The posters
were a decade too late. She circumnavigated the
dance floor again. None of the three was there.
She drained her glass and deposited it on the bar
on the way out.

Tallal was waiting three blocks away with the
horses. He had frayed the ends of his reins in
agitation. She calmed him and they moved on to
The Blow Up, a discotheque on Saad Allah Al
Diabri Street, adjacent to a park bisected by the
Kuwek River. The trees were still, but the
fountains murmured. The birds had all gone to
bed. Cass and Tallal trotted over the bridge. Their
horses' hooves bit into the wooden planks in
counterpoint to the rock 'n' roll music pulsating
from The Blow Up. Only the insects competed in
raucous disregard to the dance music, striking up
choruses of their own.

They fast-walked their mares through rows of
oleander and rose bushes, around thickets of
tamarisk and tongue plant, making for a stand of
trees to the northwest of The Blow Up. Small
pines ringed the taller growths of frangipani not
yet in bloom. White wire wickets circled the area,
but it was large enough to conceal the horses. Cass
and Tallal dismounted on the grass and led their
animals into the brush, breaking the stems of the
succulents in their path. Mabruka balked; Cass

talked her in, deeper under the boughs.

"Wait here," she told Tallal.

"No," he replied vehemently. "No one will come into the park now. It is near eleven. The horses will be safe tied to the tree."

"You promised your father you would follow my instructions."

"I would be of help to you. I can talk freely with the Syrians inside." They both lit cigarettes and scanned the terrain around them.

"And if they are there. . . ."

"You can point them out to me."

She looked into his young face. The high cheekbones offset the depth of his defiant eyes. His mouth was small and at that moment set hard, neither frowning nor smiling, in a suspension of emotion. They faced each other at equal height and like weight.

"All right, my brother, but if I tell you to go to the horses, you must. I have vowed that no harm should come to you."

He brushed that off with a flip of his head.

"By God, you must swear."

"I swear," he breathed and looked up through the feathery branches into the starlight. They did not touch.

It was a considerable walk to the discotheque, some three hundred yards. Cass paced it off silently. The entrance to The Blow Up faced out on Diabri Street, though the terrace looked out on the park, its balcony some 10 feet off the ground.

Cass checked the clip on the Corsair, then hammered it home. She put the gun back in the holster at her right hip and made sure the tail of her shirt did not impair the movement of the gun up and out of her trousers. As they entered the disco, a stout man, dressed in tuxedo and bow tie, shouted over the music for the cover charge.

Cass handed him the money.

"Your friend here. Where's his tie?"

Tallal was dumbstruck.

"He's forgotten it," Cass said.

"Can't go in without one. Sorry," he began to hand the money back.

"Have you got an extra one of those?" she said, pointing at his own tie.

The man licked his lips and looked from Cass to Tallal, then back to Cass who stood before him with her feet spread apart, both hands on her hips. She had the advantage, standing while he sat on a long-legged stool, his knees propped under him. He made to get up but Cass pushed another bill at him.

"All right," he said, opening a drawer and giving the clip-on tie to Tallal, "Just make sure I get it back."

Through the archway they walked down a long carpeted hall, feeling the bass lines of the guitar thumping under their feet. The hall opened into an inflorescence of colors and shapes, dancers swaying in and out of strobe lights, waiters dressed in black tie. They glided from table to table, raising their trays high above the heads of the dancers. Cass' eyes became adjusted to the dark and she allowed her memory to scan the photographs Vazcatchian had brought home so many weeks before. They clicked into focus like slides on a screen. She matched up the two-dimensional images of the exits, the bar, the bathrooms, with the real thing. Tallal moved in

close to her, as close as they had been since
hunched together on the trainride from Jisr Esh
Shugur. She felt his excitement and held onto his
arm, twisted him about with a smile on her face.

He was like a lamb now. It was the first time he
had been to The Blow Up, first time he had seen
the bellydance of tradition transmogrified into the
animal writhing of rock 'n' roll.

"Do you see them?" he whispered.

"Would you like a drink?" she said cooly.

"Juice," he responded. The idea of alcohol
repulsed him.

"Go out on the porch," she said. "Check the
ground around. Look north toward the horses. See
if you see anything moving out there." Then she
was gone, threading her way across the dance
floor to the bar. The main floor was dark as a cave,
though once in awhile a strobe light caught the
dancers in their fractious gyrations. A mirrored
ball sent darts of light into the four corners, onto
the tiered and carpeted areas surrounding the
dance floor where people sank deeply into low
leather couches. Their eyes were at about the
same level as their knees, which bumped the
undersides of the brass tables in front of them.
They leaned towards each other over candles
veiled in red glass. These were the wealthy of
Aleppo, the well educated. Some had gone to
western schools. Their language was a tossed
salad of English, French, and Arabic. Their
appetites were cosmopolitan, but for the most
part, their morals followed the tenets of the
Koran.

The black wood bar was set back against the
inner wall of the disco. At its far end sat two

Saudis dressed in gaudy madras jackets. Their mouths were open, white teeth flashing in laughter, but they could not be heard above the music, nor would their sins of strong drink be revealed that far from Arabia. A bottle of Scotch and a silver dish of ice sat on the bar between them, along with saucers of olives and peppers, onions and radishes. A waiter jostled Cass and elbowed past her toward his station at the bar.

The hairs prickled at the back of her neck and she moved on swiftly past two Syrian enlisted men. She found a seat near the Saudis, who immediately tried to engage her in conversation about Aleppo.

"I'm a visitor myself," she responded, "from Lebanon."

"Ah, Beirut," one of them clucked, "so sad. They are crazy there. Mad with killing. It will never be done. A waste."

Her downward glance told them to shut up.

"Orange juice, please and a Scotch on the rocks."

"I'm sorry, I can't hear you," the bartender said leaning toward her. His white shirt stood out like a blank billboard under the black light. Paisleys swam on the wall in Day-glo colors.

"Scotch with ice and a glass of orange juice, please," she said louder though forcing her voice to remain in the lower registers. She put a cigarette to her lips and immediately two lighters appeared under her nose. The Saudis were determined to please.

She thanked them while running her eyes like a searchlight through the darkness.

"Looking for someone?" one of the Saudis said.

"My younger brother."

"No sisters?"

"Sorry," she smiled and slid from the barstool and serpentined her way over the dance floor and onto the outside porch. Tallal was leaning against the concrete balustrade, a potted palm tickling his back. He hung in the corner like a boxer waiting for the bell. When he saw Cass coming he could barely contain himself.

"They are pagans!" he said.

"Drink this, Tallal. I think maybe you need a sip of mine, though."

A breeze had come up off the Kuwek. There was a pause in the music, and Cass could hear the palms rattling. A lizard popped into view, bobbed his head up and down, and disappeared when Cass put her finger under his dry belly. An argument was brewing at the southern end of the porch, beneath the paper lanterns. Cass had her back to it. Tallal was watching. A wiry man with an open shirt sidled into the group and raised his voice above the others.

"He isn't wearing a tie," Tallal said indignantly, toying with the clip-on at his throat.

Cass looked over her shoulder, then pivoted around with her hand at her gun.

"Moustafa Sheik," she hissed. Tallal snapped to attention and stayed her right hand. She was like steel under his grasp. Sheik's sudden appearance had struck her like the spikes in an iron maiden, straight through her brain, dispatching sensations sharp as razors through her body. Her stomach flip-flopped and her shirt was wet against her, wet against her breasts and constricting the beat of her heart. Her hatred of him was palpable. She

could taste it on her tongue, feel it in the burning
behind her ears, but the time was not right. The
argument had erupted anew thirty paces ahead of
her and Sheik knocked another youth hard against
the balcony rail, then brought him up close to his
face, clutching the other man's shirt about the
throat.

"Hey, by God," a low voice sounded from
within. Sheik let his victim drop back against the
rail.

"No trouble here, *maitre*. No trouble at all."

Cass did not see Mohammed or Nahass, his
bravos, but she did not have long to wait. They
pummeled people out of their way and strode to
Sheik's side. Two waiters contained the argument.
Another shouted for a boy to set the music going
again. Sheik went peaceably onto the dance floor
and out, his two companions in tow.

"Go on," she said to Tallal. "Go on," she said
again, her voice rising now, her body unmoving,
frozen in the moonlight. Grey shadows sculpted
her features. "Find out what you can. Find out if
he'll be back. Ask about his friends. Ask what the
*maitre* knows about him. Where he lives, what he
does, anything. Go. I'll be with the horses."

She looked about her then, saw all attention
directed toward the dance floor, and vaulted over
the balcony rail, landing nearly without a sound
on the grass below. Her feet found traction and
she sprinted across the park.

Tallal arrived some twenty minutes later,
spotting the glow of her cigarette. He was all
nerves.

"I forgot to give them their bow tie," he grinned.
"They hauled me back very roughly, but I

smoothed things over. In the middle of the apologies I asked many questions. I am an excellent spy."

"Tallal."

"You have found Sheik's lair. That is for certain. The Blow Up is his stomping ground, his sanctuary. Even the cops stay away. He is free with money. He seems to own half the staff and the half he doesn't keeps out of his way."

"Ouzai?"

"The whole thing. Ouzai territory. The sound system, the lights, the alcohol. . . ." Tallal laughed. "Even the prostitutes from Cairo with the blue paint over their eyes, and the bouncers."

"They told you a lot."

"They were trying to impress me, a stupid and harmless farm boy with awestruck eyes."

She clapped him on the shoulder and they cantered homeward past the Saracen walls and the open houses where laughter tumbled out on the wind amidst the cries of children. Their horses sped on towards the Abu Sayed farm. Neither mare was willing to follow the other and they fought the bits in their mouths. Tallal rode slackly, his body echoing the rocking gait of his horse. Cass, astride Mabruka, drew the animal under her, her own fluidity inseparable from that of her horse. They rode in silence.

# THIRTY-TWO

In Beirut, Andrew Pym slammed down the phone in exasperation. He had been thwarted a third time in attempts to reach Cass at Vazcatchian's farm. He drummed on the telegrams beneath his fingertips and went over in his mind once more what Vaz had said. First she'd been out riding, later she'd been to the market with Ingrid, lastly she'd gone out for a walk.

"Bloody busy girl," he said as he returned to the bar.

"No luck," Kodak said. "Well, I haven't had any either. She just doesn't want to talk with her old friends."

"Maybe she isn't there."

"Gone back to the States? You'd think she'd tell us that."

"I dunno. I don't know, really. There's a telegram here for her from New York. You'd think she'd have the decency to check in with her chums once in awhile."

"Reclusive," Kodak said, "bloody reclusive and out of character. Maybe she's still nursing her hurts, but it beats me why she'd come back here to do it. This place is full of ghosts. Exorcising her demons, I suppose. Stubborn, silly girl. I miss her company."

"Let's hope she isn't a ghost herself," Andrew said, and regretted it. Kodak frowned at him.

"What's in your mind?"

"Another beer as a matter of fact, otherwise just plain ether between the ears. Funny just the same we haven't heard. Funny," he said again.

"Working tomorrow?"

"Damascus," Pym said, bored. "Assad's statement about the renewal of the peacekeeping forces. There may be some pyrotechnics over the Sadat thing. Rejectionist front. 'Sadat the betrayer of the Arab cause.' Same old rubbish."

"Well, I'm off the hook there. No film in Syria for this boy, but here's to a story for you."

"Mr. Pym. Excuse me, Mr. Pym. Telephone call, sir, at the desk." The bellboy in red jacket and polished black shoes led Pym to the outside lobby phone. He was there for some moments.

Kodak fed potato chips to the parrot. He was champing to get out of Beirut. The city was exploding in crime. Kidnappings, sniping incidents, but nothing he could film, nothing he could get a bead on. Just plain bad vibes.

The Christian sectors were under cover and drilling their militias under the heated oratory of their leaders. The Syrian Peacekeeping Forces were agitating to be done with the Christians who dogged their movements and prevented their passing through territories that should, by mandate, be under their jurisdiction. Syrian President Assad held them tenuously at bay, trying to calm his own domestic difficulties by keeping the young Syrians out of the line of fire, but the peace would not hold for long. The civil war was slumbering fitfully, the tension heightened by the successful Israeli airstrikes into the Palestinian strongholds. The Syrians felt impotent and hated it. The angst of Lebanon was building.

At the phone, Pym fidgeted, doodling a tangle of circular lines. His Interpol Commander was livid. The voice from Damascus wanted to know the whereabouts of Cassandra Morgan. A contract was out on her life.

"I'll check it out, sir. I'll drop by the Vazcatchian farm tomorrow and see what I can find out."

He held the phone away from his ear and bore harder with the point of his pen.

"All right, sir. Tonight. Yes, all visas in order. Your dossier on Khoury arrived today, *post mortem*. If it's her work, she's doing a hell of a job. . . .Sorry, sir. Yes, goodbye."

Pym hung up and returned to the bar to pay up.

Two hundred miles to the north, Cass Morgan was making ready.

She went outside, to sleep between the shed and the paddock, close to Mabruka. Yuessef noticed her going, for during the previous nights she had slept in the main salon with the rest of the family. By day the beds were rolled up and tucked away, the counterpanes folded, the pillows piled in stacks by the wall to make way for the preparation of food. Now her absence changed the feel of the room.

Its mud stucco walls were plastered with pictures torn from magazines and newspapers. By the doorway hung a calendar bearing the image of a beautiful Arab girl, dressed in blue silk with pearl and gold sprays offsetting her dark hair. On it black marks delineated the days when the horses' shoes should be changed, when the sales would be made, when the mares were expected to foal. Beneath the only window was a carved wooden pedestal with slender legs that held a velvet-bound edition of the Koran. In the past Yuessef's father would open it to a passage and leave it thus marked with a ribbon, finding some verse of the Islamic bible to suit the day's situation. Yuessef closed his eyes. The family room warm, convivial.

He knew Cass wished to be alone.

It was not in Yuessef's mind to try and talk her out of it. He well understood the blood feud. His family tree was full of branches lopped off by raiders and tribal disputes in the past. His own Bedouin side called for a standing off from the fight, a suspension of judgment on the matter of right and wrong, a recognition that it must go forward. His city side, the education passed down from his grandmother, called for pragmatism.

When the dawn call to Allah warbled from the muezzin's throat, Cass was wide eyed. She added a prayer of her own, though not to a vengeful God, but to the sun and the trees and the ground upon which she sat. She was a reverent pagan, almost Druidic, with her faith rooted only in what she saw and felt and tasted, the emotions that quickened in her veins, determination leap-frogging fear, resignation smothering the urge to cry out. She cherished Foster's memory as she cherished the warm earth and the wild things and the verdant pastures of green and natural spirits.

She derived potency from them. Her Sunday schooling had been simple Bible stories, more like fairy tales than testaments to the wisdom of the Almighty. The Almighty had to be tangible for her now.

There was no room in her heart to forgive those who snatched Foster's life on a whim, those who violated the order of things, the braggarts and the bullies and the murderers who shattered the sanctity of the spirit and upset the cycle. She would kill them or be killed. It did not matter. The wheel must turn full circle.

Yuessef came out and watched the girl grooming her horse, cleaning out the hooves and pulling the mare's mane free of tangles. The tail was well combed and swished from flank to flank. Mabruka's hide shone like polished silver, the tarnished darker spots in her skin oily black under her swift moving hands.

Tallal, with more abrupt gestures, was caring for his mare, not the chestnut horse from the south, but his own grey. Yuessef left them to it in silence, overseeing the boys who worked the other pastures, making sure the feed was right, watching for signs of pregnancy among the mares and for signs of ardor among the studs. His wife kept to herself, caring for the children, baking the bread for the evening's meal, soaking the vegetables in olive oil and airing the mattresses behind the house. She was not singing, though, as she normally did.

The day crept on steadily, like a shadow across a sun dial. The desert's subtle shades shifted away from them toward the Euphrates, bruising the valleys with blues and greys.

Cass ate little of the supper put before her. Only out of courtesy did she take small bites of meat, pushing the food about on her plate, bucking the insult that might be felt by Yuessef's wife.

Tallal ate heartily, wolfing everything down, giggling sometimes in nervousness, his features bright with expectation, while gloom crept into his mother's soft brown eyes and pinched the corners with impending loss.

Cass excused herself and went to the paddock where Mabruka was saddled and ready. She pulled her black jacket from the pommel, beat the dust out of it with the flat of her hand and donned it as Yuessef and Tallal came out through the door.

Yuessef encircled his son's waist with a braided belt and a bedouin dagger in a sheath of beaten silver encrusted with lapis and turquoise. Over Tallal's shoulder he slung the black cloak of the high-born Bedouin and, on his head, a white keffeyeh. They had words, but Cass did not listen. She was heeding her heart.

Her blood ran hot but her brow was cool, as was her mind. Her mouth was set square, her thoughts her own.

"My son will see you safely to Aleppo, and God willing he will see you safely back. This vendetta is yours alone, not his. If one hair of his head is disturbed, if he is soiled by those men whom you seek, I will hunt you down myself. I am charging you with the life of my eldest son. I am charging him with your safe journeying, but if the ugliness of your task should spread I have ordered him to take no part but in his own defense."

Cass nodded and without a word swung up into

the saddle. She was slim as a reed and toughened by her training. Mabruka danced under her.

"I would not have you involved," she said looking into Yuessef's good eye. "I would not have your son hurt for the world."

Yuessef's hand flickered to hers.

"In the eyes of God I wish you well." His palm was hard as elephant hide, dry as leaves, but heavy on hers with the weight of responsibility. She caught sight of Tallal's mother, a shadowy image, and she waved, then spurred Mabruka east down the curving dirt path. Tallal was close behind her. They swung west on the airport road and cantered evenly toward Aleppo.

Again she drilled instructions into Tallal. Again he balked at a woman giving him orders, but swallowed his pride in memories of his father's parting words. His spare frame grew in intensity under the wings of his black cloak. His white keffeyeh shone like the moon as they galloped down the highway. A few trees broke the horizon, tamarisk and acacia, little diversion between the Arabs and their heavens. Vaporous lights burned at intervals along the road. A few cars ventured by, but neither horse started when the vehicles roared past them.

At the Saracen walls of the city they slowed to a trot. Half-naked children, aroused by the hoofbeats, watched them pass. Parents gazed upon them and were cheered by the proud figure of Tallal, his high blood mingling with his high-bred Arab mare. His companion, a stick figure in black western clothes, gave them no pause. The riders followed the culverts of the Kuwek up to the park that bounded the Blow Up Discotheque and Tallal obediently quartered the horses. He shook Cass' hand as a westerner does, then bowed low at the waist in a thousand sa'alaams.

Cass returned the honor with Arab formality.

She took her father's watch from her vest pocket, weighed it a moment and handed it to Tallal.

"If I do not return by one o'clock, ride home, take Mabruka with you, and do not look back. There is nothing that you can do for me except bring your father's wrath upon me if you are wounded in some misguided attempt at rescue. The Ouzais are many and strong. My only weapon is surprise and my ability to move, singular, one person through the crowd. Sirens and shots. They will be part of the night's diet, but it will be my supper, not yours. I do not wish to share what is rightfully my own, especially if it be death."

She strode away over the grass and followed the music to the discotheque entrance. A number of Mercedes and Peugeots lined the street on both sides. Arab women in glimmering silk were led by their husbands or brothers to the mouth of the restaurant. Cass waited behind one such group, her nostrils filled with the scents of amber and musk. She watched the flashing of desire pass between the men and their women. It was Thursday night, the eve of the Islamic sabbath, and the disco was crowded with celebrants.

The man at the door grunted recognition at Cass as she passed him the cover charge. Two men stood behind him like monoliths, arms crossed over their chests.

"Where's your brother?" he said, fingering the tie at his throat.

Cass just raised her chin. "Not here tonight."

The doorman let her pass down the hallway and she followed the charged particles of voices and vibrations of feet against the dance floor. The reza, the Arabic meal of several dishes, was being cleared from the low brass tables and the clinking of metal plates were like the ching of finger cymbals in the waiters' hands. Every stool at the bar was taken. The dance floor was crowded and the couches were thronged.

She circled the periphery, apologizing as she bumped into people on the way. Every muscle was ready, every nerve wired to capacity. Her inner ear penetrated the music's percussion and sought out male voices, the rough and raspy tones of Moustafa Sheik. She wore Foster's shirt tucked tight at the waist. The small breasts that belied her masculine disguise were flattened by her tailored vest. The shoulders of her black jacket were square, giving her a broadness of stature.

She loosened her tie and her hand roamed in back of her to the gun. She pulled it round to her hip. Her eyes travelled over the crowd and locked on the face of Moustafa Sheik. He sat ringside, enveloped in a knot of comrades. Mohammed was there, but not Nahass. Two girls with them had their heads together, their glossed mouths opening with laughter over bright white teeth. The human bodies on the dance floor were economized in the black light, a morass of white shirts, white belts and swirling skirts.

Cass stood twenty paces from Moustafa Sheik. He sat there so smugly alive, breathing while Foster's body lay still in the Florida sand. She lurked in the shadows, watching, following the pattern of Sheik and his companions. The two girls would rise to the dance floor taking Mohammed with them. Sometimes Sheik himself would spring to the floor, undulating promiscuously before his sycophants. Then with a snort, like a blade across a strop, he would return to his table and another glass of scotch. He was careless; that was good. He was exposed; that was even better.

The black lights switched off, and the strobes began to stroke the dancers. Phaser lights twirled at each corner. Sheik's table was engulfed in blackness. Figures moved as phantoms to and from the dance floor as the music throbbed relentlessly onward.

Cass listened to the songs, ignoring the words, but paying strict attention to the beat. The lights played in concert with the percussion. She hung back in the darkness. Sheik seemed disturbed, nervous. Maybe he felt Cass' eyes upon him.

The Syrian women, who had danced modestly at first, became emboldened in the darkness, and the slow rotation of the belly dance of their youth parried for favor with the hustle, spinning out from their partners then back with just the hint of a fleeting caress as they wound into the arms of their men. The males were agile, their heels striking dramatically against the floor. Cass moved to the music and began drum talking, scatting each measure, comparing the beat of the drums with the approximate report of the Corsair Unique. Her fingers tapped the butt of the revolver as she slithered closer to Sheik's table. Her hatred of him leapt over the confines of fear for her own life.

She laughed to herself, "Ha, what a crusader I am. Don't give a damn about the narcotics they're dealing. Don't give a damn if all hell breaks loose here. I only care about Sheik and his thugs, seeing them dead. Swift and final."

Mohammed got up from the table and excused himself. Cass fell back a pace. The two girls walked off toward the ladies' room. Moustafa Sheik sat alone, singing into his glass of scotch. Cass moved in behind the couch. She squatted down in the darkness, resting her arms on the back of the couch and leaning close to Sheik's ear. The tables behind her were empty. The heavy acid rock had compelled all to the dance floor. Skin drums, timpani and bone-shaking bass lines had taken over. The fever was on the rise. Sheik himself began to stand, but Cass stayed him with her hand firmly on his shoulder. He slumped back down.

"Hullo," she said in English.

Moustafa Sheik turned around smiling, one gold incisor glittering in his mouth. But his lips curled back against his teeth and his expression hardened.

"I don't know you," he said as if vermin had come to call.

"Ah, but you do,' she said, feigning hurt. The gun was already drawn in her right hand, scraping along the leather of the couch dry and hard as a reptile.

"Get away from me," Sheik said thickly. She shoved him hard with her left hand against the pillar as the drum solo soared in four/four time. She counted the beats as blood coursed to her trigger finger.

As he bounced back against her intruding left hand she raised the gun to the base of his neck and fired a bullet into the back of his brain. The light smack of the missile was lost in the din of the speakers that banked the wall of the dance floor.

He collapsed like a marionette whose strings had been cut, but she righted him and leaned him back gently against the plush leather couch as the life drained out behind him. The trajectory of the bullet boring through the tissues and plates of his skull had sent it ceilingward, to lodge in the asbestos tiles above. She rose as if sapped of strength and shook the adrenalin throughout her body. She fumbled for a moment, then slipped an envelope full of heroin into the pocket of his jacket. She did not bother to look around her. She headed briskly along the edge of the dance floor, avoiding the swinging arms and the frenzy of the dancers. Her gait was even, measured on the metronome of her free left hand. Her right hand held the gun that the Palestinian had given her. When she got to the men's room door, Mohammed was just coming out. She pressed him backwards with her left hand on his chest.

"Excuse me a minute," she grinned, "but aren't you Mohammed. . . ."

"Rawzi," he snarled. "What do you want?"

"Just a brief conversation. It began in Latakia several weeks ago. Then at the citadel when you shot down a friend. . . ."

Mohammed stepped backwards, giving himself room to get to the gun in his shoulder holster, but she already had her own trained on his face.

"A little unfinished business, that's all." His expression of horror checked her only for the fraction of a moment.

"No! Don't, I—" She pulled the trigger. The slug knocked him back into the booth and he slid to the floor beside the porcelain basin. The bullet had pierced his face between the eyes, above the bridge of his nose. It went in cleanly, but exploded from the back of his head against the white tile wall in a mat of blood and hair. The blinding light of the bathroom bulb exposed his mortality, gruesomely. She drew another glassine packet of heroin from her vest pocket. Rawzi's body jerked. His arm moved and the blood gurgled in his throat.

She felt the scream building inside her. She was annoyed with him. Sheik had died quietly, politely in the darkness. Her fingers were wet now, dripping with perspiration. Her skin was raw, her nerves racing with sensations. She ran her sleeve over her forehead and seemed to lose some of the hatred that had fueled her actions. Somebody opened the outer restroom door, but she threw her body against it.

"Just a moment. Wait a little, please. So embarrassing. I'm being sick." She ran water into the sink, splashing it in her face, rubbed her hands on a paper towel and wadded it up and jammed the booth door closed with it. His feet barely protruded, but blood was pooling around him, finding its way in rivulets along the grout of the tiles.

The music was still pounding. The bass rhythms beat heavily against her sternum. A high-frequency guitar solo began to soar and as it built it crescendoed into a woman's scream. Cass heard it loud and clear and knew it was time to go. In

disgust she shoved past the man who waited
outside, who had turned away to see where the
scream had come from, as he turned back once
more he saw Cass pass out through the emergency
exit.

"Hey," he shouted. The music kept spinning
dizzily out of the speakers. It irritated him. The
strobe lights flashed on and off like heat lightning,
then Nahass Ghourdri, the last of Foster's three
assassins, opened the door to the men's room. It
took him a split second to realize his friend was
dead, and he yelled to the other members of the
Ouzai to help him. No one paid any attention. All
eyes were at ringside. Feet were pounding across
the floor, figures frozen in terror as the plug was
pulled on the music. The lights blazed on.

"Hey, for the love of God!" Nahass shouted,
"He's getting away!" But all the women were
screaming now, shreiking at the face of Moustafa
Sheik who stared out at them open mouthed. A
young girl swooned and the Ouzais rallied around
the body.

Nahass didn't wait. Impatient and swelling with
anger he lit out after the running man in the dark
suit. The Latakia explosion played like fireworks
in his brain. He believed he was in the grip of an
assassination plot devised by the enemies of the
Ouzai.

Cass heard his shoes hit the pavement as he
plunged from the emergency exit. The door
slammed behind him on the clamor within. Her
own arms pumped, her thighs contracted and
expanded with each lengthening stride.

"Enough, enough," she said to herself.

"Hey, you! Hey, stop that man!" But there was

no one in the street near Nahass, even the parking attendants had abandoned their posts at the first sound of alarm from the Ouzais.

Cass was broken now, her limbs working on the sheer will of self-preservation. She had gotten Moustafa Sheik and Mohammed. She had nailed them, blown them away as was her intent, but the third man now gave chase. "Fool," she yelled. She could not turn eastward toward the park or she would endanger Tallal.

"Stay where you are, Tallal," she murmured as if the nightwind would carry her message back to him. "Stay where you are."

Nahass was closing in now, his lithe body moving more swiftly then hers. She turned a dark corner, rounding the serrated trunk of a palm. She could hear his steps, feel the pursuit of his panting breath, feel his own chest heaving and she turned to fire her revolver, leveling her gun between both hands, but as she did an about-face her heels caught the curb. Her weight was thrown violently off course and as she tumbled backwards and down she let fly with one round. The second went wild as her head hit the concrete and the gun clattered away from her grasp. She was stunned as the night sky moved in like a pair of hands over her face. Nahass had his gun drawn now and checked himself momentarily as the dark shape ahead of him sprawled on the ground. It was his last mistake.

Andrew Pym stood in a doorway twenty paces away aiming his .38 at the back of Nahass' head. Cass did not hear the shot, only saw the man before her stagger under its concussion. The first bullet burrowed deep into his back like an angry hornet. The second struck his head. All Cass knew was his falling upon her, pinning her to the pavement out of reach of the Corsair. She caught her breath, and shook off the dizziness that strangled her movements, and pushed him away from her. Swimming in sweat now, she regained her gun and stood over the body, just as the first siren's wail shattered the night. She held the gun above Nahass' head to complete the kill, but waited. His body did not stir. She felt the gun's potency beneath her trigger finger, but she held her shot, thinking forward now to life, not death. Escape. She flashed on her own image as if on a television screen, scrambling over a rooftop, howling like a mad woman with a gun in her hand. She was mad now, crazed and drunk with killing. Her medulla cried for more, but her forebrain told her to stop.

"Move, girl. Now." Pym spoke under his breath. "You're free. Get out of here."

She reacted as if she had heard him and he melted back into the doorway. She threw the last packet of heroin to the ground, the last condiment of her killing, and raced for the park, switching direction as if a marksman trained his gun on her retreat. Her head was splitting with the whoop of police cars. She saw the rotating light of an ambulance and and the redness of it made her run all the harder into the treeline, beyond the spikes of Spanish bayonet that tore at her clothing.

Tallal was frenetic with fright, swaying back and forth, his knife upraised as she approached.

"Ride," she said, "We're out of here, now." Both bolted for their horses, Tallal swinging his cloak behind him like a black wave. Not bothering to catch their stirrups, they dug in with their heels and galloped pell mell to the west, their horses' hooves sending up clumps of turf.

The city was coming alive. Lights switched on. Alarums sounded, people poured from their homes, a writhing mass of flailing arms, shouting over the noise to find out what all the noise was about.

"Hey boy, what's going on?" one man yelled to Tallal.

"There's been an accident on Diabri Street," he said drawing his horse down to a proper pace. Cass fell in beside him, reining in the panic, wiping the fear from her expression. The sirens grew fainter. The darkness threw its arms about them.

They rounded the great fortress, the citadel, and Cass looked only once at the stone ramp that had held Foster's bleeding body. She raised her fist, but caught herself, lost the anger at whatever God had kept her alive. They thundered down the road, cutting across the desert to Nayrab with the demons of fear dogging them on. The full moon fled before them. Within an hour, they were home.

"Father, Father," Tallal called. He jumped down from his horse.

Yuessef burst from the darkness. He had sat all this time in the dust beneath the tamarisk tree.

"It is done, then. It is done?"

"It is done, Father," said Tallal. He grabbed Mabruka's reins and held them as Cass slid to the ground.

"It is done," she said, afraid to say more. She held her hands before her in the moonlight. She threw off her jacket and tore the tie from her throat.

Yuessef spun her around and clapped his hands on her shoulders. "It is finished, girl! Finished. Allah be praised that you are still alive."

"It's all right," she said pulling away. "Thank you. I'm all right. Your son is a good soldier."

Yuessef's wife came out of the house with Hamdy mewling in her arms. Tears streaked her cheeks, and she looked in horror upon the American girl. Cass felt like poison then, the disruptive spirit, the blooded assassin.

But Tallal sung her praises as if she had just led the Jihad through the heathen hordes with scimitar slashing. Her body shook uncontrollably and Tallal's mother brought water, her own eyes softening again as she saw the warrior's strength ebbing from her guest. Cass sat down and let Tallal paint a vivid picture of things he had not seen. His mother gasped. Mabruka pawed at the ground beside her and she rose again to unfasten her girth. She peeled the sweat-soaked blanket from Mabruka's back and wiped the foam from her horse's chest. Then she walked the mare around and around in circles, cooling her out, cooling herself out, and as she walked her thoughts paraded back to Lebanon, back to take up her life without Foster. She was giddy, repulsed by her success, yet free from the burden of her revenge.

"It is finished," Yuessef said quietly.

# THIRTY-THREE

The Aleppo newspapers headlined the discotheque killings the next day. They conjectured
that a gangland contract had been put out on
members of the Ouzai by other drug-dealing
tribes. "Eye witnesses" were interviewed, each
giving a different description of the supposed
assassin. Police knew from their ballistic tests
that the gun that had killed Sheik and Rawzi was
not the same weapon that had felled the third
victim. This astonished Cass. She had believed
that by some stroke of luck her own bullet had
found its mark.

"It is Allah," Yuessef said.

"I don't think Allah carries a .38," she responded and peered into Yuessef's eyes. He
shrugged.

"Not I. I took no part in this."

Witnesses told police they had seen a car
speeding from the scene, but no one could
remember its make. Too much excitement, they all
said. Too much confusion. Cass wondered if some
gardener might go to the police when he found the
hoof tracks across the park and the broken plants
in that girdle of trees where Tallal had stood with
their horses. She knew she must get out of Syria

soon and made ready to go, again by train, this time taking the Damascus line to within reach of the Lebanese border.

She told Tallal she could go it alone, that he had already endangered himself enough, but Yuessef interceded in the dispute and invoked the law of the desert, that Tallal must accompany her to the border and see her safely through.

They compromised. He would be by her side only until she disembarked from the railroad at Tall Kalakh on the eastern spur from Homs.

As they were leaving the Abu Sayed farm, Yuessef read to them aloud from a newspaper editorial in an Aleppo newspaper.

"The evil of heroin, the befuddling stupor of narcotics, must be rooted out from our country. . . ."

Samir, the little weasel, stood beside him and laughed. They rode away from the farm in good humor.

The train from Aleppo to Damascus was crowded with soldiers soon to reinforce the peace-keeping troops in Lebanon. Three carloads of tanks, armored cars and jeeps were attached to the end of the long freight and livery train. Heat-seeking SAMs, anti-aircraft guns were packed in crates carelessly draped in canvas. Presents for the Israelis, no doubt.

Cass and Tallal rode in the livery car, once more, suffocating in the heat and stench of flocks of sheep and goats. The wound on Cass' arm from the Latakia blast had hardened and nearly healed. Her mind was not at peace, though. She was troubled by the killings, troubled by her many miles from home.

Tallal sought to cheer her with desert songs and the legends of the Bedouins. Then he grew serious and spoke of his impending conscription into the Syrian Army.

"Yes, I suppose you can't run to Canada from here," she said.

"What's that? I will be a good soldier," he said.

"Yes, probably."

Tallal's mind would be steeled against the Israelis, against the Lebanese Christians, and he would be trained to wear two faces where the Palestinians were concerned. This lively boy who had aged ten years before her eyes might lose his life before he ever held a woman in his arms. He was trapped by the traditions of Islam, waiting for the decisions to be made for him, for the family to chose whom he should wed. She felt a warmth for him that confused her, but put it aside! She wondered if anyone would touch her again as Foster had. His absence clutched at her belly, and her mind returned to her gun. She saw herself shooting, again and again.

The train lurched to a halt in a cloud of dust. Soldiers came back and rapped their rifle butts against the livery car doors. Farmers and shepherds leapt to the ground, chattering about the delay. Tallal and Cass followed. It was a long stop, just outside the Homs, to uncouple the military cars. They sat by the railway bed and shared tea with the soldiers. Cass kept quiet and her eyes cast downward at all times. One soldier tried to strike up a conversation, but Tallal barged into it and assuaged his curiosity about the silent boy.

"My brother," Tallal said, "a little tetched, you

know. He has been ill. The army won't take him, but I will be a soldier."

"Where will you be posted?" one of the men said.

"In Aleppo, at the academy."

"Ah, that is good. Much better than Damascus." Another agreed.

Tallal reached into Cass' pocket and pulled out the pack of cigarettes and handed them round. Cass contracted further into the folds of the white gelebeya which had been a gift from Yuessef; she had given him her black jacket. Tallal's mother had also presented her with a gift, new tassels on the saddle blanket and a woman's scarf which was now packed away in the saddle bags. Cass pulled the checkered keffeyeh away from her face as she sipped tea and grinned crazily at the soldiers. They kept their distance.

The train whistle blew. The ramps were hoisted up through the doors and they embarked again for the ride to Tall Kalakh. Cass counted the miles.

When they arrived her body ached with exhaustion, with bumping and jarring of the bare railway floor. The saddle blanket did little to buffer the jolts that now invaded her limbs. Tallal swore to God almighty that he would purchase a cushion for the return trip. Cass laughed uproariously, teasing him about having a woman's tender behind. To that Tallal spat back she was a she devil, a demon without feelings, that she sat on her brain and wore a hat on her ass. They began thumping each other like children. Spying a bakery shop with confections crusted with flies, they gorged themselves on cakes soaked in honey and laced with slivers of almond.

They found an inn four blocks from a stable on the outer fringes of the town. They fed their horses and returned to their room. Beds made of hemp rope slung across wooden frames stood in each corner a thin mattress on each. Cass was not anxious for company. She paid for all four cots, and gave the innkeeper some extra to find a bottle of wine and cigarettes. They took cold showers in their turn, scraping the grime from their bodies.

Though weary, Cass could not feel the draught of sleep coming over her. It was a still night. When the lights were off, she sat by the window and watched the brick carts pass in the streets. A new building was going up, its steel struts bared to the sky. New upon old. Concrete upon mudbrick. Tallal, too, was restless and disoriented, so close to this strange woman. He refused the wine and drank water instead, inhaling deeply on the cigarette Cass had given him.

"Will you return to America, now?"

"To see my mother, yes. But I don't know whether I will stay there."

"You won't go back to Egypt," he said with some vehemence.

"No," she laughed. "I don't think this part of the world is very healthy for me anymore."

"Will you take a husband? I know that you lost your betrothed, but what more can you do? You are a woman. You are getting old."

She threw the pack of cigarettes at him.

"Well, not too old, I suppose," he said and scratched his chin. "But you have no children, no husband, no brothers to keep you."

"What about you, Tallal? Soon to be a soldier. Aren't there any girls in your life?"

"No," he said absolutely. "I'm young yet, and in Nayrab they all look like horses. I would sooner have a horse. A woman's only trouble to me." He peered at the ticking of the mattress as if he might find something valuable written there.

"Like me, for instance."

"Oh, no, you are different, but never in my life will I understand you. As my father said, you fell from some star and you'll return there. I'll never see you again, but I will think of you. I look on you as a brother, by God, and it is the strangest thing. What do you look like without that thatch of short hair? What do you look like in a dress, without those boots and without a man's gelebeya covering your body?"

"You're too young to find out," she said and came over to his side of the room. She tousled his hair and he caught her hand. She jumped as if she had felt an electric shock, but he held onto her. She began to pull away but he held her wrist, gently, but firmly.

"I'm thirsty, Tallal."

He poured her another cup of wine, contented himself with taking one sip of it and holding it in his mouth for some time before he swallowed.

"Camel piss," he said and took one more swallow. He cocked his head and looked at her steadily. Her sleeves were rolled up above the elbows. Her feet were bare. The only light in the room came from a streetlight that filtered through the curtains. He ran his fingers up her arm and she shivered.

"Are you cold?" he said. "Are you nervous? Am I too bold?"

"You think me a whore, Tallal. That is no good."

"You belong to no man," Tallal said quietly. "You cannot belong to the dead."

"I'm a murderess."

"Yes, but your gun is over there," he said, pointing to her cloak. It lay in a heap over the holster. He caught hold of her other arm now and she felt his heat running down to her own loins. She bent forward and kissed him just above the eyes.

"By God, woman," he snorted, "You kiss me like my mother. Be gone." He flushed with embarrassment and twisted away from her toward the wall, trying to conceal the swelling beneath his gelebeya.

"Tallal," she said softly, and put her right hand on his shoulder. He turned toward her slowly, rising on one arm and catching the nape of her neck with the other. He pressed her to him and kissed her hard on the mouth. She resisted.

"Shweya, shweya, slowly, slowly." She kissed him again, parting his lips with her tongue. As she did so she unbuttoned her gelebeya.

His mouth strayed from hers and roamed down her neck to her collar bone. His groans swept like a balm through her veins and relaxed her muscles. She kissed his hair as he burrowed and she buried her face as tears stole into her eyes.

His fingers found her right breast. Her nipple was small and hard, standing erect against his caresses. His mouth roamed further but the cloth of her robe got in the way. She pushed him away and stood before the bed. She lifted the robe up over her head and let it fall to the floor.

He eyed her body, then the door, and with haste pushed one of the beds against it. She stood outlined in the light, about the same height as he, the manliness of her was now replaced by the feminine lines of her hips, her breasts and the triangular patch of hair at her thighs. She trembled when he came close to her as he too removed his gelebeya. He covered his manhood with his hand.

She put her arms around his shoulders and felt him shudder. They fell onto the bed and she rolled beneath him and he kissed her again, on the mouth, hard, urgently. She slowed him down. When her hands reached him he sighed, then took her breast in his mouth.

She stroked him as he kissed her, but he could barely contain himself. Cass guided him home, and with a few deep thrusts he collapsed in her arms, kissing her again and again on the throat, on the lips, on her forehead. She clasped him to her and he slept on her shoulder.

At dawn she roused him gently from his sleep. He caught her form in the daylight and sighed again.

"You are very beautiful."

"You are very beautiful yourself," she said and he looked down and quickly covered himself with his robe.

"Was it good? Was that the way?"

"It was very good," she said and turned away from him as she dressed. The innkeeper had left them a basin and pitcher of water at the door. Cass returned from the bathroom and sponged the cool water over her face and neck. She adjusted the gelebeya and strapped the gun once more to her hip. It felt alien and cold now, an intruder. She threw Tallal a towel and said, "Hurry. The sun's up. You've a long way to travel and so do I."

He ignored her and sat on his bed.

"Listen," she said, easing herself into her boots. She stamped her right foot, then her left and stood up.

He caught her hand and said, "I want to sling you over my saddle and take you home. You are mine now."

"Your father would not approve," she answered quickly.

"It has nothing to do with my father, God forgive me."

"Forgive you for what?"

The question made him wince, but he nodded and smiled at her.

"A thousand thanks, my friend."

"Peace and health be with you, my brother."

"But what will I tell my wife?" he asked, as if the idea had dropped in his lap from the sky.

"You haven't got a wife . . . yet. Why don't you worry about that when the time comes?" She looked down at his puzzled face and could not help but laugh. He joined with her.

"Just don't be too serious about this. You haven't sinned. Or I don't believe you've sinned. Christ, we are a dreary pair of outlaws."

"You turned me into a drinker," he said with mock sternness, heaving the bottle into the wicker basket. "But I will think of this as in a dream."

They parted on the Dabbussiyeh road. "God's peace to you and your family," she said. He and his mare stood as she cantered away from them. She waved once, over her head but did not turn around. He, too, waved and called out, "May God be with you." He waited until she disappeared over the hillside.

The morning sun beat upon her head. She hiked the gelebeya high up over her boots so that air could flow to her legs as she rode. She began to sing out loud, but found she was singing in English and looked around to see if any ears had heard her. At her mistake the heaviness was on her again. She was still in Syria.

"Wait! Wait!" It was Tallal's voice, she wheeled around in the saddle and brought Mabruka to a halt.

"Your watch!" Tallal called out. "You've forgotten the gold watch."

"Oh Tallal. It's yours. I have no more trains to catch."

"No," he said, "it was your father's. You must keep it with you." His face was bright, open in the sunlight.

"Will you come back with me?" he implored. "Will you come back? My father would welcome you. My mother . . . well, we could build a fine stable of our own."

"Tallal, you know it cannot be so. We are kin, now, but from different worlds. I'm sorry."

"But you belong to me. Your life was in my keeping and mine in yours. We have . . . coupled. We are one, under God."

"Tallal. It is enough. More than I hoped for. Goodbye and God keep you well."

Pride stopped any other appeal and he murmured, "God keep you well." He spurred his horse hard and she bucked under him. Then they were gone in a clatter of pebbles. This time Cass watched him disappear before she trotted slowly away.

# THIRTY-FOUR

The grass under her belly was tough as railroad spikes, dried brown under the sun's glare. Lizards darted back and forth between the aloe stems and dung beetles lumbered over the stones, pushing ahead of them bits of goat droppings. The sky was an uncompromising blue, hedged to the west by a dark wadding of clouds. White snails had petrified on the lower branches of the thorn bushes as if some forgotten wave had washed them ashore and then departed, leaving them to their fate.

Mabruka grew drowsy. A few skinny brown birds chirruped to each other. Cass lay still and considered the patrol for a second time. The jeep crawled along the barbed wire with two Syrian soldiers inside, both sun-drugged and sleepy, with a rear-mounted machine gun bolted behind them. Cass was about fifty yards away, under cover, behind the lava formations. The jeep groaned and lurched further down the track, spitting up dust for some time before Cass got up off the ground. She wiped her wet face on her keffeyeh and gained Mabruka's attention with a snatch on her rope.

She led her mare out of the shelter of rocks and into the open listening for the grind of any motor nearby. Mabruka followed her lethargically to the barbed wire fence. Cass rapped the top wire with her hand and showed it to her horse, then she swung her cloak over it so Mabruka would know exactly where her heels should fly. Hurriedly, she anchored the cloak with stones so it would not flap, then gathered some dried brush and shoved it against the fence for substance. She mounted, testing the footing at a canter and made a large circle before the wire. The jeep invaded her thoughts and the throb of its engine made her snap rigid in the saddle. A warning bullet buzzed over her head as the front grill of the vehicle jarred the scenery to her right.

She pressed Mabruka onward with her knees, galloping toward the barbed wire and the cloak, praying that the mare would not spook as gunfire zinged around them. She twisted in the saddle three paces from the jump and peered into the eyes of death. The Syrian soldier had trained his machine gun on her and her heart leapt out over her horse's neck.

"Yes, now," she commanded, not to her horse, but to the Syrian soldier. He yelled once, but she did not hear and digging her heels deep into Mabruka's flanks they lifted off the ground over her cloak and the barbed wire fence into Lebanon.

The machine gun jolted again, but the jeep was still rolling, diverting the soldier's aim. The spray of lead crossed over them, then lowered. As Mabruka's hooves hit the dirt on the other side the bullets struck into the mare's hind leg and into Cass' thigh.

"Yes, yes," Cass cried, "now, finish it." Her horse bucked and steamed, reared and shrieked as only a wounded animal can, but Cass held her seat.

When the Syrian soldier realized the apprition before him was mortal, bones and flesh, he stayed his shot. Like a glittering coin from some ancient past this image had been tossed before him. His own heart cheered and his eyes welled with involuntary pride. Too fine, too wild to dispose of at the point of a gun. There was an Arab grace astounding as a living canvas flying before his eyes. The blood on the horse only enhanced its savage beauty like a sash of honor.

The other soldier knocked him from his bewilderment, but not before the gunman had flung the machine gun out of range on the circumference of the tripod. His compatriot shouted at him and pounded him with his fists, but the soldier stood dumbly, watching the ghost. For the rest of his life he would remember the mighty arch of the grey steed and the thudding of hooves, and the rider so regally appointed, so gracefully astride the mare.

Cass struck the mare's neck with the slack of her reins and the horse shook like an engine revving, gained power and then lunged forward. They careened down the stone embankment as the machine gun ripped up the ground behind them. They galloped on the fine edge of control, plunging headlong through the narrow defiles and winding round the ledges that seemed to reach out in attempts to pluck Cass from the saddle. Mabruka's pace was uneven, disobedient to the tug on the reins.

At the barbed wire behind them, the duty bound Syrian soldier barked into his walkie-talkie and communicated with the Syrian troops on the Lebanese side of the border. His partner leaned against the hood of the jeep, still dazzled, not feeling the scalding heat of the metal through his uniform. He bore his companion's epithets with a glorious indifference.

Cass was riding into Christian territory now, along paths no tank could follow and no patrols would dare tread. She rounded a crucifix set in a pile of stones, then negotiated a steep gully gingerly. The trees keened as she sped by, the rocks murmured under the scudding hooves. Down, down into a grassy field Mabruka churned on, then finally broke and hurled her rider to the ground. The horse bellowed and sent tremors through the earth. Only then, from the dirt, did Cass realize how close the bullets had come. Blood was gushing down her mare's right rear flank. A slug had passed through her own thigh, but strangely there was no pain. It was an abstraction in a world spinning on the fulcrum of her horse.

"Mabruka, Mabruka. Easy girl. Come here to me." The mare's eyes gleamed with an unearthly light. Her flanks heaved and froth was thrown from her mouth.

"Don't go down. Don't go down here, girl. I'll get you back!" The mare shuddered and hopped on her three good legs and as she swung her head toward her wound, Cass sprang forward catching her reins. The mare dragged her some thirty paces and then came to a halt. Cass unwound the keffeyeh from her head and staunched the blood flowing from Mabruka's ravaged quarter.

"Oh, Mabruka," she was sobbing, "be still girl, be still." She drew her gun with trembling fingers. Her horse was in pain. She must put her down, end the misery. She could not see anything through her tears and she threw her arm violently across her eyes. She raised the weapon to her horse's head.

"No, don't!" The voice raked across her and she held her shot, spinning in its direction. Three men on foot stood clustered by a stand of pines.

"Help me!" she yelled. "Help my horse, for God's sake!" She felt the weight of her pistol in her hand and turned it once, listlessly, in the sunlight, then put it back inside her belt.

"Sorry," she said. "I wouldn't shoot you. My horse. . . ." Tears splashed down her face. A red stain began to expand like a blossoming flower at her right thigh.

Mabruka shivered and jerked at the bridle. Cass caught the horse's head between her hands and stroked it gently, speaking to her, calming her.

The oldest among the men, a giant of a man with bushy white eyebrows, strode forward steadily. The younger men held their shotguns halfway between heaven and earth, suspended at ready. With deft fingers the old man looked over the horse's haunch and said, "It's just flesh, no bone damage. No terrible wound, do you understand me? Your mare will be all right. We will get the bullet out."

She nodded in unspoken gratitude. Blood trickled down her thigh. The cloth of her gelebeya was glued fast against the skin.

One of the young men brought out a canteen of water, thrashed through the undergrowth and came up with a packing of leaves which he mixed with the fluid. He made a mud poultice and strode toward her.

She dodged him and said, "No, no. The horse first. Mabruka. You must help her. She is in pain. I am fine." The young man glanced at her as if she were moonstruck.

"All right, Matthew, lad," the old man said. "Here, give me her head." The young man pressed the packing of mud and leaves against the horse's rear leg. They laid a cloth over it as Cass untied the halter rope from behind the saddle and tried to bind the wound with it, tight against the horse's leg, but it would not hold.

"There, there. Take it easy. We haven't far to go, but that bullet will have to come out," the old man said, matter-of-factly, as if he had seen such things before.

"Here?" Cass said, "Now? I have a knife. We could fire the blade."

The young man wiped his hands on his trousers, cleaning them, and said, "Come on, boy."

"What happened?" the other young man said. "Who shot at you?"

She gave him a puzzled look. Both young men were dressed in leather jackets and jeans. Their hair was dark and long pushed back in heavy waves from their broad foreheads. The older man wore the more traditional garb of the region, the black mutton-leg trousers and white blousy shirt.

"My sons," he said quietly. "Matthew and John. I am also named John."

Cass could no longer distinguish who was talking. Wherever she moved she was rocked off balance. Her head was light as helium and dizzy in the sunshine.

"This is so absurd," she babbled, "I. . . ." She began to fall forward and the ground loomed before her eyes. The younger John caught her up with a laugh and threw one of her arms around his shoulder. He hoisted her into his arms and waited for marching orders from his father.

She awoke to a stab of pain in her right leg.

"It's all right," the old man said. "You've lost some blood, but you'll be all right." She flinched as the blade went into her flesh again, probing.

"I'm not the best of doctors," he said, "but I'm not sure we want to trouble the authorities about this one. Ah . . . there." He dropped a bullet on the bedside table.

"Mabruka. My horse, is she all right?"

"Yes," the old man said. Cass focused on him. He was standing over the bed. He dropped another piece of lead. "Matthew took that out of her haunch. Same place as yours," he grinned. "She's fine. Hungry even. She's eaten through half my barley already."

"Oh. Wait, I'll pay you for that. I've got some money," and she stopped, confused. She blushed, for she was no longer wearing the gelebeya and vest.

"My wife's nightgown," he said. "I hope you don't mind, but your clothes needed a wash."

"Mind?" She looked around her and the chairs and the tables clicked into her vision. She was lying in a small bedroom, on a mattress that was enormously soft and bulging with an excess of feathers. The room smelled faintly of rose water and alcohol.

A woman walked softly through the door. She was large with kind eyes and a full bosom. Gold earrings caught the lamplight through a profusion of black hair and she tossed it back without vanity.

"Now what in God's name were you doing in a man's getup, riding this part of the Lebanon? You are not even Arab, girl. Your skin is European."

Cass waited for inspiration, but none came, and she looked at the woman silently.

"A drink, perhaps. Some tea?"

"I don't think tea will do the trick, Mother," said John. "Brandy. I could use some myself."

"My wife, Magda," he said to Cass as the woman walked out of the room. "She is a very good girl. Inquisitive, perhaps, but so am I. You look like you've been through a war, though I suppose they're not hard to find in this part of the world." He chuckled as he sat down in the chair by the foot of the bed.

"Here you go," Magda said pouring out a glass for Cass and one for her husband. Then she, too, settled into a chair and waited.

"Thank you for this. For your care. How far is Becharre from here?"

"About fifty kilometers. Is that where you came from?"

"I have friends there. They will be worried. Have you got a telephone?"

"No, but I can send one of my sons to get a message to them if you like. There is a phone in the village. Matthew. Matthew!" His son appeared in the doorway.

"We've an errand for you. Go to the coffee house and call this woman's friends."

"Chuck Vazcatchian, in Becharre, or his wife Ingrid." Cass said. "Their number is 966371. Please tell them I'm safe and well and hoping they can find a van to carry Mabruka back to L'Aiglon, their farm. Here, wait, you must need some money." The old man quieted her with a sigh.

"Now girl, if you've got some strength, we'd like to hear how you came to this."

"I'm sorry, I'm being very rude. . . ."

"And you don't want to talk about it."

She smiled gratefully.

"Well, you are a surprise. You bring back all the worst memories of the war. No, no, I don't mean you. It has been more than a year since we saw any trouble here. During the war hundreds of people from Tripoli fled here to the mountains, Moslems and Christians alike in their panic. They have returned now to their homes by the sea. We have all lost someone, or something, only we continue to talk about it, again and again stirring up the torment as if we cannot leave the dead to rest in peace. Two villages away to the east, twelve men of the town were lined up and executed by the Moslems."

"Without cause?"

"No, not without cause, I suppose. The Phalangists blew up one of their buses. Killed many children. So stupid, so tiresome and now it may begin again."

"Aren't you angry?"

"I'm too weary to be angry. I leave that to the Cedars. They patrol here now. We pay the militia for our protection and the mountains remain clear."

"What about the Syrians?"

"Oh no," he laughed ruefully. "They wouldn't dare. We are a pocket of serenity. They don't wish to disturb us."

He poured himself another brandy and, with Cass' permission, refilled her gass. Magda had not said a word.

"My name is Cassandra. I am an American. I've had some personal trouble, but I believe it's all finished."

"You are not a spy, are you?" Magda asked.

"No," Cass said evenly and plucked at the sheet pulled up around her.

"Well, that is all right, then," Magda announced. "You are welcome to stay here until you are well. I do not know what trouble you have been in, but we cannot ask too many questions. You are here and safe, that's all."

"That's the part I can't believe," Cass said excitedly. "That I'm here. In Lebanon. God." Lightning rent the sky outside and a boom of thunder made her jump. She swung both feet to the floor.

"A passing storm," John said. "Not manmade. We've been waiting for weeks for the mountain rains. Now you have brought them. The vines have yellowed and grown old before our eyes. The rivers are low and murky." Cass rose to her feet and wobbled and fell back on the bed. The clouds split open like sacks of grain and spilled their wet kernels on the roof.

"You're not running from a man, are you? An angry husband?" Magda asked.

"Oh, no," Cass laughed. "It's not that at all. Oh dear. I'm not really trying to be mysterious. I just want to forget the whole thing. It's better that you don't know. I'm sorry."

Curiosity pinched Magda's face. Her husband sat back in his chair with his hands folded across his big belly.

"This friend of yours, Vazcatchian. He is Armenian, yes?"

"Yes. One of my best friends."

"The he is welcome, too."

"You are running from the police. You have stolen something?" Magda said.

"No, no," Cass said and Magda sat back once

more, confounded.

"Leave her alone, woman. If she wants to tell us something she will."

"You must be hungry?"

"No, thank you, I'm not. I'm quite content with this brandy, but no, I'm in your bed. Where will you sleep?" Cass said miserably.

"We've other beds. Rest now. Come, Mother, it's time she got some rest. Don't bother her with all your questions. You act as if she were a criminal."

Magda rose reluctantly to her feet. The rain was splashing down the tiled roof, running along the gutters and puddling at the sides of the house. Another streak of lightning severed the sky and thunder growled in the hills.

"All right." He patted Cass' hand. "Sleep well and feel safe. There is no one here who will harm you."

"Good night and a thousand thanks for your hospitality."

"It is nothing," Magda said, holding her hand over the glass bell of the kerosene lamp. She turned down the flame until it sputtered and died. Only the lightning brightened up the room. She bent down as if to kiss Cass on the forehead. The girl was startled.

"It's all right," she said gently. "I have never had a daughter, so I do not know what things they get into in this day and age. I know I would go to the cupboard myself and pull out my husband's shotgun should anyone threaten me or mine. You are a good girl, I believe. I saw many such as you fight during the civil war. Your gun, by the way, is here." She opened the drawer in the bedside table; the holster and pistol lay there. She shut it again.

"Come, Mother," John said from the doorway.

"Yes, Father." Magda padded to the door on bare feet, taking with her a scent of rose water. She turned once and smiled at the girl, then she and her husband left Cass alone.

The storm howled and the rain thudded across the roof. A door slammed, and Cass sat bolt upright in bed. She swung her feet to the floor again, wincing at the bandage on her thigh. John's head peeped through the doorway.

"Your friend is coming tomorrow. Matthew said he was very excited and thankful that you are safe. It seems we must have a feast tomorrow. A young lamb. Magda, she is an excellent cook. We shall have meat on your bones in no time, girl." He waited anxiously for some response. She managed a feeble salute. He returned it with a grin and was gone.

The cool bare floor under her feet soothed her. A wet wind was blowing from the window and the embroidered cloth on the bedside table fluttered. She picked up the two bullets and let them drop again, then poured herself more brandy, sipping it slowly. She found her cigarettes and watched her own hand shaking as she lit one. Never did she feel more bereft, more empty than she did at that moment when she settled back into the pillows and the muffled thunder beat against her ears. In the pale smoke that tendrilled out of her mouth she saw the face of Moustafa Sheik, alive. She blew him away and stubbed out the cigarette. Her eyes closed, but they opened again and again, fighting the rain that mesmerized her. Exhaustion tugged at her through her skirmishing thoughts, and like the towline of a ship pulled her down into the depths of sleep.

# THIRTY-FIVE

Mabruka loped around the paddock at L'Aiglon with Varmint in panting pursuit. The mare shook her head and threw her tail in his face, but he bit her on the neck and nearly got kicked for his advances. Cass rested her chin on her arms and watched them for a long time. Vaz and Ingrid stood by.

"More work for you, I guess," Cass said.

"Not work," Ingrid replied. "She'll be in foal before you know it."

"A colt," Vaz said with some assurance.

"A filly would do nicely," said Cass. "Less petulant. More loyal. . . ."

"Stubborn as mules," Vaz said reaching out and corraling his women toward him. "We'll take good care of her until you've got a place to keep her."

"Yes, but the foal's yours."

"Come on, Morgan. Get your gear together. We've got a plane to catch."

"All right, Kodak. Coming. Just saying so long to Old Paint here." She limped slightly as she made her way into the house. It smelled fresh and cool.

"One more phone call and we'll be off."

"Make it snappy then."

"Yes, sir!" She threw herself down into the cowhide chair and dialed her mother's number.

"Hello, Mom."

"Cassie!" Her mother's voice sang on the other

end of the wire.

"You sound terrific, Mom. How's your jaw?"

"A little stiff, but that won't slow me down a bit. You should see me, Cassie, slender as a swan. I haven't been this thin in years . . . dog years. That liquid diet, should have gone on it a long time ago. McKee says I look like a young girl."

"When do you go back in?"

"Oh, in a few days. Nothing to worry about, the doctors say. Just a little mending around the ears. It isn't bad, hon, I'm going to be fine."

"Mom." Cass held the receiver a little way away.

"When you coming home, Cassie?"

"Not for awhile." Cass waited but there was no reaction. "Mom, I'm going to Bangkok. The paper's been on my tail for weeks now. Vietnam/Cambodia, you know, they're sort of thin staffed with Iran exploding at the same time. Bangkok's as close as we can get to Cambodia right now. Kodak says we'll all have to become avowed Communists."

"Jesus, Cassie, first it's the Arabs and now it's the Asians. I do believe you're unAmerican."

"Now, it's just too tame back there for me. What's new with you anyway?"

"That Brooklyn antiques dealer, Khoury, has been arraigned and charged. His bond's been set at a quarter of a million. He could get twenty years to life on the possession of heroin alone, but the feds are coming down hard on him for . . . the bomb. I don't know whether they can get it to stick, but he certainly won't be walking the streets anytime soon. McKee's bought me a dog. Did I tell you? A spaniel. Some watchdog, huh? I'll be glad when he stops piddling on the oriental rugs. You okay, Cassie?''

"Aw, Mom. I'm fine. I'll send you a postcard."
She looked up and Kodak winked.

"It's all right," her mother said, "I've got a
subscription to that rag of yours. I'll know where
you are."

"I love you, Mom."

"Goodbye, Cassie. Consider yourself hugged.
And don't worry."

"I won't, Mom. Bye for now." Cass hung up the
receiver and jumped to her feet. "Well," she said,
patting the pockets of her khaki jacket to make
sure she had everything, "ready."

"Come on, you tart, the bordello of the east
awaits you."

"Can't wait," she said, snatching up her suitcase
and the old typewriter that had stood for weeks,
unused, in the hall. Kodak noticed her limp, but he
did not pry. It was not his way. He hustled after
her out into the sunshine. Vaz and Ingrid hugged
her and bade farewell with promises to write
about Mabruka.

"God, I'll miss that horse."

"Come on, cowgirl."

They wheeled out on the coastal highway and
sped toward Beirut, where Andrew Pym met them
at the airport for a couple of drinks before their
flight. He carried with him the possessions Cass
had left in the Commodore Hotel.

"Hello children," Pym said, dropping the bags
to the floor with a groan. "Getting too old for a
pack mule." He blew a wisp of white hair out of
his eyes.

"You're a sweetheart," Cass said and pecked
him on the cheek.

"What, that's all I get?"

"Come with us," Cass said.

"No, no. Can't teach an old dog new languages, you know. By the way, my dear, someone's looking for you."

"I figured they might."

"And who, pray tell, is they?" Kodak asked.

"It's time your luggage was passed through security. Then we'll have a little drinkie, no?"

"Sure," Kodak said. "I'll handle it. Be right back."

With some ceremony Pym took Cass' arm and led her into the bar. The tables were all covered with Formica. The wide windows looked out on the tarmac. An MEA airliner was on the ground with sunlight bouncing of its wings. Pan Am was just making its last turn before landing, spewing black trails from its engines. Down at the far end of the runway near some Quonset huts were the French troop carriers, the swell-belly planes in camouflage colors. Nearby was a line of U.N. jeeps, whitewashed, with blue insignias. A cross wind whipped the windsock on its mast.

"Cassie, a message here, forwarded to you at the Commodore. Couldn't help but notice the Interpol letter head."

She unfolded the paper and her face blanched, then filled with color. Silently she handed it back to Pym.

"But this is good news, Cass. They're dead. All the men who were involved in Foster's murder are . . . gone."

"And poppies shall spring from their graves." She looked at Pym without seeing him. "No, you keep it."

"Cass."

"Oh, Andrew," she said, her face brightening, "just one more thing." She reached into her satchel and drew out a brown paper parcel. "You know B. over at the PFLP. When you stop by there, could you drop this off? It's something I borrowed; I promised to return it. He'll know who to send it to."

"Feels like a gun," Andrew said lightly.

Her expression narrowed as she peered directly into his eyes.

"Well, I won't drop it," said Andrew. "But I certainly wouldn't walk through security with it."

"What are you packing these days, anyway, Andrew? A .38, perchance?"

"What, me? No, no, girl. I'm a pacifist." His eyes sparked with mischief.

"Andrew, when I was—"

"Hullo, Kodak. All ready, then? Where's Sally? I thought she'd be here to wave goodbye."

"She's gone back home," he said venomously.

"Don't tell me," Cass said. "She's found her oil-rich Saudi and decided to have a last binge before returning to her desert kingdom."

"Ooooh," said Andrew, "you know more about this than I do."

"She does not," Kodak snapped. "She's gone off and married a Goddamned stockbroker."

"Well, all's not lost," said Pym, "now you've got ears in the money market. When to buy, when to sell."

"Sir," said Kodak, "It does not become you to take matters of the heart so flippantly."

"Matters of the heart ceased to concern me years ago," said Pym. Cass suppressed a giggle.

"Oh, yes. I can see I'll have a lot of sympathy from your quarter. Well, then. A drink before we go."

The round came and they sipped their drinks while the loudspeaker hummed over the list of arrivals and departures. Cass was lighting one cigarette off another, but Kodak didn't seem to notice. Andrew did.

She leaned toward him. "Does anyone at the Commodore know I'm going?"

"As far as they're concerned, you're already gone. I gave Omar the amount you requested. Money makes life so much easier. Discretion, my dear. They respect it as long as their palms are greased."

They lined up for the Pan Am flight via Delhi to Bangkok. "You'll miss this place," Andrew said to the two of them.

"Like a hole in the head," Kodak said.

"Goodbye, Andrew," Cass threw her arms around him and whispered in his ear, "I hope they pay you extra for hazards above and beyond the call of duty."

"I think you missed your calling," he said holding her away from him and peering at her through rheumy eyes. He pulled a handkerchief out of his rumpled seersucker suit and gave a sniffle.

"You old fraud," she murmured.

"Come on, Morgan, we'll miss our plane," Kodak said. "No need to be mawkish about this. We've got to be filing your stories by tomorrow P.M." He hoisted the camera over his shoulder and propelled Cass forward through security.

"I wish I could get Australian television, then I

could keep up with you two."

"Come to Bangkok!"

"A thousand salaams," Pym said in Arabic.

"Peace be with you, Andrew," Cass replied in the same tongue.

"Yup, see you again," Kodak jumped in, "when all hell breaks loose."

"You won't have long to wait," Pym shouted as they ducked out of sight. "You never have long to wait here." He tapped the package which contained Cass' gun. The Corsair Unique carried the Aleppo clip—four bullets gone. Baba would come to his own conclusions about how they had been spent.


"Hey, Pym." A man smelling of talcum powder in a dark suit and dark shoes stopped Pym at the airport entrance.

"She's off," Pym said abruptly.

"Pity," the other man said, his eyes flashing furtively. "She was quite useful really."

Pym pressed by him, then hesitated. He heard the unmistakable thud of flesh against concrete. He didn't turn around. He cocked his head in that direction.

"Oh," the man said. "Saiqa. Caught him on the tarmac. Seems he had a scope. Could have picked her off on the gangway. Couldn't allow that."

"No, couldn't allow that."

"I've got a commendation for you from the commander."

"Keep it," Pym said and stalked past him. Maybe Bangkok would be a nice change of pace, he thought. His step grew lighter as he strode out under the Middle Eastern sun.